Before I could do anything, a high-pitched scream came from the woods. The party went on for another second, as though the scream hadn't happened, but then someone turned off the music and the scream came again, this time joined by other screams. The sounds ripped through the smiles of the partygoers as everyone shot one another questioning looks. A moment later Clare's sister came barreling out of the woods, her eyes wide with terror.

"Run!" she screeched.

As if on cue, a low guttural snarl came from the trees as a huge shadow loomed from the woods, furry and fanged.

Also by Laura Martin

HOAX FOR HIRE

LAURA MARTIN

HARPER

An Imprint of HarperCollinsPublishers

Library of Congress Control Number: 2018964874
ISBN 978-0-06-280381-8

Typography by Ellice M. Lee
20 21 22 23 24   PC/BRR   10 9 8 7 6 5 4 3 2 1
❖
First paperback edition, 2020

Because my heart belongs to four people,
so does this dedication.

For Josh: my forever best friend.
Thank you for being the left brain to my right.
We are a good team unless we are trying to paint a room,
at which point it's every man for himself.

And for my three kids: London, Lincoln, and Levi.
I didn't know my life was missing so much
joy and chaos until you three came along.
I love you three to the moon and back
and more than you ever wish.

"The most beautiful thing we can experience is the mysterious. It is the source of all true art and science."

–Albert Einstein

Cryptid: An animal whose existence or survival is disputed or unsubstantiated, such as the yeti.

CHAPTER ONE

"Should I be worried that I can't feel my toes?" I asked as I shuffled my flipper-covered feet. I'd never had to pull off a hoax that involved water this late in the season before, and the murky Altamaha River was a new level of cold that I was pretty sure only polar bears could appreciate.

"Suck it up," Curtis said, yanking hard on the straps that held my air tank on my back as he finished the last of our safety checks. "Everything looks good," he said. He came around to stand in front of me, his knee-high boots keeping *his* feet wonderfully dry and warm. He put a hand up to adjust my dive mask, and I slapped it away.

"Stop it," I said. "I know how to put a mask on. Gramps gave me the same scuba lessons he gave you. And if I remember right, I was better at them, so stop acting like that."

"Like what?" Curtis asked.

Like an obnoxious know-it-all, I thought, but I just shook my head. There were some things you didn't say to your older brother when there wasn't an adult around to make sure you didn't get smeared. I stared past his smug face toward the churning river. The water was moving fast, probably due to a recent rain, and I wondered idly what camera lens would work the best in this hazy light. Of course, my camera wasn't here—it was never allowed at a hoax, not since I'd gotten in trouble over those Loch Ness Monster pictures. I was here to work, not have fun, a point my dad would have made if he were here.

"Are you sure you don't want to trade me jobs?" I asked Curtis.

"No way," he said, and grinned. "I like my toes. They happen to be one of my best features."

"You aren't funny," I said.

"Matter of opinion," Curtis said. When I continued to frown, he sighed and rolled his eyes. "Grayson, knock it off. We've been over this. You've never organized eyewitnesses by yourself before, and we can't afford to mess up this job. You know that. Dad and Gramps know that. I'm sure even the real Altamaha-ha knows that," he said with a jerk of his head toward the river. "This whole hoax has a lot better shot of working if you're under the water and I'm on land doing the hard stuff."

I sighed. He was right. I didn't like that he was right. But he was. "I just wish that Dad hadn't double booked us with the Loch Ness Monster sighting in Scotland and that Gramps hadn't gotten held up in the Congo."

"You and me both," Curtis said. For a second his cocky demeanor slipped a little, and I caught a glimpse of the nerves he'd been hiding ever since our grandfather had called two days ago to tell us that we were going to have to do this one on our own.

It wasn't the first time Curtis and I had pulled off a hoax without Dad or Gramps, but it was the first time we'd had to do a sea monster hoax by ourselves. Those were always trickier, what with the scuba gear, the actual logistics of assembling a twenty-foot monster and sinking it in the water without any unwanted eyewitnesses, and then timing the eyewitness sighting you actually did want. Okay, so maybe Curtis's job on land wasn't easier, but I'd still trade him. I took a deep breath and released it through clenched teeth. Man, I hoped we didn't screw this up.

3

I come from a long line of cryptid hunters. Which is a fancy way of saying that my family is ridiculous and they managed to make it a career. A cryptid by definition is a creature that may or may not exist, like Bigfoot or the Chupacabra or the Loch Ness Monster. It's a thing that lives primarily in legend, eyewitness accounts, and footprints in the mud but nowhere else. Every McNeil as far back as anyone can remember has strapped on boots and gone out to hunt for the creatures that seemed to live only in the tallest of tall tales. Most no one has ever heard of and will never hear of because they've never been discovered for a reason: they don't actually exist. My Scottish McNeil ancestors grew up in a village on the shores of the legendary Loch Ness, where stories of a sea monster have been told for hundreds of years, so I guess cryptid hunting seemed like a viable career option. It was a life filled with adventure, travel to exotic locations, unbelievable stories, and no paychecks.

Floyd McNeil—I think he was my great-great-great uncle or something like that—is the one who figured out that if you couldn't catch the real thing, then faking it could bring in enough cash to fund the next exploration. Although, not to give him too much credit, the whole thing was completely by accident. He was hunting the Cadborosaurus, or Caddy, as the people of British Columbia called the sea monster supposedly living in Cadboro Bay, in 1815. Caddy was allegedly as long as seventy feet with flippers like those of a sea lion, a head like a horse, and a fan-shaped tail. It was also supposed to be able to swim wicked fast. Why Uncle Floyd thought he had a shot of catching something that big is beyond me, but he wasn't the only one trying to catch Caddy.

Cryptid hunters and adventure seekers were flooding into the little town on the edge of Cadboro Bay, and good old Uncle Floyd was feeling a bit crowded. Apparently, the mayor of Cadboro was feeling the same way, because over one too many drinks, the men decided to fake a Caddy sighting three towns over. Uncle Floyd agreed to arrange and execute the hoax if the mayor would pay, and it worked. Everyone chased the red herring, and Uncle Floyd got a pocket full of cash. And so the hoaxes began, and the McNeils went from wackadoodle cryptid hunters to wackadoodle cryptid hunters with a side of fraud thrown in for good measure.

For every real trip a McNeil made in search of a cryptid, they made two more to create a cryptid hoax. It was a win-win. They muddied the waters for the other cryptid hunters, successfully sending them on wild-goose chases while simultaneously funding their own hunts. They staged sightings, made footprints in mud, left hair samples, created odd sounds in the night—you name it, they did it.

Barnum and Bailey bought their taxidermy Feejee Mermaids and two-headed cows. Town mayors and officials slipped cash into my ancestors' pockets to create "sightings" that would attract tourists. Political figures seeking to disgrace their opponents hired them to stage UFO sightings and create crop circles in their opponents' yards. Husbands trying to discredit their ex-wives hired them. The list went on.

My family had found a niche, albeit a criminal one, and we weren't the only ones. According to Gramps, there was another family somewhere out there doing the exact same thing we were: the Gerhards. A fact that bugged him and Dad to no end. Anytime something cryptid-related hit the news, Gramps would watch the footage obsessively until he could determine if "those blasted ninny-headed, flapjacks-for-brains Gerhards were involved." Curtis and I always watched this performance with barely concealed grins. For a veteran hoaxer, Gramps sure worried a lot about a family located thousands of miles away in Germany.

My dad was the first McNeil to dump the cryptid-hunting part of the tradition completely and focus only on the hoaxing, a fact that disappointed Gramps more than he let on. Gramps was a true-blue hunter, but he never passed up a good hoax, and he'd have given anything to be standing next to me in the freezing cold Altamaha River, which was kind of ironic since I'd have given anything to be anywhere else.

Curtis checked his watch and nodded. "It's go time. Don't screw up."

"Thanks for the vote of confidence," I said before grabbing my regulator and jamming it between my teeth.

"I'm serious," Curtis said. "We have a lot riding on this."

I grunted at him as I sloshed through the river in my flippers, lifting my knees comically high in my best impression of a deranged duck, until I was deep enough to submerge completely. I had a date to keep with a sea monster.

CHAPTER TWO

Within seconds of going under, my dive mask started to leak. I swam toward the middle of the river, thankful that I didn't have to dive that deep today, especially since my leaking mask had me a little rattled.

Curtis and I knew how to scuba dive, thanks to Gramps and the key he'd "borrowed" for our town's pool. Curtis and I had spent many moonlit nights under water learning every scuba trick in the books. I'd loved paddling around the dark pool, with no sounds but my own breath and heartbeat in my ears. But there was a huge difference between diving in a warm pool and diving in a swiftly moving river, a fact that I was well aware of as I headed toward the spot where our sea monster was tethered and waiting.

The sea monster decoy, one of our versions of the legendary Altamaha-ha, was suspended by bungees, cables, and heavy-duty steel carabiners. I remembered with a twinge of guilt that it had been Curtis who'd tethered her here while I stayed in the van—warm and dry. Stretching a good twenty feet from nose to tip, the Altamaha-ha decoy—or just Altie, as we affectionately called her—consisted of a gigantic crocodile-like head and a long snakelike body that could be controlled from below using a system of ropes and pulleys so that she undulated realistically in the water. She wasn't my favorite sea monster decoy. For one thing she was ridiculously long and unwieldy to control, especially on your own. But since Dad had shipped our best decoy to Scotland to use for his Nessie hoax, I was stuck with this clunker.

"She's more authentic than the Nessie decoy, anyway," Gramps had said as we dragged Altie out of her crates to start assembling her last week. "You've gotten too soft with all the high-techy junkity-junk your dad's done to Nessie. Corrupted a classic if you ask me. Lady Altie here is good old-fashioned hoaxing, that's what." I shook my head. Gramps did always see the bright side of things.

Okay, girl, I thought grimly as I swam down to begin feeling along Altie's belly for the first loop, let's get this over with. I'd asked Gramps once why all of our sea monsters were girls, and he'd said something about them being like boats, which were apparently also always girls.

My cold-deadened fingers searched for the first loop. Finding it, I managed to detach the carabiner that kept Altie tethered to the five metal anchors resting on the bottom of the riverbed. My hands slid along her side, and as I searched for the next loop and clip, felt the ridges of the recycled tires my grandfather had melted down and stretched over a chicken wire frame to make the creature. If you believed the stories, it was a definite upgrade over the decoys Gramps and *his* dad had used, but as a general rule, I didn't really believe most of my family's stories.

I unhooked another carabineer, mentally counting in my head. Only three more and the long neck and alligator-nosed head of Altie would rise to the surface. I found the last clip and barely had time to grab the trailing ropes before Altie started her ascent. Our Nessie decoy did this on her own using a pressurizing system that Dad had developed, but like Gramps had said, this decoy was old-school. I was going to have to stay under water, pulling on the ropes like a puppeteer in just the right pattern and with just the right timing so that she'd appear to be swimming across the river. At least the head is upgraded, I thought, grateful I didn't have to worry about making Altie's mouth open and shut or her eyes blink. Which is when I remembered that I hadn't turned the head on.

I'd have probably muttered a few choice words if my mouth hadn't been full of the regulator, so I had to content myself with a good mental butt kicking for being so careless as I dropped the ropes and kicked hard to get close to Altie's head. She was only about three feet from the surface when I reached her and hit the large black button under her jaw. Whirling, I swam back down to reclaim my ropes, leveraging them so that Altie would emerge like the monster of the Altamaha River legend and not like a rubber duckie. Her head broke the surface a second later, and I started my rope-pulling routine. Yank rope A, wait a half second. Yank rope B. Now Rope C and D. Repeat. It was exhausting and tricky and it made my brain hurt.

"Come on," I muttered, willing the pager on my hip to buzz. "Get on with it." The eyewitnesses should have seen Altie by now, their cell phones raised in shaky hands to document what could only be the famed sea serpent that had been spotted on this river for more than two hundred years. But I knew all too well that *should* was a very dangerous word.

Finally, after what felt like a lifetime of pulling ropes, I felt the pager buzz. I paddled hard for the bottom of the river, the ropes clutched loosely in my hand. I needed to get Altie back under water, fast, but I wasn't strong enough to do it without the help of our anchors. When I was far enough from the surface, I flipped on my headlamp, and the beam of light ripped through the dark water. Where were the anchors? They should have been directly below me, but the riverbed was empty.

If I couldn't find those anchors, the whole hoax was going to be a bust. Worse than a bust, we'd be found out. Dad and Gramps would probably go to jail, and then what would happen to me and Curtis? I could just picture the headlines: *Family of Frauds Found Out* and *Sixth Generation of Hoaxers Finally Comes to Justice.* My pounding heart decided to relocate itself from my chest to somewhere near my tonsils as I frantically scanned the seemingly vacant riverbed.

After what felt like hours but probably wasn't more than a minute, I spotted an anchor. It had tipped over, and the Altamaha's sandy bottom had done its best to swallow it whole. Diving down I grabbed it, and bracing my feet on the bottom, pried it out of the sand to stand upright again. With no time to waste, I looped the rope connected to Altie's head through it and started pulling. My arm muscles burned at the effort, but slowly, slowly, the shadow above me of the monstrous and completely fake Altie started to make its way back toward the bottom of the lake.

The panic that had clamped around my chest moments before eased as I saw her finally sink completely below the surface. All that was left to do now was to hook the ropes to the rest of our specially made anchors that had become a bit of a McNeil family heirloom over the years. I snorted, sending a shower of bubbles up past my mask. What kind of family were we that our heirlooms were twenty-pound anchors created specifically for pulling a sea monster hoax? Weird, I decided. It made us weird.

Now that the crisis was over I could feel the adrenaline of the hoax slipping away, allowing my body's awareness of the freezing temperature to sink back in. My feet and hands were so cold that they felt like foreign objects only vaguely related to me, and I struggled with the knot that I'd so easily made just moments before. Minutes ticked by, and I knew I was pushing it with my air tank, but there was no way I was going to swim all the way back to shore just to have Curtis hand me a fresh tank and send me right back down here to tie Altie up the right way. It didn't matter that we'd be back for her later. It made no difference that it was freezing or that it was a Thursday and three hundred miles away my school was starting right now without me. All that mattered was the integrity of the equipment, the perfection of the plan, the completion of the hoax.

Finally I had Altie tethered once more to the bottom of the river. My sigh of relief bubbled up around my still-leaking mask, and in a moment of goodwill I swam over to give Altie a pat on the nose like she was a golden retriever who'd performed a trick well. The rubber of her head felt rough even to my frozen hands, and I took a second to admire the new paint job Dad had done to make the mottled gray-brown skin look appropriately scaly. Inside Altie's jaws were two rows of pointy teeth, which, unlike the rest of her, were actually real. Gramps had spent hours mounting the alligator teeth he'd bought on eBay into the monster's jaws one painstaking fang at a time. I noticed one of the back teeth was sitting sideways. It must have been knocked loose when we were transporting her. Reaching into her jaw, I tipped the tooth up and shoved it down into its socket. One of Altie's big animatronic eyes chose that moment to blink.

I'd never turned the head off.

I yanked my arm backward, but it was too late. Altie's jaws came down hard on my hand. I jerked as I felt those teeth penetrate my glove and sink into skin as a rush of bubbles exploded out of my mouth in a silent scream. Grabbing Altie's jaw with my free hand, I attempted to pry it upward, but all I managed to accomplish was knocking my mask off, and I was blinded instantly by the muddy waters of the Altamaha River.

My hand was on fire, and the feeling reminded me of the time Curtis had accidentally slammed my fingers in the van door, except worse because the van door hadn't stayed shut. Panic clouded my brain, and I felt light-headed. For a second I thought it was from pain before I realized that my regulator had fallen out of my mouth when I screamed. I reached for it with my free hand, but it was just out of reach, twisted behind me and stuck on my air tank. My lungs burned. I was going to die down here.

Frantic, I gave my hand another ineffective jerk, but Altie had me in her jaws and wasn't letting go. I remembered the button under her jaw, but I knew from past experience that turning her off wouldn't open her mouth. However, at that moment my lungs were starting to do that weird heaving thing inside my chest like they could bust through my rib cage and out if they just tried hard enough. Logic didn't really matter anymore. I fumbled around for the button; my eyes burned as I tried to see through the murky water. Finally I found it and brought my free hand down on the button again and again, the water making everything feel like it was in slow motion. When Altie's jaw still didn't budge, I fumbled for the button and pulled downward. It resisted for a moment before springing free and bringing a trail of twisted wires after it. Altie's eyes began blinking frantically, and I pushed my fingers inside her head, grabbed a wad of wires, and pulled backward again. Black spots were starting to appear in my vision, and I knew I only had seconds left before I lost consciousness. All too aware that this was my last shot, I pulled back and decked the sea monster right in its giant blinking left eye. Altie opened her jaws, and my hand popped free.

I fumbled wildly for my regulator and shoved it in my mouth, inhaling the best mouthful of air in the history of ever. Crisis one solved, I used the mask-clearing skills I was now grateful Gramps had insisted I practice over and over on those nights in the pool. Blinking the last of the water out of my eyes, I held my hand up for inspection to the light from my now-crooked headlamp. My scuba glove was mangled and my hand was bleeding from a few small puncture wounds, but all my fingers were still there, and considering I'd just been bitten by a sea monster, I was going to consider it a win.

I turned and swam for shore, my injured hand held tight against my chest.

CHAPTER THREE

I actually expected some sympathy when I dragged myself dripping and half frozen out of the river, bleeding hand held piteously against my chest. Which just goes to show that a prolonged lack of oxygen can really do things to your brain.

"Took you long enough," Curtis said, grabbing the tank off my back.

"You're kidding," I said. "And here I thought the empty air tank, impending hypothermia, and mangled hand were just perks of the job." I gingerly worked my shredded glove off my hand and held it up to see the damage. It had started to swell and turn an impressive purple color, although my skin had a blue tint to it from the cold so it was kind of hard to tell. My insides felt like one big frozen block of ice.

Curtis glanced at my hand, confirming that it was still there, I guess, and slung my air tank over his shoulder. "You'll live. Now hustle. The EWs could be back here any minute, and you aren't exactly inconspicuous."

I considered telling him that I could give a sea monster's backside about the eyewitnesses and whether or not I was inconspicuous after my near-death experience, but I knew it wouldn't do any good. I'd spent the majority of my life swallowing the things that I wanted to say, and today wasn't the day to change that habit. Sometimes I imagined myself as one of those gigantic dormant volcanos: peaceful on the outside but lots of hot angry lava hidden away on the inside.

I was just turning to give the darkening river one last dirty look when something moved in the bushes off to my left, and I froze. Gramps always said there was nothing worse than an unaccounted-for eyewitness, although after almost dying at the bottom of the river, I found that hard to believe. I waited to see if something moved again. Was my mind playing tricks on me, or had I really just seen a pair of eyes? Should I call Curtis back? If someone was watching, we would have blown the biggest sea monster job Dad had ever been lucky enough to land. I blinked the last of the water from my eyes and stared at the bushes. A moment later a squirrel came running out of the underbrush, and I sagged in relief. It was just my oxygen-deprived imagination seeing things like blond hair and binoculars. Behind me Curtis let out a shrill whistle to hurry it up, and I turned and jogged after him on numb legs toward our van.

The van was one of those long white, windowless eyesores favored by kidnappers, drug dealers, and my dad, and Curtis already had it running by the time I managed to finally haul myself into the front seat. He'd turned the heat to full blast, and I almost groaned as the hot air hit my frozen skin. Before I had a chance to peel off my wet suit to really get the thawing-out process started, Curtis was gunning the van backward through the trees and away. It was a rule that you never hung around the scene of a hoax in case any EWs decided to come poking around, but I still found myself caught off guard as I was thrown forward, barely avoiding a head-on collision with the front windshield.

"Easy," I yelped, fumbling to secure my seat belt with my good hand as he took a turn way too fast. Curtis didn't respond. His blue eyes held no hint of their usual humor. I knew he'd been nervous about pulling off this hoax without Gramps and Dad, but

I'd underestimated how serious my normally easygoing brother could be when he suddenly found himself in charge. Curtis's mouth was pressed into a grim line that made him look a lot like our mom used to. Even though she'd been gone for years, I could still remember her wearing that exact expression, usually when Dad was explaining his next hoaxing job or when he'd come home with bullet holes in the back of the van.

A few minutes later Curtis pulled into a gas station and parked. "Let me see your hand," he said.

"Don't start acting like you care now that we are away from your precious EWs," I said as I struggled to remove the wet suit that had welded itself onto my body. This must be what a snake feels like when it's trying to shed its skin, I thought as I twisted and flapped my arms in an attempt to free them. Curtis reached across and gave the suit a firm yank that popped my arms free. I breathed a sigh of relief as the van's heat finally hit my bare skin.

Curtis grabbed my arm and held up my injured hand, examining it like he actually knew what he was doing, which he didn't.

"What the heck happened?" he said.

"Altie bit me," I said. "Hard."

Curtis raised an eyebrow at me. "Altie bit you?" he repeated. "As in, our fake sea monster decoy?"

"No, I ran into the real thing down there," I said, cold and wet and irritable. "Don't be dumb."

"I'm not being dumb," Curtis said. "You could have. Gramps swears he saw the real Altie when he was my age."

"Right," I said dryly as I poked gingerly at one of the deeper wounds. If this injury ruined my chances at the Culver photography scholarship, I was going to personally turn that Altie decoy into mulch.

"Flex your fingers," Curtis commanded. I complied, wincing as the movement made a few of the punctures bleed sluggishly. I could probably still type, I reasoned. No one said I had to draft *all* my essays by hand before I typed them up. But my final piece was due to the scholarship board in less than a week, and between getting hauled across the state for the Altie job and now this, it would be a minor miracle if I finished it on time.

Curtis was still examining my hand, and I sighed and raised an eyebrow at him. "Feeling guilty that you cared more about the EWs than your brother's hand?" I asked, wondering if I should tell him about my moment of panic when I thought I saw someone in the bushes, before deciding against it. What was there to tell? That I saw a squirrel? I was already looking pretty stupid for letting a fake sea monster bite me.

"Not feeling even a little guilty," Curtis said, letting go. "Just wondering how the heck you're going to explain this to Gramps without getting a lecture and his boot up our you-know-whats."

I groaned. I hadn't even thought of that yet, although Curtis was exaggerating. Not about the lecture—that was a sure thing—about the boot. The only thing Gramps stuck his boot up was a very tricky Yeti suit he'd had to wear in Tibet once. Now that Curtis had freed my hand, I sat up and started working at the bottom half of the wet suit. The sooner it was off, the sooner I'd be able to feel my frozen butt cheeks again. The temperature gauge on the car said it was fifty degrees outside, and I knew in the big scheme of things that wasn't *that* cold, but I was a Georgia boy, and we didn't *do* cold. Not really.

"I wouldn't take that all the way off if I were you," Curtis warned.

I glanced up at him and frowned. "Why's that?"

"Because you're just going to have to put it back on again in a few hours so we can disassemble Altie and pull the anchors. And there's nothing worse than putting back on a cold, wet wet suit."

I held up my mangled hand. "I beg to differ."

Curtis snorted. "It's your own stupid fault if Altie bit you." I stuck my tongue out at him as he climbed past me into the back of the van to get on his own wet suit and check out the remaining air tanks. Hurt hand or no hurt hand, disassembling Altie was a two-man job. Feeling resigned, I leaned my head back against the battered seat of the van and shut my eyes as I let the top half of my body bake in the glorious blast of the heating vents while my lower half stayed frozen in soggy misery. Man, I hated sea monster jobs.

CHAPTER FOUR

Eight hours later we were on our way home, and I was finally starting to feel my toes again. I sat with them pressed against the heating vent like they were hot dogs over a fire, and it was awesome. The fact that Curtis hadn't even mentioned the strong foot smell that had permeated the entire van meant that he was either still too frozen to notice or too tired to care—probably a combination of both. Behind us, Altie's dismembered body was strapped to the inside of the van with bright red bungee cords, meticulously disassembled and loaded. I found myself giving her ugly crocodile mug dirty looks from time to time as my hand throbbed. I'd won our battle, but that fist-sized dent in her head and the mess of ripped-out wires were going to be really fun to explain to Dad. I'd have to really play up the near-death experience, but even that probably wouldn't get me completely off the hook for mangling one of his precious monsters. While I'd been worried about hiding my injury from Gramps, I was more worried about hiding the wrecked equipment from Dad. I sniffed. Dad wouldn't notice an injury unless it included a full body cast, and even then somebody would probably have to point it out to him.

Curtis glanced at me. "Should we go to the hospital to see if you need stitches? Or an X-ray or something?"

I shook my head. I was pretty sure nothing was seriously wrong with my hand. "No, we just need to get home. Besides," I snorted, "can you imagine trying to explain it? Somehow I don't think we could just cruise in there and tell them that a sea monster tried to take a chunk out of me."

"Are you sure?" Curtis asked. "Because if your hand turns green and falls off or something, Gramps will never let me hear the end of it."

"I'm sure," I repeated, although *that* lovely possibility had never actually occurred to me. "How did meeting the client go?" I asked. In the rush to get Altie out of the lake, I'd forgotten to ask the most important question: Had we done the job well enough to get paid?

Curtis nodded. "I was a little worried at first because the beach was deserted when I got there. Luckily an entire busload of field-tripping kids showed up before I had to resort to any kind of drastic measures to draw a crowd."

"Gramps doesn't approve of drastic measures," I said.

Curtis shrugged. "I needed everyone's attention on that river when Altie made her appearance, so I was prepared to get all kinds of drastic. Especially since our client was there to see it all go down. We've never had that before. Talk about pressure."

"But you did it?" I said, wanting the clarification.

"Done and done," Curtis said. "It was just a matter of directing the loudest kid's attention to the river at the right time, and I let him do the rest while I supervised the situation and made sure everyone remembered to document the amazing occurrence by yelling things like, 'Where's my phone? Get a picture of that thing! Is that a sea monster?' You know. The usual stuff. Anyways, the thirty grand will get wired to Dad's account once he completes the final sea monster hoax."

"Then what's in there?" I asked, jerking my chin toward the fat envelope Curtis had shoved between the front windshield and the dash. "You were just supposed to confirm with him that we pulled off the third hoax to his specifications."

Curtis nodded. "I did that. He wasn't very excited to see me and not Dad, but he cheered up when I told him that, for a bonus five hundred dollars cash, I'd get him an extra two eyewitnesses. The more people who got an eyeful of Altie, the bigger the headlines would be. And you know that's all he really cares about."

"Was that what took so long?" I asked, feeling slightly annoyed as I remembered my excruciatingly long wait in freezing cold water.

"Five hundred bucks is five hundred bucks," Curtis said. "You know the rules. Always go above and beyond, or they will find someone else to hire."

I glanced over at Curtis and scoffed, "Do you really believe that garbage Gramps says about the Gerhard family?"

He shrugged. "I do. Dad said they put in a bid for this job too and lost. Why else would Dad and Gramps be so twitchy about keeping our jobs and contacts secret?"

"Here's a thought," I said. "Because everything we do is illegal?"

"Well, Gerhard family or no Gerhard family," Curtis said, "Altie is one of our recurring gigs and the easiest since it's practically in our backyard. So a few extra EWs is always a good thing."

"I guess," I grumbled, not sure five hundred dollars

was worth risking hypothermia for.

"I guess?" Curtis said. "You and I both know that if we screwed this up, then we'd be eating the tickets to Scotland and Africa for Dad and Gramps. And the last thing we need is to be spending money we don't have."

"I know that," I said, thinking about all the overdue notices from the bank that had been coming in the mail. Hoaxing in general didn't pay well or even at all sometimes. Half the time Dad did hoaxes for a couple hundred bucks or less, and even those jobs had been getting harder and harder to come by recently. Curtis was convinced that hoaxing was going to die out completely if we didn't take the business digital, but that suggestion always got shut down hard. So it was no wonder that a payday this big had snapped Dad out of his usual preoccupied fog. I could still picture the way his eyes had lit up as he told us about the Sea Monster Grand Slam. He'd called it the hoax job of the century, and it was definitely the best-paying one we'd ever had by a long shot.

Sea monsters were pretty run-of-the-mill cryptids for us, second only to the many variations of Bigfoot when it came to popularity, but there were a few sea monsters that stood out above the rest. Apparently this deep-pocketed client wanted my dad to pull off a grand slam and hoax the four big ones to drive up interest in some movie they were producing. The kicker was that all the hoaxes had to be done in one week. In order to get paid, he had to pull off a Mbielu-Mbielu-Mbielu hoax in the Congo of Africa, a Loch Ness Monster hoax in Scotland, the Altamaha-ha hoax we'd just completed here in Georgia, and finally a Champ hoax in Vermont. The amount of travel involved alone made it nearly impossible, but the alternative was our house getting foreclosed, so Dad had agreed to the ridiculous time line.

The plan was for him to deal with the Loch Ness Monster and Champ. Meanwhile Gramps would handle Mbielu in Africa and then fly back to help us with the Altamaha-ha job since it was closer to home. Of course, Dad hadn't planned on Gramps getting stuck in Africa and us having to pull off the Altie hoax all on our own.

"By the way, Gramps called when you were in the river," Curtis said, snapping me back to the present.

"Checking in?" I guessed.

Curtis grinned and nodded. "Of course. It killed him that he missed this. He lives for sea monster gigs."

"I'll be glad when he gets back tomorrow," I said, stifling a yawn. "The house feels weird with him and Dad both gone."

Curtis nodded. "Agreed. He said Africa was a

success, though. He pulled off the Mbielu hoax and even had a chance to do a little Mokele Mbembe hunting since he was apparently near some tribe that had a recent sighting."

"Let me guess," I said with a sniff. "He talked to some very informative natives who described detailed sightings of a living dinosaur. They pointed to the pictures he showed them of a prehistoric brachiosaurus and told stories of disappearing villagers. And on top of all that, he even thinks he found a partial footprint."

"Close," Curtis said. "Dung."

"Dung?"

Curtis nodded. "According to Gramps a verifiable Mokele Mbembe pooped, and he found it. He's got a big old sample of it he's bringing home to run tests on. Although with his luck, it's probably just a poor elephant that had the runs." Curtis laughed at his own joke, and I cracked a half-hearted smile. Gramps was a true-blue cryptid hunter, just like his father and grandfather before him. There was nothing he loved more than being on the trail of an elusive legend like the Mokele Mbembe, although he loved a good hoax when the opportunity presented itself, like it had last week after Dad had already left for Scotland.

"Saddle up, boys!" Gramps had said, barging into the kitchen. I'd been sitting at our table, my social studies books spread across its battered surface, trying to study for tomorrow's test. I glanced up to see his arms overloaded with grocery bags. My brain was still trying to remember the date World War I began when Curtis came into the kitchen, taking the bags out of Gramps's arms.

"Grayson and I went shopping before Dad left," Curtis said, plunking down in an empty kitchen chair to peer in the closest bag. "Why did you buy more groceries, Gramps?"

Gramps waved a hand dismissively. "The slop you picked up shouldn't be eaten by human beings. Hamburger helpsie-doopsie or some garbage like that. Tonight I make you a real meal, a Scottish meal."

I put my hands over my eyes in mock horror. "Oh, please Lord, don't let it be haggis again."

"No haggis," Gramps said, sticking his head into the remaining sack. "The blasted butcher at Kroger looked at me like I was the five-headed Karfunkle when I asked for a sheep's stomach. No, my boys, tonight we eat Cullen skink just like your blessed grandmother used to make."

I raised my eyebrow at Curtis and mouthed, "*Karfunkle?*"

"*Cullen skink?*" he mouthed back.

"It's a soup that will stick to your ribs and put hair

on your chest," Gramps said. "Besides, I can throw it together and leave it to simmer while we prep for the job your dad so kindly forgot to mention."

"A job?" I asked warily, glancing at my watch. It was already four o'clock, and if I had a prayer of doing well on the test the next day, I needed the rest of the night to study.

Gramps nodded. "I'm sorry it's on a school night, but it can't be helped. I'll need both of you along for this one. It's a Bigfoot job, seems fairly straightforward, and we should be home by ten at the latest."

"Sweet," Curtis said, bounding to his feet. "I'll start loading the van."

"Does it have to be tonight?" I said, cringing a little as the words came out more whiny than I'd intended. "I've got homework."

Gramps clapped me on the shoulder before thumping a strange array of smoked fish and onions on the countertop. "Can't be helped, my boy. Can't be helped. I'm not overly pleased about your dad scheduling this while he's off hoaxing in my motherland of all places, but I leave tomorrow for Africa so it's got to be tonight. Pack up your things; you can study in the van on the way there."

Knowing a lost battle when I heard one, I started shoving my books back in my bag. It was then that I noticed the pile of mail Gramps had brought in along with the grocery bags, and I paused to shuffle through the stack. The familiar white envelope with our bank's logo on the front wasn't there, but I could see the tip of it sticking out of Gramps's back pocket as he bent over to rummage in the fridge. He and Dad seemed convinced that Curtis and I had no clue what was going on with our finances, and without ever really talking about it, Curtis and I had decided to let them continue their charade. At least after the Grand Slam we'd have the bank off our backs for a little while. The rest of the stack proved to be just junk mail and a few magazines, and I felt the familiar tug of disappointment that the letter I'd been hoping for was conspicuously absent. I sighed and tossed the lot back on the table.

"Problem?" Gramps asked.

I shook my head. "No problem." There were a lot of things that I could talk to Gramps about, but this wasn't one of them. I'd have to eventually, if I got in, but I was just chicken enough to put that off for as long as possible. The only person who knew that I'd applied to Culver Academy was my school's guidance counselor, and while she'd been encouraging in that way school counselors were supposed to be, even she hadn't seemed exceptionally hopeful. Not only was Culver one of the only private boarding high schools left with a killer photography program, but you usually had to have a trust fund and a few thousand shares of stock to be considered. I had neither. However, every year Culver let in a few select students on scholarship, and I wanted to be one of those select few. Bad. I'd already made it past the first round of applicants, thanks to the photography portfolio I'd submitted, but I wasn't accepted yet.

I needed to get out of the family business, and that wasn't going to happen if I stayed here. I'd seen Curtis skip school left and right, his grades suffering as he spent late nights with Dad in the basement putting together some elaborate hoaxing plan or helping Gramps with the details of his next cryptid expedition. Hoax for Hire was a black hole, and I wasn't going to get sucked in. If I got into Culver, I would walk away with an education that would get me a scholarship at any college I wanted. It was my ticket out of a life I'd grown to hate. That is, I thought with a sigh, if I could keep my grades up, which seemed to be harder and harder these days with Dad and Gramps traveling all the time. An hour later I followed Gramps out to the garage, where Curtis was loading the last of the equipment.

Gramps peered into the back of the van and then turned to Curtis. "Did you remember to pack the feet?" he asked.

Curtis shook his head. "I knew I was forgetting something." He slid the bin he was holding into the van and jerked his head at me. "Go grab them, will you? We need to get going."

Turning on my heel, I headed back into the house. The door to the basement was usually hidden behind a huge bookcase, but since Curtis had just been down there, the bookcase was swung open on its thick metal hinges to reveal the gaping doorway. Some kids found Narnia behind their wardrobes, Gramps used to joke, but we found Bigfoot behind a bookcase. It wasn't really a funny joke. But the bookcase did its job of concealing some very incriminating evidence that we wouldn't want to have just lying around.

The wooden steps creaked as I descended into the dimly lit room that smelled like mold and spiders. The space had never been finished, although Dad had paid big money to have it dug to twice the depth of a normal basement so that it could accommodate the large-scale decoys and costumes that were required for our elaborate hoaxes.

Above me dangled the large outstretched wings of the Owl Man costume that had resulted in Dad's broken leg two summers ago and the curved python-like body of the Nguma-Monene decoy that took three hours to disassemble and reassemble on site. Complicated bungees, ropes, and pulley systems that worked only part of the time kept all the big stuff up and out of the way while wooden shelving units lined the walls full of bins with faded labels. In the middle of the room was the worktable, a large wooden monstrosity that weighed about a ton. One of our models of the infamous Chupacabra was currently stretched across its scratched and battered surface, a project left half completed when Dad had decided to drop everything to attempt the Sea Monster Grand Slam. About eight feet in length, the Chupacabra looked like someone had crossed a dog with a hyena and maybe a mountain lion. I leaned over to inspect where mice had eaten away at the neck, revealing the chicken wire construction my great-uncle Bart had been notorious for. Dad was attempting to patch it with thin pieces of rubber that he melted with a welding torch. The honk of a horn made me jump, and I glared up at the ceiling. If Curtis was in such a hurry, he should have come down here himself.

Turning my attention back to the dusty row of bins on my right, I hurried past Mapinguari and Ogopogo sections to get to the biggest section: Bigfoot. The collection was extensive, since Bigfoot was a hoax known worldwide in different forms. Some people called it Sasquatch; up north it was the Yeti or even the Abominable Snowman. Two bins were missing, already loaded in the back of the van, and I examined the remaining bin labels. Hair samples, DNA vials, audio-video supplies, soundtracks, and finally, on the very last bin, just one word: *FEET*. Bingo.

I slid it out just as Curtis honked the horn again. The feet were inside, huge and hairy, and I picked them up gingerly. Gramps claimed they were real Bigfoot feet, found in a bear trap in the eighteen hundreds and sold to my great-great somebody-or-other for a side of salt beef and a pint of whisky. I was ninety percent sure that he was full of it, but with my family that last ten percent was always a bit iffy. The toes were long with thick yellow nails that grew to points barely visible beneath the dense layer of brown fur that covered them. If they had belonged to a living person at one time, the guy had had one heck of a time finding shoes. I thought about asking Gramps about them again, to see if his story would stay the same or get wilder with the telling, but ultimately decided it was better not to know.

Grisly prize in hand, I headed back up the stairs at a run. The sooner we got this over with the better. The smell of Gramps's Cullen skink soup was wafting from the kitchen, and I made a mental note to have Curtis stop at a McDonald's on the way to the hoax. Curtis and Gramps were already in the van, and I jumped in the back seat as Curtis put the van in gear and pulled out into the dark Georgia night.

"You navigate," Curtis said as he tossed his iPhone over his shoulder at me. It smacked off my head with a thunk and landed in my lap. Curtis laughed. "You gotta work on that hand-eye coordination, man."

"What's the address?" I grumbled as I rubbed my now-throbbing forehead. Curtis rattled it off, and I quickly programmed it into the phone.

"Would you like to read the information for the job or shall I?" asked Gramps, holding up a familiar blue file folder.

"Can you do it?" I asked as I rummaged around in my backpack for my study guide.

"Of course, my boy," Gramps said, patting his front pocket. "I forgot about that test of yours." He slapped at his other pocket, frowned, and looked inside of the brown corduroy jacket he always wore on jobs.

"Forgot your glasses?" Curtis asked.

"Guilty as charged," Gramps said, and handed the file back to me.

I grabbed it and flipped it open, using the glow from Curtis's cell phone to look at the contents. Inside was the normal stuff—contract, town map, contact name, and description of the desired hoax.

"Looks pretty standard," I said, flipping through the first few pages. "Mayor trying to draw tourism to a dying small town. Doesn't care where we do the staging, but he recommends near the houses of a few different little old ladies who will be sure to raise a fuss and get some publicity."

"Payment method?" Gramps asked.

"There is an address where we can pick up the cash. We get half now and the other half mailed to Dad's PO box if it makes the news."

"Man." Curtis shook his head. "Please tell me we're making decent money off this?"

I flipped through a few more pages, scanning the information. "A thousand bucks." I shrugged. "Not horrible. But not worth jail time either."

Gramps whistled and shook his head. "That's it for a Bigfoot job? In my day we'd get twice that."

"In your day there wasn't an internet," I said.

"And we were better off," Gramps said, and I immediately regretted the comment. "The only thing that belongs on a web is a spider, and I wouldn't even allow the J'ba Fofi to stick his giant hairy leg into that technology cesspool."

"J'ba Fofi?" Curtis repeated. "Giant spider? Or Jabba the Hutt's fancy French cousin?"

I snorted, and Gramps narrowed his eyes at us for a second before letting his face spread into a wide grin as he shook his head. "You boys and your *Star Wars*."

"You grandfathers with your Congolese Giant Spiders the size of school buses," Curtis said, perfectly mimicking the same amused and exasperated tone our grandfather had just used.

"Now that," I said with a shiver, "is much scarier than a giant slug thing that can't even move."

"The giant slug thing had Princess Leia in a bikini," Curtis said. "So the slug thing trumps the giant spider."

"So what will it be tonight?" Gramps asked, settling back and taking a sip out of his ancient silver thermos that I knew contained his favorite spiced tomato juice. "The story of the Beast of Bodmin Moor or the Dobhar-chú?"

"What about the time you were in the Congo and spotted the tracks of the Emelu-Ntouka?" Curtis asked, a familiar grin spreading across his face. I slumped back in the threadbare seat and sighed as I pulled out my study guide. Even though we're siblings, Curtis and I felt like different species a lot of the time. Although, to be more accurate, I felt like the giraffe that had accidently ended up in the monkey pen. Curtis couldn't wait to follow in the McNeil family footsteps, and because of that he never put much time or effort into school, since practically nothing he learned in a classroom would ever help him pull off a successful Kraken hoax or track down a Kongamato in Africa.

Not me, I thought stubbornly. Everything I was going to need was going to be learned under the roof of a school building.

Gramps was gesturing enthusiastically, his deep voice filling the interior of the van as he wove his tale of exotic places and creatures. I tuned him out to stare through the smudged window. The glass felt cold against my forehead as I watched house after house whiz past. Their windows glowed warmly as, inside, normal families went about making dinner and doing homework. It didn't seem fair, I thought, some people having all that normal when others didn't have any. I shut my eyes as Gramps started in on his famous Emelu-Ntouka story.

"How's that studying going, Ace?" Gramps asked, and I jumped awake, wiping a line of drool off my chin.

"What time is it?" I asked as I attempted to locate my study guide in the dark. Instead my hands came across the mummified feet that must have shifted while we were driving, and I yelped and gave up.

"Took a little catnap did you?" Gramps said. "All ready for that test tomorrow?"

"He was probably ready for it a week ago," Curtis said, taking a drink out of a large Mountain Dew. I stared at it for a second, befuddled. Had we stopped at a gas station while I was sleeping? Wordlessly, Curtis handed back a bottle of lemon-lime Gatorade and a cold Big Mac. I grunted a thanks as I washed the taste of sleep from my mouth and unwrapped what was probably once a pretty good sandwich but was now soggy and congealed into something only slightly better than Gramps's Cullen skink soup.

"Not this time," I admitted, deciding not to bring up the jobs I'd had to help out with, prep for, or clean up after over the last few weeks. If I had to hear one more lecture about staying one step ahead of those blasted Gerhards, I was going to puke.

"What's this test on, anyways?" Gramps asked.

"World War One."

"Do your books mention the U-28 Monster?"

"No," I said. "What's that?"

"Haven't I told you guys about that one?" Gramps asked. "It's what started those stinking Gerhards hunting and hoaxing."

I rolled my eyes and stifled a groan. So much for avoiding the Gerhard topic.

"Actually," Gramps went on, "maybe that's why I never told you. Anything to do with that lot gives me heartburn."

"Hoax?" I asked.

"No," Gramps said, shaking his head. "The U-28 was the real deal. A cryptid sighting so unique it has never been seen again. Even that arrogant Forester Gerhard couldn't identify it, although I have some guesses."

"How do you know it wasn't just one of their hoaxes?" I asked. "Aren't the Gerhards known for some pretty elaborate stuff?"

"I know," Gramps said, and there was something about his tone that made it clear that we weren't to pry any further.

"So what happened?" I asked, thinking that, if this was even a tiny bit historical, I might be able to incorporate it into a short answer response and earn an extra credit point or two for originality.

"Well," Gramps said. "It was 1918, and Forester Gerhard was a crew member on a German U-boat called U-28."

"What's a U-boat?" Curtis asked.

"It's a submarine," I said before Gramps could respond.

"Very good," Gramps said. "You might do better on this test than you think. So anyways," he went on. "They torpedoed a British streamer called the *Iberian* that was loaded to the gills with expensive and heavy cargo. So when it got hit, it went down faster than you could spit. Moments after it sank beneath the surface, it exploded, probably the boilers or just a lot of built-up pressure. Whatever the reason, it shot debris and water into the air, and it shot something else too."

"What?" Curtis asked, his eyes on Gramps instead of the road.

"Focus," I said, giving him a smack on the back of the head. He shot me a dirty look in the rearview, but I was grateful to see his eyes return to the dark road.

"That's just it," Gramps said. "Nothing had ever been seen like it before or since, and trust me, I've looked. There was a ship full of eyewitnesses, and they all saw a sixty-foot-long creature get blown almost one hundred feet in the air, flailing about like the dickens. Most described it as looking like a gigantic crocodile with webbed feet and a pointed tail. It landed, thrashed a bit amongst what was left of the poor *Iberian*, and sank beneath the ocean again. No one had ever seen anything like it."

"And what do you think it was, Gramps?" Curtis asked, knowing full well that our grandfather would have a theory a mile long.

"I believe there are two equally likely possibilities," he said, and even though I couldn't see his face in the dimly lit car, I knew those blue eyes of his were twinkling happily as he hypothesized. "My first guess is that it was a mosasaur, left over from the time of the dinosaurs."

"Like how everyone thinks that the Loch Ness Monster is a plesiosaur?" Curtis said.

Gramps nodded in approval. "Exactly, my boy, which is why we use that majestic creature as a model for all of our Loch Ness hoaxes. But since the animal that flew out of the water had webbed feet and a pointed tail instead of fins, I think it was more likely a Thalattosuchia."

"What in the world is that?" Curtis asked.

"A prehistoric sea crocodile known to grow to massive proportions," Gramps said in that way he had of making the obscure and absurd sound like they were common knowledge.

"If there were that many eyewitnesses, why isn't the U-28 Monster more widely known?" I asked, thinking of the fame a single eyewitness account could bring to a cryptid.

"The U-28 went down in September of that same year, and it is reported that only one of the eyewitnesses to the monster survived."

"Reported?" Curtis asked with a knowing grin.

Gramps smiled back and clapped him hard on the shoulder. "Good to see you're paying attention, my boy. You're right: another undocumented survivor walked away that day, Forester Gerhard."

When I was about to ask Gramps how he knew for certain that this mysterious creature wasn't just an unfortunate whale that had gotten its face blown apart by an explosive boat, the cell phone in my hand squawked directions and Curtis made a fast lane change and exited off the highway. I sat up, stretching the kinks out of my back as the squirmy unease that always came before a hoax settled into my stomach.

"Remember the rule about eyewitnesses, boys?" Gramps asked, his tone no longer the easygoing one of a storyteller. It was time to work.

"Eyewitnesses are the bread and butter of the business," Curtis and I chorused together. Other kids learned nursery rhymes; we learned con artist catchphrases. Ours was a very classy childhood, I reflected.

The first stop was to pick up our cash. Curtis pulled into the back alley of a huge house on Main Street, and I yanked my black ski mask over my face before jumping out and running to the back door. I was about to knock when I saw the envelope shoved between the screen door slats. *HOAX FOR HIRE* was written in all caps. I grabbed it and hustled back to the van before opening it. Inside were five crisp hundred-dollar bills. I sighed as I handed them up to Gramps. Part of me had secretly been hoping that the payment wouldn't be there so we could just turn around and go back home. No money, no hoax. It was another catchphrase I'd grown up with—although that one was more of a family motto.

"Suit up, squirt," Curtis said over his shoulder as

we bumped across the potholes in the alley toward the outskirts of town.

"It's your turn to wear the suit," I said. "I did it last time."

"I'll do the suit," Gramps said. "No need to argue about it, boys."

Curtis glared at me in the rearview mirror, and I sighed. "It's fine, Gramps. I can do it," I said, dragging the musty thing out of the bin behind my seat. "You need to help Curtis with the evidence. Remember how he messed it up last time?" Curtis shot me another dirty look, and I stuck out my tongue at him.

Curtis and I may not have agreed on a lot, but we always agreed about Gramps. Dad was flighty, always planning or plotting the next hoax, never around enough physically or mentally to really be relied on. And even though Gramps was still traveling and hunting cryptids, we knew it was only a matter of time before his age finally started to show. Enough of our friends' grandparents had broken hips or shoulders and gone into nursing homes, never to come back out again, to have us spooked. We didn't want that for Gramps, not if we could avoid it. So if that meant I had to wear the suit, then I'd wear the suit. Bigfoot in particular was difficult, what with the stilts built into the legs to add the extra height.

"Right," Gramps said, sounding a little deflated. "The evidence. Can't mess that up. One of the most important pieces of the hoaxing puzzle."

I gritted my teeth as I struggled to unzip one of the legs on the Bigfoot suit. Some of the fur had gotten stuck between the zipper's metal teeth, and I wiggled it back and forth gingerly. I didn't want to be the McNeil that finally busted the stupid thing. The suit was old enough that the smell of roadkill had almost worn away. It had been cobbled together by my grandmother with the remains of the rabbits and raccoons who'd never learned the lesson about looking both ways before you cross the road. Despite her limited sewing skills and semi-decayed materials, the thing was pretty legit. The brown hair dye had made it one uniform color, and if you caught sight of someone walking in the suit, hunched and apelike, you'd be convinced you'd either lost your mind or that Bigfoot really did exist. We had a few other suits in rotation, but this was the best of the lot. Bigfoot was one of the oldest hoaxes my family could take credit for. Not that we *could* take credit for any of them without getting arrested. It was a downside to the whole hoax business. That and having to wear roadkill.

Curtis turned off the headlights and pulled the van into a dark parking lot beside a forest preserve.

"Ready?" he asked, unbuckling his seat belt. He pulled his own black ski mask out of the pocket of his hoodie and pulled it on over his head.

Gramps did the same, turning in his seat to inspect me. He gave a short nod of approval and held out a hand. "Feet," he said. I gingerly handed them up, doing my best not to visibly cringe. Gramps hefted one in each hand and grinned, his teeth shining white in the dim light of the van.

"Evidence container," Curtis said, matching Gramps's commanding tone, and I narrowed my eyes at him. A four-year age difference did *not* make him an adult or my boss, a fact I'd have pointed out if Gramps weren't there.

I pawed through the pile of Tupperware containers lining the wall of the van until I spotted the container labeled *BIGFOOT* in my dad's handwriting and shoved it a bit too forcefully at the back of Curtis's head. He grabbed it and shot me a look that promised vengeance. With that he and Gramps slipped silently from the car. I sat back, the head of the Bigfoot costume sitting in my lap as the sounds of crickets filled the van. Ten minutes later they were back, slipping silently inside the van and pulling off their masks to reveal identical flushed faces and shining eyes. It was the adrenaline— a hoax high. I'd seen it enough times to recognize it, but there was something about seeing it on Curtis that always felt wrong. Didn't he want more than a life of lies and cash in envelopes?

"Showtime," he said. My stomach lurched. There was no hoax high for me. You had to enjoy it to get that kind of rush.

"Good luck," Gramps said. "Remember to keep your eyes up, and tread carefully on those stilts; the terrain is rough."

I nodded. There was no use delaying the inevitable, so I jammed the Bigfoot head on, opened the van door, and slid out into the warm night. The suit itched, and sweat immediately started pooling between my shoulder blades, but if I breathed through my mouth, the smells of rotten leather and burned hair weren't that bad. Curtis cleared his throat loudly, and I turned to see him giving me the "get on with it" hand flap as he slipped back into the woods on my left just as Gramps disappeared to my right. So I did. Bending at the waist, I began the hunched-over lope my father had forced me to perfect at the age of eight. My arms were loose and low, my shoulders curved, my feet moving with an animal-like grace despite the suit's built-in stilts that made me a whopping eight feet tall. The sounds of the night silenced as I made my way through the trees. The forest had never seen anything quite like me before.

When the small white house came into view, I hesitated. I hated this part, but I gritted my teeth and lumbered forward. The quicker I got this over with, the quicker I could get out of here. I made sure to step on every twig and dry leaf as I shuffled toward the house, making the noises that were supposed to sound like a Bigfoot. Some kids learned "Row Row Row Your Boat," but I'd learned how to sound like a barfing moose.

Sure enough, the lights flicked on. I banged a bit against the side of the house and then began my shuffle back toward the perimeter of the woods. I caught sight of a woman's face peering out into the night and froze. A man's face appeared next to the woman's, and their twin expressions of terror were almost comical. Uh-oh, I thought. This wasn't good. We'd been banking on only one eyewitness. I waited another half second, until the flash of a camera had lit up the night, and I heard Curtis and Gramps whistle simultaneously, sending me the signal that the EW was a success. Then I turned and lumbered into the cover of the trees. The woman's terrified scream cut through the night, quickly followed by the sound of a man's excited shouting and a door slamming. I took two more shuffling steps, ensuring I was out of eyesight, and then I took off through the woods, running as fast as the stilts would allow just as the sound of a shotgun being fired rang out—

I was jerked back to the present and out of my memory of last week's Bigfoot hoax as Curtis hit a pothole hard, and I lurched in my seat. This time I was in the front seat, and there was no Gramps there telling stories about sea monsters and exploding World War I submarines. I glanced over at Curtis to see that his face was just as closed and drawn as my own felt.

"You should try to get some sleep," he said. "You have school tomorrow."

"So do you," I pointed out.

"But only one of us actually cares about staying conscious for it," he said.

"I don't think I'll be able to sleep," I admitted. "I still feel frozen solid."

"Same here," Curtis said. "Dad should really charge more for sea monster gigs when the water's that cold."

"At least he has to do Champ," I said, stifling a yawn. "I bet Vermont is freezing right now."

I woke up as we pulled into the garage. The overhead lights were harshly fluorescent, and I sat up blinking. My neck hurt, my butt was numb, and my mouth tasted like I'd been licking someone's shoe. Sleep had made my eyes crust over, and I rubbed at them to peer at the clock; it was well past midnight. I groaned as I untangled my legs and climbed out of the van.

Still half-asleep, I stumbled to my room and fell facedown on my bed. And I should have just crashed like that, but I felt gross and gritty from my swim in the river and hours spent cramped in the van. Besides, Curtis's talk about my hand turning green and falling off had me worried. So I dragged myself into the bathroom and dumped an entire bottle of hydrogen peroxide over it, clamping my teeth down hard as it bubbled and fizzed in the angry red scrapes. When I was little, my mom used the stuff liberally any time we skinned a knee, and she'd always pretend like somehow watching your open wound bubble made the sting worth it. It didn't. A fast shower and a freshly bandaged hand and I was back in bed less than ten minutes later and instantly asleep.

CHAPTER FIVE

My alarm went off at five a.m. I grumbled at it and hit the Snooze button, but I didn't go back to sleep. I never did. I lay in my nice warm bed and lectured myself. The lazy part of my brain protested that I'd had a late night, that I could sleep another hour if I really wanted, that missing one day wouldn't hurt anything. The other part of my brain argued that I would regret it if I slept in.

So despite the hour and the dark and the late night, I showered and shrugged into a hooded sweatshirt. Curtis thought I was a real freak for showering in the morning *and* at night, but I thought it was gross that he didn't. After grabbing my writing notebook out of my backpack and my camera off the shelf, I made my way into the living room to boot up our ancient desktop computer.

Usually I took a walk around the neighborhood in the morning before school, taking pictures in the early predawn light as the world was just waking up. The portfolio I'd sent off to Culver for scholarship consideration had been chock-full of pictures taken less than a block from my house. I loved the early-morning calm with nothing but me and the soft click of my camera. They weren't the pictures I wanted to take, of exotic locations, but they would do for now. Just like the ancient camera I'd inherited from Gramps would do until I had the cash to buy something that didn't look like it belonged in an antique store. Luckily the people at Culver had assumed my pictures' aged quality had been an artistic choice or I never could have competed against the other entries with their fancy digital cameras.

There would be no picture taking this morning, though, and I flexed my fingers, thankful again to be alive and not stuck on the bottom of the Altamaha River, a fact that I'd downplay significantly when Gramps forced the story out of me. I pushed the thought away along with my urge to forgo working on this awful essay and sat down. I preferred writing by hand instead of typing, but despite the fact that my hand felt better than it had the night before, it was in no shape to write. As our computer finished booting up, I flipped open my notebook to my page of ideas for the scholarship essay. I was a scholarship finalist based on my photography, but the second part of the application was an essay. If I didn't get started on this thing and soon, there was no way I'd get it in by the deadline, and I could kiss Culver goodbye.

I craved a life of adventure and travel just like every other McNeil before me, but unlike the rest of them, I wanted one that I could actually photograph and tell people about. What was the point of seeing amazing places and doing cool things if it had to be kept an undocumented secret? The scholarship to Culver Academy was my ticket out of a life I'd grown to hate.

Speaking of tickets, Dad's receipt for his stupidly expensive, last-minute ticket to Scotland was still sitting next to the keyboard. I picked it up, wondering which credit card company had allowed him to spend that much when he hadn't paid them back yet for the last expensive ticket he'd bought to who-knows-where to pull off who-knows-what hoax that he may or may not have gotten paid for. It was a downside of doing something illegal for a living: who could you complain to if you didn't get paid? Scotland, I thought with a sigh. I'd only been there once, four years ago when I was eight, and I wanted to go again but not as a hoaxer. Never again as a hoaxer.

The day Gramps had taken us to Scotland I'd been unable to contain my excitement. Unlike most trips, Dad was actually coming with us on this one. Usually he preferred to travel and hoax solo, pulling off complicated jobs with the help of elaborate plans and technology rather than a partner. Mom had been gone only a few months, and he'd already started the transformation from *Dad* to *Guy Who Hung Out in the Basement a Lot*, but there was still enough of the old Dad left that I'd felt hopeful about the trip. I wasn't sure if I thought that going to Scotland was going to somehow snap him out of the funk he'd been in or if I'd just been looking forward to seeing the legendary Loch Ness that Gramps had been telling me about, but I'd barely been able to stay in my seat as we waited for our plane.

"If you need to use the bathroom, you should do it now," Dad had said, looking up with barely concealed annoyance from the book he was holding.

"I don't have to go," I'd said.

"Then why are you squirming like a fish on a hook?" he asked, his thin mouth turned down disapprovingly. His face had changed dramatically in a short amount of time, the lines around his eyes and mouth deepening as his once round face thinned out, leaving overly prominent cheekbones and eyes that always looked tired. I hadn't known that it was possible to age years in a matter of months, but apparently grief and loss could etch themselves into skin just as easily as the heart.

"Just excited, I guess," I apologized, making an effort to sit still. Inside my blue backpack was a book I'd checked out from the library all about the infamous Loch Ness Monster. I was planning to read it on the plane so I could impress Gramps with all my knowledge about Nessie sightings, even if I knew for a fact that over half of them were orchestrated by my own family. I was also planning to use it for the report our teacher had assigned me to complete over our spring break. She'd given each of my classmates and I one of those yellow disposable cameras and instructed us to document our reports, and I just knew that the photos I would take would put my project over the top. The best report was going to get a prize, and I was bound and determined to win it.

"Do you think we'll see Nessie?" I asked.

Dad snorted in response, turning his attention back to his book.

"But Gramps says that this is the perfect season for

Nessie sightings," I said, unable to let it go.

"The only Nessie I've ever seen is the one I helped your grandfather sink in the loch when I was only a little older than you," Dad said, his eyes still on his book.

"Can you tell us about it?" Curtis asked, leaning forward across the aisle from where he sat next to a snoring Gramps.

"No," Dad said shortly, his eyes flicking to either side of us, where our fellow passengers waiting to fly on Air Scotland sat reading newspapers and listening to headphones.

Curtis leaned back, disappointed, and we both flicked our eyes toward Gramps, who would, undoubtedly, tell us all about it later if we asked.

"Gramps said his brother is meeting us at the airport?" I asked Dad.

Dad sighed and closed his book. This was a new role for him: kid entertainer. My mom used to be the one with the snacks in her purse and the endless amounts of patience. Dad was allowed to parent from the fringes, getting called into the fray only if Curtis and I needed our attitudes adjusted. Mom had been the one who made sure our lunches were packed and our sheets were washed, that our school projects got done and our permission slips signed. Dad had no patience for any of that, and after she'd died, he'd made the unilateral decision not to attempt to fill the unfillable shoes she'd left behind. Instead he'd decided that Curtis and I were old enough to manage on our own, and for the most part, he was right. At eight I *was* capable of packing my lunch and putting myself to bed at night. But still, just because I *could* do it didn't mean I liked it.

Gramps, on the other hand, had thrown himself into our family like a Scottish whirlwind, launching new traditions, cooking strange dinners, and turning all our laundry pink from his inexperienced enthusiasm. It was as though he realized that filling the mom-sized hole in our lives was impossible, so instead he created a Gramps-sized hurricane to distract us. I swallowed hard, missing my mom as my stomach turned nervously. She had always packed motion-sickness medicine for me, but I knew Dad wouldn't have thought of it, and from his annoyed expression I didn't think I should bring it up.

"Your uncle Angus is picking us up and taking us back to his place."

"What's it like?" I asked. "Uncle Angus's place, I mean."

Dad shrugged. "It's small, near the loch, smells a bit like fish." He turned back to his book, clearly dismissing me, and I swallowed the rest of my questions and decided to dig out my library book to get a head start on my research.

I was totally immersed in minutes, trying to commit sighting dates to memory, when Dad sniffed, practically in my ear. I jumped, not realizing he'd put down his own book to look over my shoulder at mine.

"So he got to you too," he said as he gave my book a disgusted look before turning the same glance to my sleeping grandfather. "The sooner you realize that Gramps's stories are just that, stories, the happier you'll be. Learn the hoaxing business, because all his stories and adventures do is drain his bank account. He's been hunting cryptids his entire life, Grayson. And stories he can't tell anyone but us are all he has to show for it."

Just then our flight was called to board. Gramps woke up with a start and looked around confused for a moment before grinning and asking me to give him a hand out of his seat. Curtis had hurried back to grab his stuff, his pockets full of candy he'd later eat on the long flight while I filled an impressive amount of barf bags and sat with my head against the window, wishing I could die.

Despite the puke bags, the trip had been a good one. We'd met Gramps's brother, Angus, who was just as cryptid crazy as he was. We'd seen plenty of Loch Ness, but Dad had been right. The only monster we saw while we were there was the one we assembled. Despite that disappointment, I'd written an impressive report on the Loch Ness Monster and taken some awesome pictures of the loch. It was the first time I'd looked at the world through the viewfinder of a camera, and I'd fallen in love. Hard.

I remembered how proud I'd been of those pictures right up until Dad had discovered them and thrown them away along with my library book and report. Cryptids were not something we were allowed to talk about, even in a book report. I'd had to scramble to find a new topic and my report had been crummy and earned me my first C minus.

Gramps was the only one who'd noticed the tears I was trying and failing to hold in, and he'd pulled me aside that day after school and given me the old Nikon camera he'd taken as payment for a Knobby hoax way back in the day. As I'd sat in my room that night, poring over the yellowed instruction manual in the camera case, I'd decided that the only adventures I wanted to go on were the ones I could photograph. Period.

If I got the Culver photography scholarship, I could document my adventures. The only thing standing between me and that dream was one crummy essay. The essay prompt stared up at me from the top of my notebook. It was one of those purposefully vague monstrosities that smart people thought made them look smarter but were really just obnoxious. *What Does the World Need?* What did that even mean?

An hour later the smell of bacon and scrambled eggs wafted from the kitchen, and I gave up my dead-end essay idea about the world needing more recycling centers so that I could investigate. Curtis stood over our stove still wearing the same clothes from the night before, a pencil stub stuck in his messy hair.

"Hungry?" He yawned as he plunked Mom's old cast-iron skillet down on the table—without a hot pad. I quickly grabbed one out of the drawer and, using the sleeve of my sweatshirt as a pot holder, slipped it underneath.

"You didn't have to cook," I said.

"No problem," Curtis said. He grabbed for a piece of bacon and yelped when he burned his fingers on the hot pan.

"Now that smells like a million bucks," boomed a voice behind us, and we both turned around to see Gramps shouldering his way through the door, battered tan duffel bag in tow. Tall and lean, our grandfather was an older version of our dad, but while Dad's hair was a reddish-blond like mine, Gramps's had gone white years ago. His once broad shoulders were a little stooped now, but at six feet four inches, he still filled a room.

"Gramps!" I said, jumping up to give him a hug.

Gramps chuckled and hugged me back so hard my ribs hurt. Usually I didn't greet him like an overeager puppy, but I'd almost died on the bottom of a river the day before, and, man, was I glad to have him home.

"How are my McNeil boys?" he asked, ruffling Curtis's hair and dislodging the pencil before sitting at the table. It was Mom's old spot that he always sat in, although I don't think anyone had ever told him that.

"Good," Curtis said.

"Tired," I yawned, sitting back down.

"I can't believe you got up to do homework this morning," Curtis said, shaking his head. "I feel like I blinked and it was time to get up. But what are you doing home, Gramps? I thought your flight didn't land until this afternoon. We could have picked you up."

Gramps waved a dismissive hand. "Never you mind that," he said. "I would have been home days ago if my good-for-nothing bush pilot hadn't decided to wager his plane in a bad game of poker. That's the last time I trust a man named Steve, I'll tell you that much." Gramps rolled his eyes in disgust, and Curtis and I grinned at each other. Typical Gramps. "Anyway," Gramps said. "I knew I'd never make it home in time to help with Altie, but when I heard that a bush plane had landed two tribes over, I decided to see if I could catch a ride. It beat a two-hour jeep ride through the Congo to the nearest airport. My old joints appreciated the cushier accommodations."

"How did the Mbielu-Mbielu-Mbielu hoax go?" I asked.

"Breeze," Gramps said. "My old friend Bintu was more than happy to help me out since a Mbielu spotting would give his village's tourist trade a good kick in the rear. We pulled it off in front of an entire convoy of Americans and their iPhones. Glorious. We went on a spectacular Mokele Mbembe hunt afterward too, and I swear we were so close to catching the beast I could practically smell it. Which reminds me." He reached down and pulled a small metal toolbox out of his duffel bag and plunked it on the table beside the bacon. He produced a small key, inserted it in the front lock, and threw the lid back. I wasn't close enough to see what was actually in the box, and I never got the opportunity because the smell hit me a second later, and I gagged on my mouthful of bacon. As though we'd choreographed it, Curtis and I both pushed back from the table simultaneously. Curtis shoved so hard that his chair tipped backward dangerously before he caught his balance.

"What is that?" I choked, holding my shirt over my nose.

"That," Gramps said proudly, "is a sample of Mokele

65

Mbembe droppings." He leaned forward and grabbed another piece of bacon as though the overpowering smell of decaying diarrhea wasn't about to make him gag.

"Gramps, seriously," Curtis said as he flapped a hand in front of his face. "Can you get that out of here? At least while we're eating?"

"Right, right," Gramps said, picking up the offending box and disappearing with it into the garage. I jumped up to wrestle open our ancient kitchen window while Curtis stood by the kitchen door, opening and shutting it to bring fresh drafts of air into the house. Slowly our kitchen stopped smelling like the inside of an abandoned porta-potty, but despite the definite improvement, I kept my shirt pressed firmly over my nose. Gramps was back a moment later, reassuming his seat at the now-vacated kitchen table. "Sorry about that," he said. "I've gotten used to the smell—a few hours in a small plane tends to numb the senses."

"You're lucky the pilot didn't pass out," I muttered.

"That's a pretty awesome find," Curtis said, scooting his chair back up to the table and helping himself to more eggs. How could he possibly eat with those fumes still floating around?

"It is," Gramps said excitedly. "But," he said, smacking me hard on the knee, "I want to hear about how your first solo Altamaha-ha went. I apologize again for not being back in time to help, but your dad never should have agreed to this crazy Sea Monster Slam Grand or whatever fool thing he's calling it. Too many big hoaxes to pull off in a week, if you ask me, which he didn't. I don't care how much money they offered him." He shook his head, his mouth pressed into a tight line so that his lips virtually disappeared. He always lost his lips when his only son did something that made him mad, but he was always careful not to say anything directly bad about Dad. I'm not sure if it was because Dad was his son or to shield us, but Curtis and I always knew when he was swallowing what he really wanted to say. This time he looked like he was almost choking on the words, but after a second he shook his head and forced a smile back onto his face that made the wrinkles around his eyes more pronounced. "I spotted something about an Altie sighting in this morning's newspaper, so you must have been successful."

"We were," Curtis said, not bothering to conceal the pride in his voice. "Multiple eyewitness accounts and a five-hundred-dollar bonus."

Gramps whistled in appreciation, and Curtis gave up hiding his grin. I slipped my injured hand into the sleeve of my hoodie and glanced down at the uneaten bacon and eggs on my plate.

"I want to hear every detail," he said. "But first, did your dad call?"

I glanced up, eyebrows raised. "No? Was he supposed to?"

Gramps nodded. "I talked to him twice while I was in Africa. He always underestimates the time a quality Nessie job takes. You have to sink the decoy at least a day before the hoax to avoid any unwanted attention from those bloody tourist tours that now infest most of the loch."

"Those bloody tourists are what help pay the bills," Curtis reminded him with a smile.

"I know, I know," Gramps said, flapping a hand at him dismissively. "You don't have to tell me. But all that extra kerfuffle means he will be cutting it close to get the decoy back to the States and ready for the Champ job. Especially since we always have a holdup in customs when we try to ship that thing anywhere. Those big crates tend to raise some eyebrows. He should have just used the Nessie in the Scotland annex like I told him to."

"The Nessie decoy in the Scotland annex is ancient," Curtis said. "You have to hook it together using leather straps, and we always spend half the time trying to fix corroded buckles. Besides that, it doesn't have any of the technology or upgrades of our Nessie."

Unlike Curtis, I'd never actually visited one of the McNeil family annexes, but I did know that there were ten in just the United States alone, with others located in some of our main hoaxing locations: Scotland, Ireland, Africa, and Switzerland. The annexes were full of outdated cryptid models, decoys, evidence containers—you name it. The McNeils had some major pack-rat tendencies and hadn't thrown away any cryptid gear since the Silver Lake incident in 1855. Apparently our great somebody or other had pulled off an awesome Silver Lake Sea Serpent sighting, and the town of Perry, New York, became tourist central. He made big money. The only problem was that he tried to burn the sixty-foot sea monster decoy in the attic of some hotel and did a crummy job of it because, when the fire died down, there sat an only slightly singed sixty-foot-long sea monster. It almost ended the McNeil hoaxing career right then and there. So ever since then McNeils had been storing all the old models and suits and evidence containers rather than attempting to get rid of them without getting caught. Dad called the annexes "obsolete junk collections" and preferred to transport his updated cryptid models, and with a payday as big as this one at stake, Dad wasn't taking any chances. When it came to cryptid hoaxes, Dad was the epitome of dependability, which is why Gramps's comment about him not calling felt so wrong.

"Dad always checks in on time," I said. "Do you think something happened to him?

"I'm sure he's fine," Gramps said, but his mouth pulled down at the corners and gave away that he was more worried than he was letting on. "I'll give him a ring soon." Gramps glanced at his watch and pushed back from the table. "You boys had better get a move on if you're going to make it to school on time. I made an appointment with Felix to look at my specimen this afternoon, so I'll see you both for dinner." He disappeared down the hall, humming the jaunty tune he always hummed when a hunt had gone well. But despite his easygoing manner, I felt old familiar nerves turn in my stomach.

"Speaking of dinner, we need to grab some groceries soon," Curtis said as he took a big bite of eggs straight from the pan.

"Do you think Gramps is hiding something?" I asked. "Dad always checks in on time."

"I'm sure he's fine," Curtis said around the mouthful, little bits of egg shooting out to spray the tabletop. "Gramps said so. Now, did you hear me? Groceries? Make a list, and we'll stop after school and stock up. We have plenty of cash after the Altie job. Dad doesn't have to know about that nice little eyewitness bonus I snagged us."

"Sounds good," I said, pushing away from the splatter zone. "You should hit the shower. You look awful and smell worse." But I couldn't shake the feeling of unease that Gramps's words had brought on, a feeling I knew wouldn't go away until Dad called and said everything was okay.

CHAPTER SIX

I was ready to leave for school ten minutes before we actually had to be on the road. I sat in the front seat of Gramps's ancient Mercedes, frantically studying my world history notes. It was one of my favorite classes, but I'd missed the review session for today's test because of the Altie hoax. The unit was on Greek legends, and I'd enjoyed learning about things like Cerberus and the Trojan horse. When Curtis finally made an appearance, his hair still dripping water from the shower, I was too angry to yell at him about being late. It wouldn't do any good, and it wouldn't make him drive any faster.

Curtis floored it out of the driveway, and I grabbed

the handle above my head. The seat belts didn't work, and if we got in a crash, I was going to have to literally save myself. Although I'd pit Gramps's old car against almost anything. The thing was built like a small tank, complete with a tape deck that didn't work, bulletproof glass, and a Volkswagen logo Gramps had decided was a good idea to wire to the front bumper despite the fact that the car wasn't a Volkswagen. It had been there so long that the wires he'd used to hold it in place had rusted permanently to the car and were impossible to remove. We'd tried. It felt like riding in a large bumpy boat, but it beat the bus. By the time we lumbered into the parking lot of my middle school, I was sweating. I hated being late.

"Relax," Curtis grumbled as he peered into the rear-view mirror and ran his fingers through his still-damp hair. "It's Friday. No one cares if you're a little late on a Friday."

"I care," I said, slinging my backpack over my shoulder.

"You know you don't have to be such an uptight dweeb *all* the time," Curtis said.

"Somebody has to be!" I shot back.

By some miracle I managed to make it to home-room just as the bell rang and I sat down at my desk while the morning announcements squawked over the loudspeaker. An unwelcome twinge of guilt washed over me as I pulled out my notebook and flipped it open. I probably shouldn't have snapped at Curtis. I hadn't been exactly fair. He was a slob, sure, but he did carry his fair share of the weight. He'd driven home last night while I slept, and without Gramps in the front seat telling stories, it must have been pretty hard to stay awake.

My uncompleted essay outline stared up at me from my notebook, and I sighed and ripped the page out. The idea was junk. I'd have to start over and write something new tonight. Type, I amended as I shut the notebook again and grabbed my camera out of my bag. I'd neglected it ever since the Grand Slam had taken over our lives. I held the viewfinder up to my eye to zoom in on a gum wrapper someone had dropped on the floor. A real photographer could make any subject beautiful, I reminded myself as I twisted the lens with my injured hand and winced. It had stopped throbbing, but now it just felt stiff, like my skin had shrunk a few sizes, and I was silently cursing Altie when a large honey-colored eye suddenly got in the way of my artistic gum wrapper portrait. I jumped about a foot as I looked up to discover Clare leaning over my desk to inspect my hand. How had I not noticed her arrival? I always knew where Clare was. Always. Maybe I was more tired than I thought. I fumbled my camera, barely getting it under control before it met an untimely end. I let out a relieved breath and carefully set it down on my desk. It wasn't worth much, but it was all I had, and it was from Gramps, which made it priceless.

"That looks gnarly," Clare said, her eyes never leaving my messed-up hand.

"You should see the other guy," I said, trying on a cocky grin like the one Curtis always wore. It felt unnatural, though, like I was wearing someone else's face, so I stopped.

"Yeah, right," Clare said. "Spill it. What happened?"

"Um," I said, shoving my hand back in my pocket, "nothing."

"You can do better than that," Clare said, grabbing my hand and yanking it out so she could study the hodgepodge of Band-Aids I'd used to cover up the puncture wounds. Her nose wrinkled in concentration, and I wished she wasn't quite so observant. Clare had moved here last year, and since her last name was Mayfield, she'd ended up getting assigned the seat right next to mine. On her very first day at school she'd smiled and started talking like we'd known each other for ten years and not ten minutes. At first I didn't quite know what to make of this girl with massive amounts of dark curly hair and eyes that saw a little too much, but I decided I liked having her as a friend. She was a nice dose of normal first thing in the morning, even if she was nosy as heck.

"My dog bit me," I supplied, knowing from past experiences that she wouldn't leave me alone until I gave her some excuse.

"Lame. You don't own a dog," she said. "Try again."

I rolled my eyes. "You wouldn't believe me if I told you," I said.

She raised her eyebrows at me. "Oh yeah?" she said. "Try me." And there was something about the way she said it, like a challenge, that made me want to shock her, to replace her smug you-won't-impress-me grin with one of surprise.

I leaned forward conspiratorially and beckoned her closer with a finger. When she sat forward I darted my eyes left and right before whispering, "Sea monster bite."

She sat back laughing. "Fine," she said. "Don't tell me. I don't really care anyway." She flipped her hair over her tan shoulder and the smell of coconuts and flowers wafted over, temporarily eclipsing the usual school smell of generic floor cleaner and shoes. How did girls always manage to smell so good?

"Well, if you're not too injured, Donovan's dad is letting him have a bonfire tomorrow in one of their farm fields. You should totally come. It's going to be fun."

"You know I don't go to that kind of stuff," I said. Which was true, but I didn't mention that it was because I'd never really been invited.

Sensing my hesitation, Clare rolled her eyes in mock exasperation. "Anyone can come. It's just a bonfire, and music."

"Bonfires are pointless without s'mores," I said without thinking, my brain still churning through the pros and cons of this new development.

"I'll make you a deal." She grinned, her voice playful. "If you bring the marshmallows, I'll bring the chocolate and graham crackers." Just then the bell rang ending homeroom and the room came alive with clattering chairs as everyone headed out. Before I could reply, Clare was gone.

The rest of the day passed in a blur of comforting normalcy. It was one of the many reasons I loved school—all that normal broken up by set periods of time, dictated by schedules and bells and rules. Marvelous stuff. Although today's normalcy was tainted a bit by my worry about Dad. I didn't have a cell phone, so until I saw Curtis after school, I wouldn't know if he had ever checked in with Gramps. I added it to my mental list of reasons why I *needed* a cell phone despite Dad's not-until-you-are-sixteen-and-driving rule.

If I was old enough to pull off a solo sea monster hoax, I was old enough for a cell phone, dang it.

I was hurrying outside after the last bell to meet Curtis in the parking lot when I heard someone call my name. The voice was female, and I turned automatically, searching the crowded hallway for Clare. Instead I saw my guidance counselor, Mrs. Howard, waving me down from just outside her office door, and I made my way back down the hall. This must be what a salmon feels like swimming upstream, I thought as I shouldered my way through the swirl of backpacks and talking kids all trying to exit the building as quickly as the narrow hallways of our old school would allow.

"Grayson, I'm so glad I caught you," she said, smiling one of those smiles that showed a few too many teeth to be considered pretty. She'd been Curtis's guidance counselor too. I think she got assigned all the kids whose last name started with an M or something, and he used to refer to her as Mrs. Horseteeth, which wasn't very nice of him. "Do you have a minute to talk," she asked, "or do you have a bus to catch?"

I shook my head. "No bus. Curtis picks me up, but he's always late, so it's no big deal."

"Great," she said as she stepped aside and ushered me into her minuscule office, which I suspected was a coat closet once upon a time. I took a seat in the one small chair perched mere inches from her postage stamp—sized desk. "I meant to call you down all day, but the afternoon just got away from me," she apologized.

"It's okay." I shrugged. "What's up?"

"I got a call from Culver Academy yesterday," she said, and I felt my stomach do a funny flop that couldn't be healthy.

"About me?" I asked.

She nodded. "They are looking into the potential photography scholarship students, checking in on current grades, asking for teacher references, and looking into attendance records." She said this last bit with raised eyebrows, and I felt my heart sink.

My mouth felt dry, like my tongue was suddenly twice as big as it had a right to be. "What did you tell them?" I asked.

"The truth," Mrs. Howard said. "That your attendance record leaves something to be desired. Did you know that if you'd missed even one more day of school last year, the state would have required you to take the sixth grade again?"

I nodded and looked down at the floor, blinking hard against the tears that I felt pushing against the backs of my eyeballs. It wasn't even going to matter if I wrote a killer essay for the scholarship contest. I was going to be out of the running before I even submitted my piece.

"But," she said, "I also told them that despite your absences you were caught up in every class, that you were extremely diligent about getting work that was missed and always turned it in in a timely manner."

"Thank you," I said. "I appreciate that." I had no clue if it would be enough, if all the good would outweigh the bad of a kid who couldn't manage to get his butt in his desk more than three or four days a week sometimes, but I had to hope it was.

"Don't thank me yet," Mrs. Howard said. "I know from my experience with your brother that a letter home, a phone call home, even a state-issued warning will not change your erratic attendance, so I am trying something new. And since you seem to value an education more than your brother ever did, maybe you'll heed my warning." She held up a Culver Academy brochure. "I know how much this means to you, Grayson. The portfolio you submitted shows a real talent, and I hope more than anything that you get one of those scholarship spots, but if you miss another day of school this year, I *will* report it to Culver."

I nodded, feeling a little sick. "I understand. I won't miss another day. I promise, Mrs. Howard. Really."

She smiled, her teeth showing all the way up to the

gum line. "I know you will. Have you settled on an idea yet for your essay?"

I shook my head. "The prompt is so vague it's making it tough."

"Well, I'm sure you will come up with something great," she said with an encouraging smile. "You have all weekend to work on it. Just make sure you submit it before noon on Wednesday. Now, I won't take up any more of your time since I'm sure you don't want to keep Curtis waiting."

"Thanks," I mumbled as I grabbed my bag and left Mrs. Howard's tiny coat-closet office. My shoes made an eerie *slap-slap* noise in the now-deserted hallways as I walked in a daze out to the parking lot. I felt tired—exhausted, really—and even though I'd only gotten about three hours of sleep the night before, I didn't think that was the reason.

If I hadn't been so distracted, I would have worried that Curtis was going to be bugged at me for being so late, but that worry would have been for nothing. Curtis was leaning against the side of the tank with his tongue shoved halfway down the throat of his girlfriend, Abby. He was much too busy to worry about his little brother running late. I sighed, slid into the passenger seat, and pulled out a book to read, but I couldn't seem to get past the first few sentences on the page. My conversation with Mrs. Howard swirled around and around in my head.

What if she was wrong, and Culver had taken me off the list of scholarship candidates despite her reassurances to them that I wouldn't miss any more days? When I'd submitted my portfolio for Culver, my attendance, or lack thereof in this case, hadn't even crossed my mind. Although it should have, considering missing school for hoaxes was one of the reasons I'd wanted to escape to Culver in the first place. But if I didn't get the scholarship, I was going to be stuck underneath Hoax for Hire forever. I swallowed hard and swiped at my eyes with the back of my hand, thankful that Curtis was too busy trying to locate Abby's tonsils to notice.

Ten minutes later he got in the car, a smug smile tugging at the corners of his mouth. Abby's lipstick was smeared practically to her ears, and even though I wasn't an expert by any means, I was pretty sure that kissing her must be a lot like kissing an overeager Labrador.

"Sorry about that," he said as the tank gave a disgruntled grumble before roaring to life.

"No you're not," I muttered.

"True," Curtis acknowledged. "But she's leaving town this weekend, so I had to seize the day, or her tongue, or whatever. Besides, you weren't exactly punctual yourself. What took you so long?"

"Mrs. Howard wanted to talk to me," I said.

"Uh-oh." Curtis frowned. "What did old Horseteeth want? Everything okay?"

"It's my attendance," I said.

"That," Curtis said with a dismissive wave of his hand. "You still have plenty of days left before you get the state letter and the lovely threats about having to retake a grade."

"I know," I said, "but I can't miss any more."

Curtis snorted. "Dream on. You and I both know that's not going to happen. Even if Dad gets his big payday for the Sea Monster Grand Slam and gets the bank off our back, he and Gramps are all hung up on the Gerhards stealing work, so we are booked solid for the next few weeks. Dad said we are going to be hoaxing for hoaxing's sake, which means lots of work for no cash. It's like he wants to mark his territory or something,"

I shook my head. "No."

"No what?" Curtis said. "I'm not lying. You can check the calendar and everything. Dad went a little nutso on the hoaxing jobs, and Gramps is going to have to cover more of them than I'd like."

I sighed and looked up. "That's not what I meant. I saw the schedule, but I don't care. I'm not missing any more school. Period. If it's an overnight hoax, Dad will just have to figure it out on his own."

Curtis snorted. "Yeah, right."

"I'm serious," I said. "I'm done."

"Good luck with that," he said, and it was clear from his tone that he thought I was nuts. The real kicker was that he was probably right. I gritted my teeth and ignored him. He could say whatever he wanted to say, Dad could yell, and Gramps could look hurt, but I was done missing school. D. O. N. E. Done. If Culver called again, and I prayed that they called again, I wanted Mrs. Howard to give them a good report.

"Did Dad check in yet?" I asked, reaching for Curtis's cell phone. He snatched it before I had a chance to pick it up, and he shook his head.

"Not yet. And hands off the phone. You know Gramps doesn't text. Now, did you make a list? We're here."

With a sigh I pulled the grocery list I'd made during Spanish out of my back pocket, ripped it down the middle, and handed over half to Curtis.

Even though I was only eight and Curtis was only twelve when my mom died, she'd taught us well. Hoaxing gigs were never consistent, which meant money wasn't either. So when Dad did manage to bring some home, Mom would stock the house like one of those crazy doomsday preppers you see on TV. I could remember her cramming two months' worth of groceries into the trunk of her tiny red car like it was her very own game of Tetris. Things had gotten better after Gramps moved in, since he did some of his own hoaxing on the side, but it was still a good idea to stock up when we had the opportunity and the cash.

We left the store an hour later with two overflowing carts. The tank had a trunk that could fit a small water buffalo, but we filled it in no time, resorting to cramming the remaining bags in the back seat. As we smashed the last one inside, I wondered if Curtis had noticed the marshmallows I'd snuck into my cart. They weren't just marshmallows; they were Jet-Puffed Marshmallows. The generic brand ones had been sixty cents cheaper, but I didn't want Clare to think I was cheap or didn't have any money—even if those things were true. I just wasn't about to let marshmallows out me.

The car loaded, Curtis sagged forward, his head resting on the steering wheel. "Are you as beat as I am?" he asked, yawning so wide I could see the silver filling in his back left tooth. "I feel like I could sleep for a week."

"I might just do that," I admitted, tipping my head back so I could shut my eyes. I'd passed the point of tired and was starting to feel a little nauseous. Curtis's cell phone rang, and we both jumped, already half asleep in the grocery store parking lot. Curtis glanced down at the caller ID and smiled. "It's Gramps. Dad probably finally checked in so you can chill the heck out." He hit the answer button.

"Thanks for the wake-up call, Gramps," he said. "Grayson and I just about fell asleep in the—" He cut off abruptly, and his entire expression changed in an instant. I sat up, my exhaustion forgotten as I took in the unfamiliar look of worry on my older brother's face. I'd only seen that look once before, and it had involved a misfiring nail gun during the construction of a Yeti model and had included a trip to the emergency room, sixteen stitches, and a round of tetanus shots. Dread crept up my spine as Curtis listened, his face the same off-white color as the leather seat behind him.

"Is he okay? How did it happen?" Curtis asked. "Do you know which jail he was taken to?"

And then I knew: Dad had been caught.

CHAPTER SEVEN

When I was little I used to worry obsessively about Dad getting caught, my mind going in anxious, dizzying circles as I imagined the police showing up at our door, Dad in handcuffs and a battering ram to take down the bookcase concealing the basement door. It didn't help that Mom was terrible at hiding her anxieties and worries from us. When Dad was away on a hoax, she'd stop talking almost completely, turning inward to this place where Curtis and I weren't allowed to follow. The moment he walked back through the door, though, safe and in relatively one piece, she'd snap out of it, like the sun had just come up after the longest night of her life. So I'd worry right along with her, my mind jumping to every awful possibility and conclusion. I'd squeeze my eyes shut and pray on repeat that Dad would be okay. As it would turn out, I was praying for the wrong parent.

After Mom died of an out-of-the-blue, no-one-could-have-predicted-it, what-an-awful-shame-she-has-kids aneurysm, I switched gears and actually began wishing that Dad *would* get caught. I imagined that it would end the entire hoaxing mess once and for all so he could get a regular job like a normal dad—one that didn't involve anything scary or dangerous or illegal. But I know now that was the immature wish of a kid. Normal wasn't possible for the McNeil clan. Although I was hoping that was just because someone hadn't been willing to try hard enough.

I used to lie and tell people that Dad was a plumber. It worked because ninety-nine percent of the population knows what a plumber does, so they don't ask a lot of questions. I stopped telling people that after the second grade when my teacher, Mrs. Chriswell, fell into the obnoxious one percent who couldn't leave well enough alone. She was scouting out parents to fill spots for career day, desperate to find enough warm bodies to parade in front us while she sat at her desk overdosing on chai lattes. When I'd said the word *plumber*, her eyes had lit up like I'd just announced that my dad was the president. She'd called him that night.

But my dad wasn't a professional plumber; he was a professional liar. So when Mrs. Chriswell called, he did what all good liars do. He lied. Although that was pre-Mom-dying Dad. Post-Mom-dying Dad might not have even returned Mrs. Chriswell's call. Back then, though, he was the kind of parent who attended parent-teacher conferences, checked my grades online, and helped me with my homework. So when she called, he started talking about the logistics of copper pipe versus PVC pipe in such a persuasively muddled way that Mrs. Chriswell hung up the phone convinced a bona fide wrench-slinging plumber would appear in front of her class the following Friday. And for all she knew, one did.

My dad had shown up dressed head to toe in a plumber's coveralls, toting our plunger over his shoulder for good measure. I'd sat in the back row and tried to make myself melt into the seat. He was a hit. Of course. Just like Curtis, Dad was charming and funny with a smile that made you want to smile back. Which is what my entire class did as he waved his plunger around and told stories of turtles stuck in pipes, of plugged toilets that exploded whole houses, and expounded on the virtues of a quality wrench. The performance was really good, but it still made me feel ill.

Ever since then I'd just told people that my dad was unemployed, which was substantially closer to the truth than the whole plumber thing. And really, it worked better. For one thing, he'd never been asked to speak at career day again, and I'd discovered that people never asked questions after you said the word *unemployed*, like it might be contagious or something.

"Does he need a lawyer?" Curtis asked Gramps, snapping me out of my thoughts and back to the interior of the tank. Curtis paused to listen, his jaw clenched tight. "But I thought the Champ hoax had to be done by Tuesday or we forfeit the money?" Curtis said. I reached for the phone, wanting to hear this all for myself, but Curtis just flapped an impatient hand at me as he listened to whatever Gramps was saying. I squirmed impatiently. "No, we'll be okay until you get back. You booked a what for tomorrow? Now, why did you agree to that job right in the middle of the Grand Slam? Well, do you at least have it designed already? Hold on a second, Gramps. I need to write some of this down." He glanced at me. "Find me something to write on, Squirt." My backpack was by my feet, and I rummaged around until I found a notebook and pencil. Curtis took them out of my hand, rolling his eyes in exasperation at the delay. "I'm ready," he said, the phone cradled against his shoulder as he wrote furiously on the notepad. "No, it's okay," he said. "Grayson and I can handle a job that small without you. We pulled off the Altie job yesterday, remember?"

I frowned at Curtis. "*What are we handling?*" I mouthed, dreading the answer. He'd said "tomorrow" and called it a "small job," so he couldn't mean the Champ hoax, which meant that Gramps must have booked something for this weekend or even tonight. Curtis paused, and there was something about the way his eyes narrowed and his forehead wrinkled that made my hands clench and unclench uncomfortably.

"Uh-huh," Curtis said slowly, turning his back to me so I could no longer study his face. "Our passports are up to date, Gramps. Why don't you let Grayson and me fly out there to help you? That sounds like a lot, and if the Gerhards are really involved—" He stopped short, listening. "But Gramps, even if the Gerhards are a bunch of half-brained ninnies who don't know their butts from a hole in the ground, isn't Scotland freezing this time of year?"

I tasted blood and released my bottom lip, which I'd been gnawing unconsciously as I listened to Curtis's half of the conversation. Curtis shook his head. "That sounds like Dad." He sighed. "Well, I'm sorry you have to clean up his mess. Make sure you call us when you get there or we'll worry." I could almost hear Gramps harrumphing and blustering on the other end about his years of hoaxing. "Promise, Gramps," Curtis pushed, his voice tight, and I wondered just what exactly Dad had gotten Gramps into. "Thanks," Curtis said, his shoulders relaxing. "Love you too. Be safe."

He hung up and stared at the phone for a second too long before he turned to me. "I'm thinking that we should order a pizza tonight. Pepperoni okay with you?"

"Shut up," I said. "What's going on? Dad got caught, didn't he? How bad is it? Gramps has to go to Scotland now?"

"We need to get home," Curtis said, turning the key so the tank roared to life. "The ice cream is melting."

"Curtis," I said, his name both a warning and a plea.

"Dad got caught," Curtis said, pulling out of the parking lot and back onto the road.

"I gathered that much," I said impatiently. "What happened?"

"Well," Curtis said, "Gramps doesn't have the full story, but he thinks that right after Dad got done pulling the Nessie job, some government officials showed up and conveniently stumbled upon him coming out of the loch, on private property. So they attempted to arrest him as a poacher."

"Attempted? I thought you said he got caught."

Curtis rolled his eyes. "I'm getting there. Well, apparently Dad tried to jump back into the water, since he was in his scuba gear and all, and so on top of the trespassing and poaching charges, he was also charged with resisting arrest."

"Not good," I said.

"Understatement of the year," Curtis agreed.

"This doesn't sound right," I said. "Dad's way too careful for something like this to happen."

"If you smell something fishy, it's because Gramps is pretty sure that Dad was squealed on by one of the Gerhards. Apparently they are ticked that Dad got the sea monster gig, and they decided to end the rivalry forever by putting Dad out of business and behind bars. If he can't pull off the last sea monster hoax, not only do we not get the big payday, our reputation gets trashed. The Gerhards will make sure of it."

I groaned. "The Gerhards? Seriously? Doesn't that make them traitors? I mean, ratting out a fellow hoaxer has to break some kind of code?"

Curtis raised an eyebrow at me. "A code? Our family is in the fraud business. There are no codes other than *don't get caught.*"

"You know what I mean," I said.

Curtis flapped an impatient hand at me. "Forget about the Gerhards. What matters is that Dad is stuck in some Scottish prison cell, and even though he pulled off Nessie before he got caught, there is still one hoax left unfinished." He held up his hand and started ticking off jobs on his fingers. "We pulled off the Altamaha-ha job in Georgia, Gramps pulled off Mbielu in Africa, Dad got the Loch Ness Monster, but the last hoax, Champ in Vermont, isn't done."

"And let me guess," I said, already knowing the answer. "Gramps is going to Scotland to get Dad out of jail and dredge our Nessie decoy out of the Loch so he can bring her back to pull off Champ?"

"Unfortunately, yes." Curtis sighed. "He's flying there tonight, which really sucks since he scheduled a random last-minute job for tomorrow he won't be around to help with anymore, so now we have to do it."

"He really flies out tonight?" I said.

Curtis glanced at the dash to check the time and nodded. "In a half hour, actually."

"Will they make it back in time to pull off the Champ job?" I asked. "That seems tight."

"They have to," Curtis said. "That decoy is the only decent Champ we have. I almost suggested that Gramps leave Dad to cool his heels in jail awhile and to let us help him pull off Champ using Altie. She's not a perfect Champ, but she'd work in a pinch, and then I remembered that someone I know bashed her head in yesterday." He finished by giving me a look that let me know just how dumb he thought I was.

I glared back at him and held up my Band-Aid-covered hand. "It was her or me. And I like me a lot better than I like her."

"Do I get to vote on who my favorite is?" Curtis asked. "Because I don't think you'll like those results."

"Gramps should just forget about the Nessie decoy," I said, imagining my seventy-year-old grandfather strapping on scuba gear to dive into the ridiculously deep Loch Ness in the middle of the night.

Curtis shook his head. "You know he can't. Dad sank way too much money into his new high-tech cryptid gear, and if we don't pull this off . . ." He left the sentence unfinished and shrugged. "Even if we didn't need the money, which we do, Gramps would never let the Gerhards get away with this," Curtis said. "Now it's a pride thing. Besides, if the McNeils don't pull off a contracted hoax, we're as good as sunk in Scotland."

"That wouldn't be such a bad thing," I grumbled as we pulled into our neighborhood.

"What was that?" Curtis asked.

"Nothing," I said. "Just thinking about what life would be like if Dad was a plumber."

CHAPTER EIGHT

It felt weird to pull into the garage knowing that Dad and Gramps weren't home. I could tell that Curtis felt it too, but he didn't say anything as he grabbed a bag of groceries and began cramming the garage freezer full of cheap frozen pizzas and rocky road ice cream. I piled the remaining bags up in my arms and schlepped them into the house. I never made more than one trip inside with the groceries. It was a personal rule.

My muscles were screaming when I finally slung the bags onto the counter, and I glanced down to see angry red tiger stripes zigzagging across my skin where the heavy bags had dug deep. Whatever. Still worth it. I began to unload the boxes of macaroni and cheese and cans of tomato soup onto the counter. Curtis came in and sat down at the kitchen table. Clearly, unpacking the rest was my job.

I dug through the fridge, throwing out anything that was no longer distinguishable as food, and I found myself wondering how Dad thought we got groceries. He certainly never shopped or gave us money for them. He was always too busy working in the basement on the next hoax. Maybe he believed in an elusive grocery fairy. Why not? It wasn't any less ridiculous than hunting for Ogopogo in British Colombia's Lake Okanagan.

I slid a Coke across the table to Curtis, who grunted in appreciation and popped the top.

"How long is the plane ride to Scotland?" I asked.

"I have no idea," Curtis said.

"We should look that up," I said. "That way we know when to expect a call from Gramps."

"On it," Curtis said, pulling out his phone. "And try not to worry. Gramps will figure everything out. He always does. And I'm sure Dad's fine. Until then we just have to hold down the fort. I was serious about ordering pizza earlier, and I think we should go whole hog and get the breadsticks with the cheese sauce that gives you gas."

"We just bought a boatload of frozen pizza," I said.

"We can just have that. And the cheese sauce gives you gas. Not me."

Curtis shook his head. "No frozen pizza. Even on a good day that stuff tastes like cardboard. It's the weekend, and after pulling off our first sea monster hoax, I think we deserve to celebrate. It will be just like old times."

"Pizza sounds good," I said absentmindedly as I turned all the cans in the cabinet so their labels faced out. The last thing I felt like doing was celebrating, a fact that I was sure Curtis was well aware of, just like he was aware that nothing about this situation was like "old times," where Dad used to order pizza after a successful hoax so Mom wouldn't have to worry about dinner.

"I'll make the call," Curtis said before sauntering out of the room. I glared at his back for a second before yawning so wide my jaw cracked. My eyes felt itchy, and I fantasized about climbing into my bed. Instead I turned back to the grocery bags still covering the countertops. Reaching into the closest one, I pulled out the bag of Jet-Puffed Marshmallows that I'd completely forgotten about in the revelation of Dad's arrest. I stared at them a moment, wondering what had possessed me to buy them. Of course I wasn't going to go to that stupid bonfire tomorrow night. That was something a normal kid would get to do because his grandpa would be around to drive him there instead of being on a plane to Scotland. It felt like a lifetime ago that I'd talked to Clare about making s'mores.

The thing was, though, that I'd actually really wanted to go. It would have felt nice to be just another kid at a bonfire, talking to a friend about the merits of the perfect chocolate-to-graham-cracker ratio. And now, with Dad stuck in some jail, I felt guilty for even thinking about it. The sound of Curtis's bare feet slapping on the floorboards made me jump, and I shoved the bag into the cupboard behind the mixing bowls.

When he banged back into the kitchen a second later, a familiar leather book tucked under one arm, I was studiously digging around in the junk drawer for a fifty-percent-off pizza coupon I'd seen once upon a time. Curtis plunked down the large leather logbook that Dad usually kept under lock and key, and I gave up the coupon search to lean against the countertop, eyebrows raised.

"You know you aren't supposed to touch that," I said. "Dad would flip out at you."

"Yeah?" Curtis said. "Well, last I checked Dad was in jail."

"Good point," I said, grabbing an open bag of chips off the counter where Curtis had left them the night before. The leather-bound volume was a written account, the only written account, of every hunt or hoax ever pulled off by a McNeil. The information was too sensitive to put anywhere on a computer, a fact that itched at Curtis, who was convinced that the next era of hoaxing was going to happen online—an idea that both Dad and Gramps were firmly against. The public was too attuned to the online scam, they warned. The McNeils relied on the good old-fashioned hoax, the impacts of eyewitness accounts and authentic, untampered-with photographs. The end.

Curtis flipped open the log, and I watched in silence, munching on a few stale chips, but my mind was still on the stupid bag of marshmallows shoved in the cabinet behind my back. I'd bought the biggest bag they'd had. What a waste of four dollars and ninety-seven cents.

But honestly, why couldn't I go to that bonfire if I wanted to? What was stopping me? Dad in jail? There was nothing I could do to help him thousands of miles away. If I really wanted to be a normal kid, shouldn't I make an attempt to do normal kid stuff? Especially if my alternative was sitting at home worrying about a flubbed sea monster hoax?

"Why do you look like you're constipated?" Curtis asked, jerking me from my thoughts.

"Nice," I said, shaking my head. "You know you

have a real way with words. Poetic, even."

"What?" Curtis asked, taking a long drink from his sweaty can of Coke before belching. "You do!"

"I'm thinking. It's this thing you do with your brain. You should give it a go sometime. You know, just to change things up a bit."

"That's okay," Curtis said as he chucked the empty Coke can into the sink, where it clattered off the breakfast dishes from that morning. "I wouldn't want to hurt myself." He went back to looking over the log, and I wondered if I really did look constipated when I was thinking. If so, I'd have to do something about that.

"Are you going to spit it out or what?" Curtis said a minute later. "I know you're chewing something over in that big brain of yours. Might as well tell me sooner rather than later. Is it about Dad and Gramps? Because I told you, it will be fine."

I shook my head.

Just then the phone rang, and Curtis and I both jumped about a foot. Curtis's hand went immediately to his cell phone, but the ring was coming from the wall, where our ancient pea-green house phone hung. We both turned to stare at it like it was an alien that had just landed in our midst.

"Did you know we still had that thing?" Curtis asked.

I shook my head. "I can't remember the last time it rang. I figured Dad stopped paying the bill for it years ago."

"It rang the day Mom died," Curtis said, and then winced as though he hadn't meant for those words to come out. "It's probably Gramps," he said a little too quickly. "Missed his flight or something and needs us to get online to book him another one."

Curtis pulled the handset off the wall and put it to his ear. "Hello? Gramps?" he said just a little too loudly, as though a wall phone worked differently than his cell phone. "Oh," Curtis said a second later, turning to raise an eyebrow at me. "Why, hello, Clare." I stood bolt upright. Had he really just said Clare?

"Clare Mayfield, right?" Curtis said. "Your older sister is Mallory?" He paused for a second, listening, then nodded. "She's at Purdue this year? Is she still hot?"

I groaned. Why did I have to have a brother? And if I had to have a brother, why did it have to be Curtis? He turned to smirk at me as he leaned against the wall, obviously enjoying making me squirm. I stumbled over and held my hand out for the phone, but he just brushed it away in the same way you would an obnoxious fly. I narrowed my eyes. If he kept this up, I was going to find a way to get even. Maybe by putting something really unpleasant in his bed, like a snake.

"Yeah, he's here," he said, grinning at me. "Now, what do you want with a punk like my little brother?"

I decided the snake was too nice. Dog poop would be much better. I snatched the phone out of his hand and glared at him as I put it to my ear.

"Hi, Clare," I said. "Um, what's up?"

"I just wanted to make sure you're coming tomorrow," said Clare's voice, sounding strange and hollow over the old landline phone. Curtis was watching me, an amused expression on his face, like I was a puppy that had just figured out a new trick. I scowled at him as I tugged at the stupid curly phone cord that someone, I suspected Curtis, had tied into knots at some point in time. It was then that I realized I was supposed to respond to her.

"How did you get my number?" I asked, because obviously that was the cool thing to say when a girl called you. Curtis smacked his forehead in the universal "just how dumb are you?" gesture. I turned my back to him in an attempt to create some sort of privacy.

"The school directory," she said, as though this should have been obvious.

"Oh," I said stupidly. "I didn't even know we had one of those."

"So?" she prompted, and I heard her muffle the phone as someone said something in the background.

"So what?" I asked.

"Are you coming or not?" she said, sounding impatient.

"Yeah," I said automatically. "I'll be there."

"Great!" she said, the impatience of a moment before gone. "And tell your brother that Mallory is home from college for fall break and is going to drive me so she can hang out with Donovan's older brother. You know, if he's crappy about driving you."

"Thanks," I said. "I'll do that."

"Great, bye," she said, and the line went dead.

"Where exactly are you going to be?" Curtis asked as soon as the phone hit the receiver.

"It's nothing," I mumbled.

"No," Curtis said. "It's obviously something. I feel like I should congratulate you. First time a girl called for you, and not just any girl: a Mayfield, no less."

"Do you have a date tomorrow night?" I asked. Curtis peered at me suspiciously.

"No, I already told you that Abby was leaving town." And then a grin practically split his face in two. "Why? Do you?"

"No. Don't be a putz. Clare is my friend. I was just, you know, wondering if you could drop me off at this bonfire a guy at my school is having. I was going to ask Gramps, but since he's not here . . ." I trailed off lamely, not sure where else to go with my explanation.

"A bonfire?" Curtis said again slowly as he sat back down in front of the logbook. "And you really want to go?"

I shrugged. "Yeah."

"You?" Curtis said again, as though I'd just announced that I'd like to take up flamenco dancing.

"Clare said her older sister, Mallory, will be there to hang out with Donovan's older brother," I said, the words coming out in a garbled rush.

"I see," Curtis said, and he looked so smug I could have just punched him. But then of course, I'd screw myself out of a ride. I stared back at him for a second and then threw up my hands in defeat.

"Just forget it," I said. "It's no big deal." I turned and headed for my room, but Curtis's hand shot out to grab my arm, stopping me.

"I never said I wouldn't take you," he said.

"Yeah?" I asked, not sure I believed it.

"Scout's honor," Curtis said, holding up a hand.

"You were never a scout," I accused. "You can't use that."

"Uh-oh," Curtis said, glancing around in a mock panic. "Keep your eyes out for the scout police. Wouldn't want to get busted." A second after he said it, he winced and shook his head. "Sorry," he said. "That's not exactly funny at the moment, is it?"

"Not really," I agreed. With nothing better to do, I plopped back down beside him, offering him the bag of chips.

He shook his head. "No way. If I get greasy finger-prints on here"—he gestured to the large leather book still on the table—"Dad will skin me alive. You know that."

"Right," I said, deciding not to mention that he'd just been drinking a dripping can of Coke dangerously near said precious book. Curtis turned back to the beginning of the log, where the image of our family tree spread out across two full pages. I leaned in to look. Dad and Gramps usually had the log out only at night, and they were so twitchy about it that idle reading had never been allowed. Not that I'd ever asked. Curtis was the one who was into this stuff, the one who spent hours on the internet researching cryptids and playing around with the newest version of Photoshop in case he was ever allowed to actually use a digitally altered pic-ture for a hoax. The scrawling lines of our family tree went back all the way to the eighteen hundreds. Each McNeil's name was written in small cramped handwrit-ing with a tiny line of numbers beside it. I knew the numbers matched up to pages in the book where that particular McNeil's hoaxes and hunts were recorded.

Curtis flipped to Gramps's page, and I ran a finger down the seemingly endless list of exotic locations and strange creatures Gramps had tried to track down. As the list had gotten longer, the handwriting had gotten smaller and more cramped so that the latest hunt was a barely legible smudge at the bottom of the page. I turned the aged paper over to see if his list had continued onto the back side. It hadn't. The next page was Dad's. Many of the early hunts listed on his page were the same as on Gramps's, because, of course, when he was our age, he'd gone along with Gramps on all his adventures. It wasn't until my dad was eighteen that the hunt list stopped cold and the hoax list took off. Next to each hoax Dad had written the pertinent information about the employer, the hoax requirements, and the payment. There was something about Dad's page that made me feel a little ill, and I wasn't really sure why. Maybe it was because hoaxing had changed from a job to an obsession after Mom died, or because hoaxing felt wrong, slimy somehow, if you weren't doing it to fund a hunt. I flipped his page despite Curtis's cry of protest that he wasn't done yet. The next page had Curtis's name written across the top.

"You're in here now?" I asked, surprised. "When did that happen?"

"What do you mean?" Curtis asked. "Dad put us in

here the day we were born. Look." He flipped again, and there was my name: Grayson Carston McNeil. I guess I could only blame myself for not knowing this was here. I could have looked at it anytime Dad or Gramps had it out. Of course, I'd chosen not to. But I was still surprised that my page was almost as full as Curtis's. Because there in Gramps's scrawling handwriting and Dad's slanted one were the hoaxes I'd assisted with over the years.

I scanned the list as memories of long-forgotten hoaxes resurfaced. Had I really helped with that many? There were more hoaxes to my name than to some of my ancestors combined. "I didn't know," I said.

"Because you never bothered to look," Curtis said.

"But I don't want to be in there," I said, pointing at my name with shaky fingers.

"Tough noogies," Curtis said. "You're a McNeil. You don't get a choice about being in the family history book."

I shook my head again, my stomach clenching hard.

"Relax," Curtis said, flipping back to his page, where he'd started writing down the information about the Altie hoax from the night before, detailing the number of eyewitnesses, the time of day, the payment. When he was done, he wrote the words SOLO HOAX next to the entry and grinned.

"Our first sea monster," he said, flipping to my page. "You want to write it down, or should I?"

"You do it," I said, wishing that I could rip my page out instead of adding yet another hoax to the already-too-long list.

"Suit yourself," Curtis said. When he was done, he turned back to Gramps's page. "You know," he said, "Gramps may need to add a new page somewhere else in the book. After he finishes up the Nessie job for Dad, he won't have any room left on his original page."

"Or maybe Gramps shouldn't be pulling off Nessie jobs anymore," I muttered under my breath as I rolled up the top of the chip bag and shoved away from the table. I needed to shower and go to bed.

"You sure mutter a lot for a kid who usually doesn't have a whole lot to say," Curtis said, not looking up.

"You don't want to hear what I have to say," I said. "Trust me."

Curtis sat back, arms crossed. "You know," he said, "I think I just might this time. What has your boxers in such a twist?"

I paused in the doorway, prepared to swallow down what I really thought and just go to bed like a good little dormant volcano, and I should have. But for some reason, maybe it was the lack of sleep or Dad getting arrested or the vise that seemed to clamp around my heart every time I pictured Gramps boarding that plane all by himself, but something inside me boiled over.

"Gramps is seventy," I said. "You and I both know that he has no business freezing to death in a Scottish Loch just to clean up Dad's mess."

"What else is he supposed to do?" Curtis asked. "If he doesn't get our decoy out and get it back to the states to pull off the Champ job, we don't get paid. We'll be lucky not to lose the entire Loch Ness Monster business after Dad's screwup." When I didn't say anything, Curtis's eyes narrowed.

"I know you don't give a Bigfoot's backside, but the Loch Ness Monster has been one of the McNeils' most consistent paydays for a long time."

"But why?" I exploded. "Why do we need the Loch Ness Monster? Or the Yeti? Or the Skunk Ape or the Bunyip or the Jersey Devil or whatever other names you want to call the frauds we haul out of the basement and parade around?"

"We *need* the Nessie because we *need* to pay bills," Curtis said as though he was explaining something to a two-year-old. "If we don't watch our backs, the Gerhards will take it over, and then piece by piece we'll lose every contact our family has fought to make."

"News flash!" I snapped. "Normal jobs pay bills too! Why can't a McNeil just get one of those? With tax returns and Friday paychecks and vacation days? Did you ever think about that, Curtis?" I asked. "A life other than this?" I shoved the leather book across the table toward him.

"No," Curtis said. "But I don't have to ask if you have. You make it obvious every step of the way how you feel about what our family has built."

"Built?" I practically choked on the word. My entire body felt like a stretched rubber band about to snap. "You mean the life they *built* on lies and creatures that don't exist? Because as far as I can see, that's the only thing a McNeil has ever built!" I grabbed the logbook again. "This thing? This precious book Dad loves more than us? It's the history of a family who wasted their lives chasing daydreams and lying to people. That's nothing to be proud of! Don't you see that?"

"What I see is one of the most ungrateful people I've ever met," Curtis said, and there was something so hard in the way he said it that I stopped cold. Curtis shook his head in disgust. "You know, I just don't get you. You have the opportunity to live a life of adventure, hunting undiscovered creatures and literally making history with our hoaxes, and all you can worry about is being normal. News flash, Squirt: no one remembers normal."

I threw my hands in the air in exasperation. "Don't

you get it? No one is going to remember you either, Curtis. They will remember that some poor hiker spotted a Bigfoot once and required therapy for three months to get over it. No one will know your name. You will die just as big of a nobody as me."

Curtis and I stared at each other, and I wondered if he was going to punch me. Without Dad or Gramps in the house to break up a fight, my butt would get soundly kicked.

Curtis finally shook his head and pushed away from the table. He was halfway out of the kitchen before he paused and turned back to me. "Just do me a favor, okay? You can be a jerk and run your mouth off to me all you want, but don't do it in front of Gramps. You'd break his heart."

I tried to think of something to say back, but Curtis had already disappeared. I'd just kissed my ride to that bonfire tomorrow night goodbye, and I wasn't even sorry. It had felt good to yell, even if the person I'd really wanted to yell at was thousands of miles away behind bars. That was a low blow, bringing Gramps into it. Besides, somehow I'd always classified Gramps on a different level than my dad. Gramps was a hunter, an explorer, and an adventurer. He did it for the love of it. Dad did it to escape a reality that no longer included Mom. And instead of getting a normal job like everyone else's dad, ours had gotten himself arrested. The bang of Curtis's door slamming let me know it was safe to leave the kitchen, and I realized I'd never asked him what job Gramps had asked us to do for him.

The leather-bound book of family secrets was still sitting on the table. It was kept in the basement safe at all times, and I was surprised that Curtis had left without putting it away. Maybe I'd made him madder than I'd thought. I stared at it a moment before picking it up and chucking it onto the corner of the counter with the junk mail. Curtis was right. I had no desire to follow in the McNeil footsteps. I got up to head to bed, no longer hungry for the pizza we'd never gotten around to ordering. I felt like absolute crap, and I told myself that it was just the lack of sleep and not what Curtis had said.

Our conversation replayed in my mind as I brushed my teeth, and I sighed, sending little flecks of toothpaste onto the mirror. The kid looking back at me from behind the dirty glass looked exhausted and a little mean. I guessed the problem with being a dormant volcano was that sometimes they erupted and slaughtered all the unsuspecting people. As I stood there studying my reflection, I realized that I'd been holding Culver up as my way out, when really Culver didn't matter. The endgame of the hoaxing life was jail or strapping on scuba gear in your seventies to retrieve a stupid sea monster decoy. No thanks. When Dad and Gramps got home, I was going to lay it all out on the table for them. I wanted to be a photographer and capture real stories from behind my lens. I wanted to have adventures I could actually tell someone about, not just write down in some dusty book that no one would ever read. And if the only way for me to do that was to go to Culver, then that was what I was going to do. And really, they still had one McNeil to carry on the family legacy or whatever. That would just have to be enough. Curtis could have this life. I didn't want it.

CHAPTER NINE

I woke up to the smell of pancakes. It's a good way to wake up. Gramps always made his famous cottage cheese pancakes on Saturday mornings. I stretched out in my bed and yawned so wide my face felt like it might crack in half. Saturdays and Sundays were the only days that I let myself sleep in since I could work on my scholarship essay whenever I wanted. It wasn't until I was rolling out of bed that I remembered that Gramps was on his way to Scotland, probably donning scuba gear to go for a swim in freezing-cold, peat-filled water. I reversed and tumbled back into bed, pulling the covers over my head. Sleeping all day seemed like a newly viable option that I should investigate, even if Curtis was luring me out with the siren song of pancakes. After our argument the night before, he'd probably spit in mine. I could resist.

My stomach grumbled at me not to be a hero, and I rolled over, mentally telling it to get over itself because I was going back to bed. My door flew open with a bang.

"Rise and shine, Squirt," Curtis said, grabbing my covers and ripping them off. The icy morning air sent goose bumps racing down my arms, and I made a grab for my covers.

"I'll pass, thanks," I said, managing to catch hold of the corner and pull them back up.

"Oh," Curtis said with a sigh, "if only that were an option."

"Did Gramps call? Is Dad okay?" I asked.

"Gramps is still on a plane," Curtis said. "Last time I checked, Scotland was kind of far away. Now get up and eat. We have work to do before we hit the road."

I groaned, remembering the job Gramps had told Curtis about the night before, the job I'd forgotten to ask about in the drama of finding out Dad was in jail, the shock of Clare calling, and then the messy argument with Curtis. "Do we have to?" I asked. "We got the Altie job money. Isn't that enough?"

"You don't even know what the job is," Curtis said.

"I don't have to know." I sniffed. "It's a hoax. Ergo, I automatically hate it."

"Don't start that again. And don't say ergo," Curtis said, slapping me none too gently on the back of the head. "It makes you sound like a tool. Now get dressed and meet me in the basement in ten." With that he turned and strode out the door, slamming it behind him for good measure.

I flopped back down on my bed and stared up at the ceiling, where the fan Dad was supposed to fix three years ago sat collecting cobwebs and dust. Locking the door and going back to sleep weren't options. The last time I'd done that Curtis had retaliated by taking the door completely off the hinges and hiding it. Four months later I'd finally found it stashed behind the spare Nguma-Monene decoy. Being doorless wasn't an experience I was looking to replicate any time soon. Besides, he seemed to be over our fight from the night before, and the last thing I needed was a pissed-off Curtis for the next week without Gramps or Dad to act as a buffer.

So I got out of bed, showered, and threw on jeans, hiking boots, and a yellow hoodie before heading to the basement and whatever fresh hoaxing horror the day held. I swung by the kitchen on the way and snagged a pancake off the plate Curtis had left on the table. Not that I'd ever admit it to him, but he hadn't done that bad of a job. Maybe a little too crispy, but that was better than soggy.

When I got to the basement, Curtis had already pulled out four bins, one of which he'd tipped on its side, so the contents lay strewn across the battered surface of the worktable. Three different surveyor's reels, boards of various lengths and widths, and ropes of all shapes and sizes were scattered among complicated drawings of circles and swirls on graph paper, all immaculately plotted and measured. It was a crop circle job. At least I didn't have to wear a costume for this one.

Curtis's face was illuminated by the glow of his laptop as he stared intently at the screen. The bin at my feet was filled to the brim with photographs, some in color but most in black and white, each depicting a different complicated crop circle design. I picked up a stack and shoved aside the surveyor's reels so I could perch on the tabletop. It creaked a little under my weight, but the thing could have held a tap-dancing elephant without much trouble. The photographs felt heavy in my hands, sturdy and thick in the way modern pictures weren't, and I flipped slowly through the stack, turning each one over to note the date of creation as well as the McNeil responsible for the design. Extra notes were scribbled in various degrees of illegible handwriting about the amount of iron pelts left in the field or the green lights that had been utilized to alert some poor farmer to the supernatural artwork that had been implemented in his field without his permission. There were also flight plans detailed for each hoax, because what was the point of creating intricate and impossible crop circles if no one flew over the top of them to document the event?

Curtis was still absorbed in his computer screen, biting his lip in concentration as he typed on his laptop. It was practically new, a gift from Dad in a rare moment of affection last year when Curtis helped him out of a tight spot during a Mothman hoax. Curtis had decorated the cover with stupid bumper stickers about Bigfoot. The only one that was funny was the one that said, "Bigfoot doesn't believe in you." I'd bought it for him for Christmas.

I knew better than to disturb him, so instead I glanced over at the other bins he'd dislodged, hoping for a few more clues about the crop circle hoax we were apparently responsible for. One bin contained the magnetized metal we'd sprinkle among the barley and wheat, and the other held thick manila files, some with the familiar "CLASSIFIED" label of the federal government stamped across the top. These I knew contained every wild UFO or alien encounter ever taken seriously by the United States. My great-aunt Henrietta had taken a job as a janitor in Area 51 for five years to get her hands on those. The reports were all similar: unexplainable lights in the sky, strange flying objects, bizarre crop circles, meteorite strikes, the works.

"I'm finishing up the crop circle design now," Curtis said, finally looking up from his laptop.

"Should I tell Dad and Gramps that you made the design on a computer instead of on graph paper like you're supposed to?" I said.

"Not if you like your nose where it is," Curtis said, and his tone made it hard to tell if he was joking or not. "The future of hoaxing is on here," he said, thumping his computer. "If Gramps would just let me post some of his adventures, the cryptid buzz would hit social media, and we'd be turning away jobs left and right."

"They'll never let you," I said. "Not if you woke up tomorrow with three heads and a unicorn horn." I didn't add that it was one of the very reasons I wanted to go to Culver. So I could have adventures *and* tell people about them.

"I'd look good with three heads," Curtis said.

"Right," I said, "The unicorn horn would be the thing that mucked everything up for you."

"You're right," Curtis said. "I could pull off the horn too. Now back to the crop circle job. If we leave here by four, we can be set up and be ready to rock and roll by sundown."

I groaned, slouching back against the table in defeat. "Dad isn't even here, and he still managed to ruin everything."

"Ruin what?" Curtis asked, turning back to the laptop. "It's not like you ever go out. You're practically a hobbit."

"Hermit," I corrected. "A hermit is someone who doesn't leave the house. A hobbit is short with furry feet."

Curtis looked me up and down and smirked. "No, I meant hobbit."

"Well, this hermit was supposed to go to a bonfire tonight," I grumbled.

"Oh yeah," Curtis said, sitting back to look at me with a raised eyebrow. "I forgot. Where was this bonfire at again?"

"Doesn't matter now." I sighed, pushing off the table so I could start piecing together the clunky equipment I'd be dragging around a field all night instead of going to the bonfire and making s'mores with Clare. It was going to be a long day.

We got home from the crop circle job a little before nine. Every inch of me felt itchy from stomping around in Farmer Dellinger's wheat field, measuring and then double-checking measurements before hauling my tamper around and around in circles, all the while hoping that dear old Farmer Dellinger wouldn't decide to take a few potshots at whoever was messing around in his field. And to make matters worse, we hadn't even gotten paid. Apparently when Gramps had taken the last-minute job, he'd agreed to have the paycheck mailed to our anonymous PO box after the circles had been sighted, photographed, and reported to the appropriate media outlets and tabloids.

The moon was high and full, and I stood at the window over the kitchen sink watching it for a while as I felt my muscles creak and groan. I wasn't sure if it was because Dad had finally gotten caught or I'd had just one too many nights cramped in the front seat of the kidnapper van, but I was done. From-the-tip-of-my-wheat-dust-covered-head-to-my-blister-covered-feet done.

Curtis came in from the garage, walked over to the fridge, and opened it to peer blearily in at the contents. He bent low to dig around in the back, dislodging a few stray strands of wheat from his hair, before standing and tossing something at me. My hand shot up reflexively to catch the ice-cold energy drink, and I looked at Curtis, eyebrow raised in question.

"I thought you wanted to go to that bonfire," he said. "If we hustle, we can make the last hour. Are you game?"

"You'll still take me?" I asked, thinking of our fight the night before and the uneasy tension that had seemed to vibrate between us the entire day.

"Not if your skinny butt isn't in my car in the next five minutes. I'm not sitting around all night waiting to chauffeur you around." He walked out, and I stood there for a second, staring at the empty kitchen doorway. Was he serious, or was I going to race to get dressed and hurry to the car just to have him tell me it was all some joke?

"Four minutes!" Curtis yelled. I sprinted toward my bedroom, moving so fast that I caught a foot on the doorframe and went sprawling. Wincing, I scrambled to my feet and dug around my closet for something that wouldn't make me look like a dork. What did people even wear to a bonfire in a field? Did I have time to shower? How bad did I smell?

"Two minutes!" Curtis called, and I heard the garage door go up.

"Fastest five minutes of my life," I grumbled, grabbing a plain red hooded sweatshirt and a clean pair of jeans. The horn on the tank honked, and I heard it backing out of the garage. I grabbed my running shoes on the way out of my bedroom door and booked it, stopping only long enough to shove the bag of Jet-Puffed Marshmallows into my hoodie pocket. Curtis was coasting toward the road, and I ran after him in my socks, opened the passenger door, and threw myself inside the moving car.

"Nice to see you could make it," Curtis said, accelerating out of our driveway.

"If that was five minutes, I'm a Feejee Mermaid," I grumbled.

He glanced over at me, eyebrow raised. "Don't be so hard on yourself. You're slightly more attractive than one of those."

I rolled my eyes. "Gee, thanks," I said, thinking of the grotesque creations that had fascinated spectators at the Barnum and Bailey Circus back in 1840 when my great-great grandfather had the genius idea to sew the front half of a mummified monkey to the back end of a dried-out carp and call it a mermaid. I leaned forward to put on my running shoes and the bag of marshmallows in my hoodie crinkled loudly.

Curtis's eyes focused in. "Whatcha got there, little brother?" he asked, and before I could react, he had his hand inside my pocket, fumbling for the bag. I yelped and twisted away, but it was too late. The bag ripped open and marshmallows exploded in the air.

"What the . . . ?" Curtis said. The tank swerved dangerously into oncoming traffic, and I grabbed the steering wheel with one hand to steady us.

"Nice going," I snapped as he pulled off the road and onto a small side street before stopping.

"Explain," he said as he pulled a marshmallow from his hair, inspected it, and then popped it into his mouth.

"Why did you have to do that?" I moaned as I attempted to pick up marshmallows and stuff them back into the ripped bag.

"I thought you were trying to smuggle some of Dad's whisky to the bonfire in a paper bag. That's what *usually* hides underneath someone's shirt. Loser."

My eyes burned as tears pressed against the backs of my eyeballs, but I blinked them away angrily. "It was just a thing," I said, waving a hand dismissively. "Forget it. Can you just take me back home? I changed my mind about going." Curtis didn't say anything for a moment, and then he put the car in gear and turned around. Sighing, I shut my eyes. I was too tired to go out, anyway. Clare wouldn't even miss me, not that she'd probably expected me to go.

A minute later Curtis threw the car in park and my eyes snapped open. To my surprise we weren't at home. We were at a 7-Eleven. Curtis got out without a word and stomped into the store. He was probably going to pick up one of those disgusting hot dogs that spun around on a greasy conveyor belt. It was his go-to late-night snack, and part of me was convinced that he ate them just to gross me out. My eyes slid shut again, and I leaned my head back against the seat. I was almost asleep when something soft hit me in the face. Curtis climbed into the car and headed back onto the highway. I looked down at my lap. There was a fresh bag of marshmallows. Jet-Puffeds.

"Thanks," I whispered.

"Whatever."

CHAPTER TEN

The bonfire was still in full swing when we finally pulled in. I was glad it was dark because I'd started nervous sweating. I dug through the glove box until I found Curtis's emergency cologne and sprayed it on liberally.

"You know you just made yourself irresistible to every woman and mosquito in a hundred square miles by putting that stuff on," Curtis said.

"It's better than smelling like sweaty wheat," I said. "You could have at least let me grab a fast shower."

"If we ever have a drought, you're screwed," Curtis said. "You use enough water for five punks your size."

"I need a ride home," I said. "Please don't leave without me."

"I only did that once," Curtis said, then laughed when I glared at him. "Okay, okay, more than once. But I won't tonight. Besides, I see Clare's older sister over there by the pickup truck." When I still didn't look convinced, he sighed and tossed me the car keys.

"Better?" he asked.

I nodded and clambered out of the car. Curtis walked next to me toward the glow of the bonfire, and I couldn't decide if having him beside me made me more nervous or less. He had this way of carrying himself like he was six feet tall and owned the world, and it always made me feel dorky in comparison. And tonight I really didn't need to feel any dorkier than I already did.

Donovan's brother had backed his truck up to the fire, where it sat illuminated from the flames as his speakers pumped country music. The truck seemed to be the hangout spot of choice for the handful of high schoolers who'd gotten stuck driving younger brothers and sisters while the kids from my school perched on hay bales and logs, laughing and clutching pop cans. The bonfire was blazing a good five feet high, throwing the trees bordering the field into sharp relief, their shadows stretching toward the stars before disappearing into the blackness. The fireflies were out, flashing their lights over the freshly plowed field.

Pausing at the edge of the circle of light cast by the bonfire, I scanned the crowd for Clare. I was an idiot for showing up this late, and with marshmallows of all things. What was I? Five? I wondered how mad Curtis would be if I asked him to just drive me back home. Probably pretty mad, especially since he'd made the stop for the marshmallows and everything. I did have the keys, though. I could just go sit in the tank until he was tired of hanging out on the back of a tailgate and could drive me home. He'd tell me I was a dork, and he'd be right. But at that moment, I didn't even care. I turned to head back across the field.

"Grayson? It's about time you got here! What did you do? Ride a horse?"

Jumping guiltily, I spun back to the fire. And there was Clare, hands on her hips, her hair piled into a purposefully haphazard bun thingy with little curls springing free around her face.

"You were thinking about chickening out, weren't you?" she accused.

I frowned. "No."

"Liar," Curtis coughed into his hand before flashing Clare one of his wide smiles on his way to the far side of the bonfire.

Clare raised an accusing eyebrow at me, and I sighed.

"Fine, maybe a little."

She laughed and threw an arm around my shoulders as she leveraged me toward the bonfire. She smelled like wood smoke and fire, and I wondered again how I'd been lucky enough to make this girl my friend.

"I thought you weren't going to show," she said. "The bonfire started hours ago. Why are you so late?"

"Just had to help Curtis with something," I said absentmindedly as I took in the clamor of the bonfire. It all felt so overwhelming, and I wondered how everyone just seemed to know how to act at a party like this. Did someone tell them? Were there instructions on the internet somewhere?

"With what?" she asked. "Hunting down that sea monster that bit you?"

I shot her a look, but she wasn't looking at me. I made a mental note not to joke around like that with her again. Clare was too smart for her own good sometimes.

"Did you bring the marshmallows?" she asked. "Because I have a purse full of Hershey bars and graham crackers that aren't fulfilling their purposes in life."

"I told you I would," I said, holding up the newly purchased bag of Jet-Puffeds, relieved that she'd dropped the sea monster joke.

"Awesome!" she squealed, as though I'd just

presented her with a pony instead of marshmallows. I wondered if she knew that marshmallows were made from pig snouts. Probably not. No one got excited about ground-up pig snout. She grabbed my arm and pulled me toward the warm glow of the flames. I followed. What else was I supposed to do? None of my friends at school were at this party, so it was either go with her or lurk around the edges of the bonfire like a creeper.

"This is Grayson!" Clare gushed to a group of girls sitting on one of the hay bales closest to the fire. They were all girls from my grade, and while I knew each of their names, I also suspected that none of them knew mine. Tonight they were all wearing makeup in thick layers like the frosting on a cake, and two of them even glanced up from their cell phones long enough to give me a quick once-over. Clare smiled her thousand-watt smile, and I noticed that her caramel skin was mercifully free of anything shimmery or glossy or cake-frosting-like.

"Grayson is in homeroom with me, and look!" She held up the bag of marshmallows. "It's s'mores time!" I tried not to think about the fact that Clare was treating me like a puppy at a show-and-tell, and I smiled awkwardly. The draw of chocolate was apparently enough to disengage them from their cell phones, and the girls chattered excitedly.

I'd thought that the whole s'mores idea was going to be cheesy, that Donovan and his jock buddies would take the opportunity to make fun of it and shove a marshmallow up my nose for good measure. But it was Clare's idea and not mine, so of course the s'mores were a hit. Soon the girls were standing near the flames giggling and shrieking when a marshmallow caught on fire. I somehow became the designated s'more assembler. A girl would totter over in the high heels she'd probably swiped from an older sister, and I'd smash her blackened marshmallow between the graham crackers and chocolate Clare had brought. I assembled Clare's third s'more, but instead of rejoining her friends she perched next to me. She seemed weirdly anxious, and she glanced down at the time on her cell phone before looking at me. I studied her out of the corner of my eye. Had I ever seen Clare nervous before? It wasn't a normal Clare emotion.

"Um, are you having fun?" she asked, and I glanced back down at the graham crackers I was breaking apart before she caught me staring.

"Sure. It beats a normal Saturday night."

Clare glanced at her cell phone again, and after seeming to discover that only a few seconds had passed, looked back up at me. "I bet," she said, and I could tell that she had been only half listening. Was she regretting inviting me? I wondered. That would be weird since she'd gone to the hassle of calling our house to make sure I'd be here. Something was up.

I took Curtis's car keys out of my pocket and swirled them around my fingers for something to do because my hands suddenly felt really large and in the way. Clare usually waved her hands around in the air when she talked, animated and fluttery like butterflies, but tonight she was clutching her cell phone like it was the last life raft on the *Titanic*. I twirled the keys again, a bit too aggressively this time because they flew off my finger, nearly braining the girl in front of me before landing a foot short of the fire. So much for the keys making me look cool.

"House keys?" Clare asked after I'd retrieved them and resumed my perch on the log.

I shook my head. "Insurance against my brother forgetting me." I jerked my head toward the opposite side of the fire, where I could see Curtis lounging on the tailgate of Donovan's truck. Clare's sister was standing next to him, laughing at something he'd just said. She was a taller version of Clare but with shorter hair and too many earrings.

Curtis smiled at me when he noticed me looking his way, raising both eyebrows in mock surprise when he saw me sitting next to Clare. I pulled a face at him that I hoped Clare didn't notice and then smiled. "*This is it*," I wanted to tell him. "*Look at all this wonderful glorious normal everyone is enjoying. We should have this too, all the time, not just for a stolen hour when we got home from a hoax ahead of schedule.*"

"He's forgotten you before?" Clare asked.

I nodded. "More than once too. And I really don't want to have to run home tonight." She giggled like it was a joke. I wished it were. And I wished I were funnier so she'd laugh again. It was a great laugh. Clare glanced back down at her cell phone, and I wondered if she was waiting for a call from someone. She noticed me looking and blushed self-consciously.

"Sorry," she said. "Bad habit. Just wait until you get a cell phone."

"That's not happening anytime soon," I said.

"Does Curtis ever let you use his?" she asked.

"Nope."

"Why don't you give me his number anyway?" she said. "I bet he won't care if I call every now and then, and it beats calling your home phone."

I blinked at her. She was going to call me again? Like, that was going to be a thing? I quickly rattled off Curtis's number, and she plugged it into the contact list on her phone. As though he knew we were talking about him, Curtis chose that moment to saunter over to us as though he'd been invited.

"Rumor has it someone has s'mores over here," he said, giving me an exaggerated wink. I shot him a look that hopefully said, *"Don't ruin this for me."* He ignored it, grabbed a handful of marshmallows out of the bag and tossed them up in the air. Even in the dim light, he managed to juggle five of them perfectly. It was a stupid trick Dad had taught us years ago on one of the rare occasions when he'd decided to try his hand at parenting for a hot minute. Before I could say anything, Curtis started flipping the marshmallows to me, and on reflex I caught them mid-juggle. Clare's groupies shrieked with delight. Curtis passed off all five marshmallows and started adding more, lobbing them one by one into the fray. We were up to ten, and I could feel sweat on my forehead as I focused on the small bits of white as they silhouetted themselves against the night sky. Every eye was on me, and I hated Curtis for that. He was the one who liked this sort of thing, not me. It was one of the reasons I loved photography: I was never the one in front of the lens.

Curtis grabbed something and launched it into the middle of things, and suddenly I was juggling ten marshmallows and a soda can. It went well until I flipped the can up into the air, and fizzy Dr. Pepper sprayed everywhere. The majority of it hit me square in the face, and the marshmallows I'd been juggling rained down. Leave it to Curtis to throw me an open can. A few people booed, others clapped, but I was too busy trying to wipe the soda out of my burning eyes to notice which of those Clare did.

"Sorry about that," Curtis said, throwing a companionable arm around Clare's shoulders. "Just wanted to make sure that my baby brother wasn't boring you." Clare giggled, and I wanted to kick Curtis. Before I could do anything, a high-pitched scream came from the woods. The party went on for another second, as though the scream hadn't happened, but then someone turned off the music and the scream came again, this time joined by other screams. The sounds ripped through the smiles of the partygoers as everyone shot one another questioning looks. A moment later Clare's sister came barreling out of the woods, her eyes wide with terror.

"Run!" she screeched.

As if on cue, a low guttural snarl came from the trees as a huge shadow loomed from the woods, furry and fanged. Now it wasn't just the girls screaming. A few kids whipped out their phones and tried to catch pictures of the creature, but it had already slipped back into the woods. I jumped back as marshmallows and chocolate scattered across the dirt to get trampled by panicked feet as everyone ran toward the line of cars at the edge of the field.

The growl came again, and I would have been terrified . . . if I hadn't helped record it.

CHAPTER ELEVEN

Tires squealed, throwing chunks of dirt into the air, and within moments the bonfire was deserted. I watched the last of the taillights bumping across the field and fading into the night, and it wasn't until I turned to find Curtis that I noticed Clare was still sitting on the log I'd just abandoned, apparently frozen in terror, her face white. Before I could figure out what to say to her, Curtis grabbed my arm and leaned down to Clare.

"You need to get out of here," he said. "Who was your ride?"

"Mallory," Clare said, his words seeming momentarily to break through her fog of panic, and she stood up, glancing around for her sister.

"Did she really leave without me?" she said, and I wasn't sure if she sounded panicked or furious.

I shot Curtis a questioning look, and he opened his eyes at me, trying to communicate something I was apparently too dense to get.

"Come on," he said, grabbing her arm as the growl ripped through the woods again. I could hear the faint crackling noise coming through on the soundtrack. I'd been eating a bag of chips when I'd recorded this particular piece, but that growl still sent chills down my spine. Especially since this time, I had no idea who was playing that soundtrack.

"Get her out of here," Curtis growled in my ear, thrusting Clare at me. I nodded and tugged her toward the far side of the field, where the tank was parked. A quick glance over my shoulder showed Curtis running toward the woods.

I fumbled in my pocket for the keys. This was made more difficult by Clare, who in her panic ran with all the coordination of a tap-dancing goat.

"Where is your brother going?" she asked.

"No clue," I lied. "He'll be fine. He knows how to take care of himself."

"But that thing?" she said. "I didn't get a good look, but it must have been a mutant wolf or something."

"It's probably just somebody's grumpy farm dog," I

said, my own heart pounding in my chest.

"That was no dog," she said.

"Maybe it was a coyote," I supplied. I was betting on the panic to muddle her enough that my excuse sounded viable.

I finally managed to locate the keys and began pressing the unlock button on the key fob. I knew the car was parked somewhere around here, but the night was dark, and I was worried I'd gotten turned around. Suddenly a loud bang went off directly to our left. Clare screamed and jumped sideways into me. I tripped, and we went down. Scrambling to my feet, I looked over in the direction of the noise and spotted the tank, its trunk open and the trunk light illuminating the surrounding field. Inside the trunk was a disassembled model of the Thetis Lake Monster as well as four different Tupperware containers labeled things like "Hair Specimen of a Skunk Ape" and "Sasquatch Snot" that I was supposed to have put away last week and hadn't. I lunged, slamming the trunk shut before Clare had regained her footing, my heart lodged somewhere near my tonsils. This night just kept getting better and better.

"It was just the car," I said in what I hoped was a reassuring voice.

At that moment a red Mustang came careening across the cornfield. "That's Mallory!" Clare said, jerking out of my arm to run toward the car. Mallory rolled down the window, her eyes wide as Clare dived head-first into the passenger seat.

I thought for a second that Clare's sister was going to offer me a ride, but instead she hit the gas. The last thing I saw before the car took the turn onto the road on squealing wheels was Clare's worried face looking out the window at me.

I ran back toward the bonfire just as the eerie call came again. Following the sound, I changed course and headed into the woods to the left of the fire. If Dad was in jail and Gramps was in Scotland, then who was playing our Shunka Warak'in soundtrack? The glow of the bonfire behind me threw my shadow out in front of me, making me look like the Bigfoot I'd so often imitated. "Curtis!" I yelled.

I stood still, listening for a response, just as the Shunka Warak'in call came again. It was a combination we'd made from mashing together the howl of a coyote and the shriek of a North American mountain lion, with a little wolf thrown in for good measure, and even though I'd helped make it, it still succeeded in sending goose bumps rippling down my back. I pushed the feeling away, wishing that we McNeils weren't quite so good at our jobs. Suddenly there was an angry shout, followed by the sound of a scuffle.

"Curtis!" I called, charging deeper into the woods as the bonfire disappeared behind me. The trees were thick, and brambles and weeds tore at my legs, making the going rough, but I thrashed my way through. Curtis yelled again, but his words were too garbled by the night for me to tell what he was saying. Before I had time to really think about what I was rushing into, I broke free of the trees and into a moonlit clearing.

The first thing I saw was the Shunka Warak'in lying on the ground. Dad had built it himself, forever retiring Gramps's old moth-eaten version we'd had to animate using a complicated system of ropes. Dad's used a remote control, the audio built right into it so you could change out the sound effect CD just by lifting a flap on its chest. Modeled to look like some weird combination of a dog and a hyena, we used the Shunka Warak'in only for Idaho jobs, since it was Idaho's Ioway tribe that had made this particular cryptid famous. What was it doing here?

Behind it, Curtis sat on the ground holding his bleeding nose. I barely registered the large man standing behind him until a set of strong hands grabbed me and brought me to my knees, hard. I turned to look up into the sneering, angular face of a teenage boy I'd never seen before.

"Who are you?" I asked.

Curtis spit and wiped his face with his sleeve as he glared up at the man still holding his arms behind his back. "Grayson," he said, "meet the Gerhards."

CHAPTER TWELVE

"The Gerhards?" I asked as my brain fought frantically to make sense of the two strangers that towered over us. "Why aren't you in Germany?"

The man standing behind Curtis snorted. "That's the same thing your brother said. You thought maybe Germans weren't issued passports? Weren't allowed on airplanes?" His English was perfect, although his German accent was still thick. Standing over six feet tall, he towered above my brother.

"Let's cut to the chase," the boy behind me said. He didn't have an accent at all. "Those kids are probably all running to tell their mommies about the scary monster in the woods, and I don't want to be here when the police show up." The kid had to be around Curtis's age, but he seemed older somehow. Maybe it was his impressive build, I reasoned. Curtis was no shrimp, but compared to this guy, he looked practically scrawny. Although, to be fair, the only place that kid *wouldn't* look scrawny was in a lineup of NFL linebackers.

"What *do* you want?" Curtis asked.

"To meet the rest of the fabled McNeils of course," he sneered. "We've been hearing about your family's hoaxes and hunts for years, and I wanted to see if you really did look like the ugly, rat-faced thieves my grandfather described." Reaching down, he grabbed my chin roughly and turned it this way and that in the moonlight before nodding. "Good to know the old man wasn't exaggerating," he said. I yanked my chin away.

"No one flies all the way from Germany just to look at someone," Curtis said. "And where did you get our Shunka Warak'in? Dad took it with him to pull a bonus hoax on his way back from . . ." He trailed off, his lips pressing into a thin line as it apparently dawned on him what a bad idea it would be to tell these guys what Dad was up to.

"Back from Scotland? Or Vermont?" said the man with an ugly laugh. "Oh, we know all about the Sea Monster Grand Slam. That job should have been ours, and it would have been if your dad hadn't offered to do it for a thousand bucks less than we did. But lucky for us the guys who wanted the Grand Slam couldn't care less about who actually does the first three hoaxes as long as the last one, Champ, gets done. So when your dad doesn't complete the job by Tuesday at sundown, per his contract, guess who will be pulling it off on Wednesday morning and collecting a nice fat check? Really we should thank you for doing the first three of the four hoaxes. The Altamaha-ha job in particular was nicely done, considering it was pulled off by two kids barely out of diapers."

"Wait a second," I said, realization dawning. "You were there that day? Were you in the bushes?"

Curtis shot me a sharp look, and I remembered again my moment of panic on the shore of the Altamaha River when I thought I'd seen binoculars.

The teenage boy smiled, revealing two rows of crooked teeth. "We were," he said. "I wanted to grab you both then, but my uncle said no."

"We needed them to lead us back to their house, Clive," said the man with a touch of annoyance in his voice. "When am I going to get through to you that hoaxing is about thinking ten steps ahead?"

"Sorry, Uncle Axel," said Clive, not sounding in the least bit sorry.

"You're still learning," Axel said, "but it would help

if you paid attention during your training every once in a while." He turned his attention away from his nephew and back to us. "So thank you for saving us some work, but we will be taking over the Grand Slam from here and collecting that check."

I felt like someone had just punched me in the gut. There *had* been someone in the bushes that day, and I'd been too worried about my stupid hand to investigate like I should have. And now they were going to screw up the Grand Slam. "You can't do that. It's cheating," I said, even though I knew just how lame that sounded.

"Can you really cheat on a hoax?" asked Clive with a wide grin that pulled his already narrow eyes into small slits. I stared at him, my own eyes narrowing in concentration. There was something weirdly familiar about the boy, which made no sense since I was positive I'd never met him before in my life.

"I don't know about that," Axel said with a jerk of his head toward our downed Shunka Warak'in. "But as it turns out, you *can* hoax a hoaxer."

"How did you even know we'd be here tonight?" Curtis asked.

"We have our sources," said Axel with a smile and a wink at Clive.

"But Dad's Shunka Warak'in?" I said, still having trouble putting this all together.

"Ah, your dear old dad," said Axel. "He wasn't at all happy to see us, was he, Clive?" he asked, and his nephew snorted. "It was as though he didn't want us to borrow the Shunka Warak'in."

I twisted to glare at Axel Gerhard and felt a shiver run up my spine. While his nephew, Clive, was built like a professional wrestler, Axel was smaller, with an angular sharpness to him that made him stand out against the moonlight.

"Liar. He'd never let you borrow that," I said. "He won't even let Curtis and me touch it, let alone use it."

Axel looked at me, his deep-set eyes turning pure black in the dim light of the clearing. "I may be using the word *borrow* loosely." He chuckled. "You see, we knew your dad was going to be tied up for quite some time and wouldn't be needing it. So we thought we'd give it a few test runs."

"So you stole it," Curtis said. "You waited until Dad got caught, and you stole it."

"Worse than that," I said, glancing from one smug face to the other. "I'd bet anything they're the reason he got caught in the first place." Axel smirked at Clive, and I felt something click into place. "Did Dad even get caught?" I asked. "Or was that a lie too?"

"I see this is the one with the brains in the family," said Axel with a smile as he lit up a cigarette.

"Although since you're a McNeil, I'm afraid that isn't much of a compliment."

"I don't understand," I said. "Don't you have a successful hoaxing business of your own? Why do you need to steal the Grand Slam?"

"We did," he said. "But times are getting tough, and we thought that it was high time to monopolize the market, if you will."

"The market?" Curtis scoffed. "There is no one else in the hoax market but us."

"Exactly," Clive said with a smile. "So if we take out the dumb McNeils once and for all, there is no one left to pick our pockets clean by snapping up all the choice jobs."

"We don't snap up the choice jobs," Curtis said. "And Dad didn't cheat you out of anything. You just do junky work. Gramps told me all about you guys. Practically getting caught at every turn, not being thorough with your evidence placement and your eyewitnesses. Sloppy."

I stifled a groan. Leave it to Curtis to insult the very people holding us captive. Sometimes he was just like Gramps.

"Gramps," I gasped out loud, as realization hit. I turned horrified eyes to Axel, no longer caring how terrifying he was. "Did you do something to Gramps too?"

I asked. Even in the moonlight I could see Curtis's face go white.

"The old man?" He chuckled. "Don't you worry about him. He just took a little detour on his way to the airport. As long as he doesn't cause trouble, he'll probably be fine."

"Probably?" I echoed, feeling ill.

"It was almost too simple," Axel said around the cigarette. "A bit of a letdown, really. Two phone calls and the McNeil patriarch and his son come running. Almost too easy to nab them both. The only thing left to deal with is you two, and honestly, it was just an excuse to try out your dad's robotic mutt."

"What did you jerks do to them?" Curtis said.

"The same thing we will do to you two if you don't listen and listen good," said Axel, leaning forward threateningly. "The McNeils are officially out of the hoaxing business. The cryptid hunting business too, for that matter, although rumor has it that you don't do much of that anymore."

"You can't do that," I said.

"Who is going to stop us?" Axel said, blowing out a puff of smoke directly into Curtis's face. "Please. Call the police. Explain to them that your family has been in the hoaxing business for over a century and now someone's trying to cut you out of the criminal game."

He laughed, and I clenched my fists so hard that the car keys I still held dug painfully into my palm.

Axel shook his head. "Everyone here knows that you won't risk having your family name plastered all over the headlines. You won't say a word, and if you do, you just make our job that much easier. The McNeils will be found out, and every business contact your family managed to make will come calling for the Gerhards. So in fact, please do tell, because it will just expedite things." He smiled coldly.

My chest felt tight, and I wondered momentarily if this was what a panic attack felt like. I'd wished the hoaxing life away millions of times, but I'd never pictured it getting ripped away like this. Just then a distant siren sounded, and the faint glow of red and blue lights flashed through the woods.

Axel glanced down at his watch and grinned. "Just in time," he said.

"What?" Curtis asked, glancing frantically from the toppled and lifeless Shunka Warak'in to the flashing trees and back again.

"You can never trust teenagers, you know," Axel said with smile that made my stomach hurt. "Couldn't rely on them to call the police, so I did the job for them. We don't want the delinquents who terrorized that group of poor children with their mechanical monster toy to get away. Now do we? Besides, we have a job to organize in Vermont. There is a very disgruntled client looking for someone to finish the hoax your dad so kindly dropped the ball on, and I know just the family to do it."

"Do we really have to leave it behind?" asked Clive as he gazed longingly at the Shunka Warak'in. "It's so much cooler than the one we use."

"Leave it," barked Axel. "Now get on with it, so we can get out of here."

"Get on with what?" I asked at the same moment that the keys in my hand were pulled free.

"You can't possibly drive in your condition," Clive admonished.

"What condition?" I asked just as something hard clubbed me in the side of the head and everything went black.

CHAPTER THIRTEEN

'd never woken up in a police station before, and if I never did again, that would be just fine with me. My head was pounding like tiny men with hammers were marching around inside, banging on my brain. It was a lot like how I'd felt after having my tonsils taken out when I was five. Although then I'd woken up to a sterile hospital room and my mom holding a cup of green Jell-O. This room smelled like old rubber and stale air, and I blinked as I sat up slowly.

Curtis lay on the bench beside me, snoring loudly as a line of drool dripped down his chin. A giant purple bruise on his forehead solved the mystery of what had knocked me out. The thugs had literally slammed our heads together, and I reached up gingerly to feel the large tender lump on my own head. Wincing, I looked around. We weren't in a jail cell, but I could tell immediately that we were in trouble. A tall police officer with a no-nonsense crew cut sat behind a nearby desk working on a bulky desktop computer. He looked up when he saw me moving, shoving his chair back with an ear-splitting squeak before walking over to crouch in front of me and flash a small flashlight in my eyes.

"What's going on?" I asked, my eyes watering from the sudden onslaught.

The officer sat back on his heels and raised an eyebrow. "You and your brother got picked up on private property after a few hysterical girls called about a monster in the woods."

"Monster?" I asked.

"I'm assuming they meant that thing," he said, jerking his head to where Dad's precious Shunka Warak'in lay on its side, its two front legs bent oddly out of shape as though someone had tried to force it into a too-small trunk. "Your brother is still out cold. Want to tell me what happened?"

I glanced back over at Curtis, wishing that he'd woken up first. He was so much better at lying on the fly, and we were going to need a real doozy to get out of this. "Um. No?" I said. Now that my brain was fully awake, it was spinning in frantic circles as the events of the night rushed back to me. The officer must have seen something on my face because with a booted foot he slid over a small metal trash can seconds before my insides rolled, and I bent over and hurled directly into the trash can. There wasn't much in my stomach, just the remains of the fast food we'd grabbed on the way home from the crop circle job and one lone s'more, but my body heaved and heaved again as though if it tried hard enough it might be able to send my entire intestinal tract into that trash can.

When I finally finished, I sat back, and the officer held out a bottle of water. I nodded my appreciation as I rinsed out my mouth and spit into the can.

"How old are you, kid?" he asked.

"I'm twelve," I said.

"Looks like you and your brother cracked heads," he said. "We already had a medic look at you, and other than a couple of impressive goose eggs on your noggins, you both checked out fine." The officer nudged the yuck-filled trash can out of the way with his foot. "What I want to know is why we found you both knocked out next to that wolf thing."

I swallowed hard. "We were at the bonfire just like everyone else. Just ask some of the other kids. We were there when that dog thing started howling. Curtis and I ran into the woods to see what it was."

"Wait one second," the officer said, holding up a hand. "So you're telling me that while everyone else was panicking and running for their lives, you and your brother ran *into* the woods to see if there really was a monster?"

"Um," I hesitated, wishing I were close enough to Curtis to give him a good kick. He needed to wake up and soon before I dug the hole we were in any deeper. "Yes?" I said, although it sounded like a question even to my own ears. "We aren't very smart," I said with what I hoped was a convincingly straight face. "And"—I shrugged as inspiration stuck—"there was this girl at the bonfire. Her name's Clare, and I wanted to impress her."

The officer's expression changed, and he nodded as though trying to impress a girl explained all the stupidity in the world, which it probably did.

Curtis chose that moment to wake up, sitting bolt upright with an expression of panic on his face. He whipped his head this way and that, taking in the small, official-looking room before seeing me and the officer. He rubbed at his eyes with the palms of his hands and shook his head hard, as though trying to dislodge something from his ears. I felt myself slump a little in relief. Curtis would know what to do. Curtis always knew what to do.

The officer repeated his performance of flashing his

flashlight into Curtis's eyes and supplied him with his own trash can just in time for him to hurl. Apparently that happened a lot in jail.

Curtis finally spit into his trash can and sat back, and I saw his expression change. Thank God. He had a plan. He smiled sheepishly at the officer.

"Well, we got caught," he said. "I should have known not to have my punk little brother help. He always screws up everything." He turned to glare at my gob-smacked face, then looked back at the officer. "This isn't the first time this officer has caught someone trying to pull off a senior-class prank, is it, sir?"

"It most definitely is not," he said, giving me a look that clearly showed his disapproval of my lie, since he'd just swallowed Curtis's story hook, line, and sinker. I tried to look appropriately sheepish while silently thanking my lucky stars that Curtis was such a convincing liar.

"Although," the officer said with a shake of his head, "I have to admit this is one of the weirder pranks I've ever seen. Now I just need to call your parents, and we can decide what to do with you two." My heart lurched again as I thought about Dad and Gramps, but Curtis made a face.

"That may be hard to do, officer," he said. "Our mom passed away a few years ago, and our dad and grandfather are in Scotland at the moment."

"In Scotland?" the officer repeated, but not before I saw his face do that thing that people's always did when they found out that Mom was dead. A flash of sympathy and, in this case, understanding, as though Mom dying somehow explained why we'd been found knocked out in the woods with a strange mechanical monster-dog.

"Family emergency," Curtis went on. "Our uncle got in a car accident; it doesn't look good. It was only supposed to be a short forty-eight-hour trip, but things took a turn for the worse and they got tied up there."

"I see," the officer said, and I took the opportunity to study the chipped concrete floor so that my face, whatever expression it happened to be wearing at the moment, wouldn't give us away. Curtis was doing his thing, and I just needed to stay out of his way.

"Any other adult relative in the area I can call?" the officer asked.

Curtis and I both shook our heads, and the officer huffed and sat back, glancing around the small office as though looking for inspiration. His eyes landed on the mangled Shunka Warak'in, and he turned back to Curtis.

"Why a gigantic dog thing?" he asked. "When I was a kid we just borrowed the local farmer's pig and greased it up."

Curtis shrugged. "Couldn't find a pig."

"Right," the officer said, and sighed. "Well, I have to make some phone calls to figure out what the next step is with you two. So sit tight." He turned and walked back to his desk. A minute later he was on the phone, his back toward us as he talked quietly into the receiver.

"Now what?" I whispered.

"Now you do what the nice officer told you to do," Curtis said. "You sit tight."

"If we get out of this, it's going to be a miracle," I muttered, giving Dad's Shunka Warak'in a dirty look for good measure.

"Agreed," Curtis said.

"That Gerhard kid took the tank's keys," I said, remembering the last hazy moments before I'd been knocked out.

"I think our lack of a ride home is the least of our worries," Curtis said. "Now shut it."

So I did, and it turned out that Curtis was right. Losing the tank really was the least of our worries.

Two hours later the police car pulled away from our dark house, and Curtis and I stood blinking in the predawn light. I hadn't thought it was possible to be this tired, but I was wrong. Every part of me longed to climb into my comfortable bed and stay there forever. Maybe, if I just slept long enough, the entire mess with

Dad, Gramps, the stupid Gerhards, the stolen tank, and the confiscated Shunka Warak'in would just go away. Curtis looked just as bad, his once-clean button-up shirt was puke splattered and wrinkled, and something had torn a hole in the left sleeve. But despite his appearance, I had to admire him a little. He'd talked us out of our tightest spot yet. We both now had tickets for disturbing the peace on our records with strict orders for Dad or Gramps to accompany us to court in a week, but under the circumstances it could have been a lot worse.

"Come on," Curtis said. "Let's get inside before the neighbors spot us looking like the juvenile delinquents we are." I nodded my agreement and stumbled after him toward the house. I was just reaching up to fish the spare key out of the gutter above the front door when I froze.

"What is it?" Curtis asked behind me. "Get a move on, will you?"

"It's the door," I said, taking in the inch of space between the door and its frame. "It's already open."

"What?" Curtis said, and shoved past me, almost knocking me sideways into the bushes as he barged through the front door. My exhaustion forgotten, I charged after him and skidded to a stop inside our living room. It looked the same as we'd left it, not a thing out of place.

"Maybe we just forgot to shut the door all the way the other night?" I said, even though I knew we hadn't. Everything about this felt wrong. Curtis must have been feeling the same thing, because he turned and walked slowly into the kitchen, which also appeared untouched. I was just turning to investigate the bedrooms when I saw it. The basement door was standing wide open, the large bookcase that usually concealed it torn off and cast aside onto the floor, where it lay in broken, splintered pieces. Curtis and I exchanged horrified looks before rushing down the stairs.

The only thing left was the worktable. Every single bin was gone. The wooden shelves they'd sat on stood empty, dusty outlines the only reminders of what had taken generations of McNeils a lifetime to accumulate. The ceiling was stripped clean too, hooks and ropes hanging like untied shoelaces where once full-scale decoys and costumes had hung.

"No," I gasped as I spun in a slow circle. "No. No. No."

Curtis didn't say a word. He just walked slowly into the now-cavernous space, running his hand over the empty shelves and looking around as though in a trance.

"They took everything," I said, sitting down hard on the steps. "It's my fault that they got the keys. I thought they only took the tank. I never imagined . . ."

I swallowed hard at the lump in my throat, unable to really grasp what I was seeing. "They just let themselves in."

Curtis shook his head numbly, his eyes still on the empty shelves as though if he just looked long enough, the bins might magically reappear. "Not your fault," he said, and there was something about his voice, a dead quality that sent goose bumps down my back. "A locked door wouldn't have stopped them. This was always their plan. Don't you see? It was why they brought the Shunka Warak'in to the bonfire. It's why they got Dad arrested and took Gramps. They wanted to get us all out of the way so they could rob us blind. Do me a favor, will you? Go check and see if the van is gone too."

I turned and raced back up the stairs and into the garage. The spot where the kidnapper van usually sat was empty, nothing but a greasy oil stain on the concrete left to show it had ever been there. However, parked in its usual spot, as though we hadn't abandoned it in a cornfield, sat the tank. I blinked at it in surprise before walking over to look inside. Pinned to the steering wheel with the point of a pocketknife was a note in scrawled handwriting. I gingerly pried the knife out, noting the gouge in the leather that would really tick off Gramps, before looking down at the note.

Congratulations on your retirement.

Suddenly the numbness disappeared, and I was mad. Furious to a level I didn't know I was capable of. Muttering some choice Scottish swearwords Gramps probably didn't know I knew, I wadded up the paper and threw it on the ground before stomping on it for good measure. Fuming, I scooped it up and headed inside to find Curtis. He was still in the basement, sitting on the cold concrete in front of the family safe. The thick metal door with its complicated combination lock hung limply on one hinge, apparently having been blown off. Inside the safe the metal shelves sat just as empty and forlorn as the wooden shelves that flanked it. Tears were running down Curtis's cheeks, and I stopped on the stairs, unsure what to do. I hadn't seen Curtis cry since Mom's funeral. It just wasn't something he did.

"Are you okay?" I asked, which sounded just plain stupid in my own ears. Of course he wasn't okay. I certainly wasn't.

Curtis jerked his head at the safe. "They got the family logbook too," he said. "Probably using it to scavenge for potential employers before they chuck it in the trash somewhere." He looked up at me. "Is the van gone?"

I nodded as this new blow of the logbook getting taken sank in. "Yeah. But weirdly enough they returned the tank. It was apparently too ugly even for those stupid Gerhards. Oh, and they left us this." I tossed Curtis the wadded-up note. He gave it one glance, swore, and re-wadded it into a ball before chucking it into the corner of the room.

I looked again at the bare shelves and ceiling. The sight made me feel heavy. This was wrong, all wrong. Even though I'd wanted out of hoaxing my entire life, I'd never, not once, pictured it coming to an end like this. "So now what?" I asked as I dropped my head into my hands, unable to look at all that ugly emptiness any longer.

"Now we go to bed," Curtis said.

"What?" I asked, my head snapping up. "What do you mean we go to bed?"

"You heard me," he said, getting to his feet. "We go to bed."

"But—" I protested, standing up.

"No buts," Curtis said. "Bed. We've been up for almost twenty-four hours."

"But all our stuff. The Gerhards. We can't just—" I said, my words as jumbled and confused as my brain felt.

"It's gone," he said. "They're gone. We can't call the

police, especially after what happened last night. You know that. They know that. Gramps and Dad will know that too. There is nothing we can do. I'll make sure all the doors are locked. Now get." When I didn't move, Curtis scowled and shoved past me up the stairs. "Suit yourself," he said. I stood there as his footsteps padded across the ceiling above me as he went from door to door locking and dead-bolting each one. A minute later I heard his bedroom door shut, and the house went quiet. I sat back down on the steps and put my head back in my hands.

My brain felt like someone had spun it one too many times on the merry-go-round and at any moment it was just going to barf all over someone's shoes. I closed my eyes, and a second later jerked back upright to avoid falling asleep and tumbling headfirst down the stairs. Anger and exhaustion warred inside me for another feeble second before exhaustion won, and I dragged myself up the stairs and into my room, shutting the door softly behind me. It looked the exact same as when I'd left it that morning, but somehow it felt dirty now. A Gerhard brother had probably been in here, poking his filthy hands around in my things, hunting for one last McNeil treasure to steal. No sooner had I thought it than my heart sank and I turned to my backpack and opened it with trembling hands. To my relief there sat my camera. It was no longer in its case, the spare lenses scattered among my notes on Greek history, but it was there. For a second, it was almost funny that my most treasured possession wasn't even worth the effort to steal, but the humor drained away quickly as I thought about all the things that *had* been stolen.

I flopped down on my bed and shut my eyes as the events of the night before whirled through my head. I could almost feel those keys getting pried from my hand. Curtis had said this wasn't my fault, and he was probably right, but it was heavy guilt that pulled me under and into some much needed sleep.

CHAPTER FOURTEEN

I awoke confused. I'd fallen asleep as the sun was coming up, and it appeared it was coming up again through my window. I stared at it for a second, trying to make sense of what I was seeing. Maybe I was wrong and it was going down? It was nearly impossible to tell. There was no way that I'd slept twenty-four straight hours. Was there? It didn't seem entirely impossible. I did feel better physically at least. The nauseous feeling of exhaustion was gone, and except for the fact that I was still wearing the muddy clothes I'd been taken to the police station in, I felt pretty good. Which was wrong because of course nothing was good at the moment. Dad and Gramps were in major trouble. And, oh, we'd been robbed.

I rubbed at my eyes and glanced at my alarm clock, hoping for some sort of clue. It was apparently seven thirty. Seven thirty at night or seven thirty in the morning? My mouth felt like I'd been licking the bottom of someone's shoes, and I smelled like the old shoes I'd apparently been licking. Somehow I found my feet and stumbled into the hall toward Curtis's room, hoping he could tell me what time of day it was. His door was open, and I walked in, stepping over the pile of dirty clothes and discarded textbooks, but what I thought was a sleeping Curtis under a tangle of covers was actually just his pillow and some rumpled sheets.

"Curtis!" I yelled as I headed back down the hall. The kitchen was empty too; the remains of a half-eaten pizza sat on top of the oven. My stomach let out a hungry snarl at the sight, further convincing me that I really had slept for twenty-four hours. I poked at the pizza experimentally. The cheese was ice cold, but I ate a piece anyway. It was either that or my left arm, and I was pretty attached to the arm. "Curtis!" I called again around my mouthful of rubbery pepperoni. "Where are you?"

Our house wasn't that big, so I poked my head into the garage to make sure the tank was still there. I took the opportunity to give the gouge in the steering wheel the stink eye before turning to look out the window again. The sun was still in limbo, and I couldn't tell if it was going up or going down. Weirdest feeling ever. Like waking up and not being able to tell if you were on the ceiling or the floor.

I walked back into the house, this time pausing long enough to microwave one of the pieces of pizza before eating it. This time it was too hot, and the roof of my mouth got a good scalding before I swallowed and let the pizza sear my throat on the way down. That's when I noticed the light on in the basement. Hadn't Curtis had enough of that depressing sight?

I headed down the basement stairs, and their familiar creak echoed weirdly off the bare walls. It felt like walking into a graveyard or the scene of some tragic accident. No Curtis. I was about to go back up to keep looking, but I found myself sitting on the empty worktable instead, my quest forgotten to find out what day it was. What did it matter, really? And, not for the first time, I imagined what my family's life would look like without hoaxing and failed. It was like trying to picture a fish climbing a tree or an elephant flying. Ever since Mom had died, Dad's entire life revolved around hoaxing. He loved it more than he loved us. Which wasn't self-pity talking at all; it was just the truth. What would he do now that it was all gone? Then there was Gramps, who loved the hunt more than the hoax, but if the Gerhards' threats were to be believed, even *that* had been taken away. And Curtis? Curtis wanted this life, had planned for it, and now the future he'd imagined would never happen.

I wasn't sure how long I'd sat there on that worktable thinking before I heard the kitchen door upstairs slam shut. I waited for Curtis to come down and find me, and when he didn't, I pried myself off the table and back up the stairs, my sights set on another piece of that awful pizza. I found him sitting at the kitchen table. Unlike me he'd showered and changed into a gray T-shirt and jeans. I took in the dark circles that sat like plum-colored bruises under his eyes. If I'd slept for a hundred years, he'd been awake for just as long.

"So when you told me to go to bed this morning, that was just for show?" I asked, sitting down across from him. I paused and glanced back out the window. "This may sound stupid," I said, "but it was *this* morning, wasn't it? Is it seven thirty in the morning or seven thirty at night? What day is it?"

"It's Sunday night," Curtis said absentmindedly as he spun his cell phone around in a circle on the table.

"Okay," I said. "So I didn't sleep for twenty-four hours. That's good, I guess."

"Congratulations," Curtis said, without looking up.

"Where were you?" I asked.

"Out," Curtis said.

"Well, thanks for clarifying that," I grumbled as I got up to throw another piece of pizza in the microwave.

"I think we need to call the police," Curtis said, so quietly that at first I didn't think I'd heard him correctly over the whir of our ancient microwave. I pushed the Off button and turned to him.

"Come again?" I said. "Did you just say call the police? You know we can't."

Curtis looked up at me then, and I saw something in his eyes that I'd never seen before, a dullness that made my heart feel like I'd just tied an anchor to it and tossed it into the deepest part of the ocean.

"Why not?" he asked. "It doesn't matter anymore. I've gone over it a million times in my head. We can't finish the Sea Monster Grand Slam without our stuff, and the Gerhards will make sure our reputation is ruined after we botch the job. So even if they hadn't taken everything, which they did, it would be Game Over. The important thing is getting Dad and Gramps back, and if that means we have to call the police, then that's what we are going to do."

"But Dad and Gramps would never—" I started.

"Gramps and Dad aren't here," Curtis cut in. "Look around, Grayson. We have nothing left. The log, our hoaxing gear, the van—it's all gone. We have no leverage and no way to fix this on our own. It's over."

I sat back down. "But the police?" I said. "Then everything will come out. All the hoaxing, the hunts, the— well, everything." I spread my hands out as though somehow I could encompass over a hundred years of our crooked history in one gesture.

"Don't worry," Curtis said. "I don't think it will affect your chances of getting into that fancy boarding school."

This jolted me out of my previous shock, and I narrowed my eyes at him. "How do you know about Culver?"

Curtis flapped a hand at me like I was an annoying fly he could brush away. "You've had the dumb brochure under your bed for months now, and you aren't nearly as sneaky as you think. And just for the record, when I was your age, I hid much more interesting things under my bed. But don't worry. I hear lots of the kids that go there have at least one family scandal in their past. Although it usually involves some kind of embezzlement scam or insider trading or whatever."

I stared at him for a second, taking in the fact that he'd known about Culver all this time.

"The McNeils have hoaxed their last hoax," Curtis went on. "You can throw the party later."

"I'm not going to throw a party," I said, although, truth be told, that's exactly what I'd envisioned doing if I got into Culver and never had to hoax again. It wouldn't have been a very big party, just me and an extra-large Heath Blizzard from Dairy Queen, but still.

"Save it," Curtis said. "You don't have to lie for my benefit. You finally got what you always wanted."

"I didn't want *this*," I said, then swallowed hard as the lie stuck halfway up my throat. "Well, I didn't want it this way," I clarified. "So why haven't you done it yet?" I asked.

"Because it feels like a betrayal," Curtis said, running his hands through his hair in frustration. "I need to get some sleep. I'll call them first thing in the morning. I'm sure Officer Crew Cut will be excited to hear from us."

I glanced back out the window as Curtis's footsteps faded down the hall. The sun had set, and I reminded myself that it was Sunday night. Tomorrow was a school day. A school day I couldn't miss. The thought felt absurd, like my conversation with Mrs. Howard over my attendance had taken place two hundred years ago instead of only two days ago. The pizza I'd eaten sat uneasily in my stomach, and I put my head down on the table and shut my eyes, actually wishing for the previous few days' exhaustion. Slipping away into sleep would be a welcome break from everything battling inside my brain. I was just as worried about Dad and Gramps as Curtis was, and I had to admit that the police seemed the best option. The Gerhards had been pointedly vague about their plans for Dad and Gramps, simply insinuating that they would be kept out of the way until the Champ hoax was over. Thinking about the Champ hoax set my teeth on edge, and I clenched my jaw as I stared at the battered wood of our crappy kitchen table. We'd been one hoax away from getting the bank off our backs, and now Curtis and I couldn't even attempt it ourselves because every single piece of hoaxing equipment we owned was gone.

Resting my head on the table was doing nothing but giving me a headache, so I sat back. The kitchen was a wreck, so with no clue of what else to do with myself, I started washing the mountain of dishes in the sink and disposing of the layer of clutter that had accumulated on the countertops. I was working on autopilot, my brain still churning with images of the police walking around our empty basement as we reported what had to be the most bizarre robbery in the history of ever, when I moved a stack of papers to reveal a leatherbound book I didn't think I'd ever see again.

There on the counter sat the family logbook, exactly where I'd chucked it after my fight with Curtis the other night. I stood there staring at it for a second and almost called Curtis before I remembered how exhausted he'd looked and stopped myself. I picked up the log. Dad and Gramps never let us touch the thing, let alone hold it, and its weight felt unfamiliar in my hands. My feeling of elation at seeing it fizzled a little as I carried it over to the kitchen table and sat down. It didn't really fix any of our problems. If anything it was just something for the police to label as Exhibit A when they started collecting evidence tomorrow after Curtis called them. I wondered momentarily if I should destroy it, burn it, or shove it piece by piece down the garbage disposal. Instead I opened up the front cover.

I'd expected the log to start on page one with the account of good old Floyd McNeil's accomplishments when he first made a deal with the Cadboro mayor to pull off that first sea monster hoax. It would have made sense, considering he was the one who had gotten the McNeils into the hoaxing business to begin with, but instead the front page contained an intricate drawing of an old Scottish coat of arms. Our Scottish coat of arms, I realized, the McNeils'. Gramps had the exact same one tattooed across his back and shoulder blades, a fact that had intrigued me a lot right after he moved in with us, but I couldn't remember the last time I'd really noticed it. Although, admittedly, the tattoo had gotten covered up by thicker and thicker layers of back hair as Gramps had gotten older, so looking closely at it wasn't really encouraged. Now I leaned closer to the page to get a better look. In the center of the coat of arms was a shield divided into four separate compartments, each with its own tiny picture perfectly drawn inside: a ship, a lion, a castle, and a red hand facing palm out. I had no idea what any of them meant, but I couldn't help but feel like that palm must have something to do with getting caught red-handed. Why hadn't I ever asked Gramps about it before?

I flipped the page, still expecting to find Floyd McNeil, but instead I found only one line of official-looking writing. The ink had started to fade with age, and I squinted so I could see it better.

Keep the Legends Alive.

I read it three times before sitting back in my chair. I'd never heard the phrase before, but there was something about it that twisted inside me. My family had been in the business of creating and chasing legendary creatures for over a hundred years. Because of what my dad and grandpa and great-grandpa and so on had done, there was still mystery in the world. People wondered about creatures like Bigfoot and the Yeti, little

174

boys and girls pored over grainy images of sea monsters, and camp counselors told scary stories about the Chupacabra and the Bunyip. A lot of that could be credited to my family working behind the scenes and keeping the legends alive.

We were the great and powerful Oz, I realized, remembering the scene from *The Wizard of Oz*. Dorothy and her entourage finally made it to the Emerald City and came face-to-face with the great and powerful Oz, or at least his weirdly floating head. If Curtis turned this book in to the police tomorrow, it would be like Dorothy pulling back that curtain to reveal that the great and wonderful wizard was nothing but a sham. The police would comb through the thick yellow pages of my family history and connect my ancestors to hundreds of unsolved mysteries. They would debunk every legend, explain away the unexplainable, and essentially ruin the cryptid hunting industry forever. If this book came to light, no one would ever believe in the mysterious or the unknown again. And was that really fair? I may be as un-McNeil as they came, but in a world dominated by instantaneous Google searches and smartphones equipped with the technology to answer any question you asked, wasn't it nice that there were still things the human race hadn't quite figured out? I no longer believed there were mysterious creatures out there just waiting to be discovered, but did that mean no one else should either?

I leaned back, reading and rereading those words over and over. I wasn't sure how I really felt about this new realization. It sat uncomfortably with everything I'd thought about the hoaxing business for the majority of my life. What did it say about me that it took losing everything for me to see what Gramps, Dad, and Curtis had probably known all along? Even though I still wanted out, I suddenly realized that I didn't want the McNeils' hoaxing career to end. Not like this.

If Gramps were here, he'd know exactly what to do, I thought angrily. He'd never let the Gerhards outsmart us. But, I remembered with a pang, Gramps wasn't here. He was being kept somewhere by the Gerhards until they had a chance to pull off Dad's Champ job and cement the end of the McNeils' hoaxing forever. I knew that his safety was the real reason Curtis was ready to turn over everything to the police. I gnawed on my bottom lip in frustration. Gramps had a rather vulgar way of describing situations like this involving a river of poop and a canoe with no paddle, and I had to think it was probably the best description of our current dilemma. Saying the cards were stacked against us just sounded too tame.

My brain was starting to hurt, so I turned back to

the log and flipped to the next page. I'd been right: it did start with Floyd McNeil, who was apparently a really lousy coal miner before the whole hoaxing gig landed in his lap. As the evening turned into night and midnight came and went, I dug further and further into the log, reading about the details of hoax after hoax and hunt after hunt. The hunting reports were all pretty much the same as my ancestors chased down legends, always finding some bit of evidence or small clue that kept their hopes alive until they could earn enough money hoaxing for the next hunt.

The hoaxes were more interesting as the years progressed, becoming more elaborate and high tech. Every few pages I'd find a diagram of an early cryptid model or costume design. Some weren't even attached to the log and were simply folded in half and tucked in between the pages. I unfolded these gingerly, particularly enjoying the diagrams of some of the early attempts at the Hell Hound and the Kraken. Compared to what we used now, they were pretty basic but still impressive, considering my ancestors had been cobbling them together before Henry Ford had figured out how to engineer his first Model T. It wasn't until I found one of the first working models of the Loveland Frog, created back in 1955 by an overachieving uncle, that I noticed the small word written in red ink in the bottom right-hand corner of the page, *Annex D*, and stopped cold.

The Annexes. How in the name of Bigfoot had I forgotten about the annexes? Every old piece of cryptid hunting or hoaxing junk had been stashed away in one of the family annexes. If we could just get to the Vermont Annex, there was bound to be something there we could use to pull off the Champ job. And then my excitement and hope got hit by a double-decker bus. There probably was an annex in Vermont, but the only people who knew where that annex was were either in jail or missing. I sagged in disappointment and looked back down at the log.

Now that I'd spotted those small red words, I started to notice red writing all over the place. There apparently were an Annex A and B and even an Annex Z. Almost every cryptid diagram had an annex listed on there somewhere, and even a few of the hoax accounts had a small red A written behind them. The annexes are taunting me, I thought bitterly. Why had I never thought to ask Gramps or Dad about their locations? But even as I thought that, I knew the answer. It was because I'd never cared.

It wasn't until I got to the back of the log that I found what I'd been secretly hoping for. I shut the log and sat back, a plan already forming as I carefully folded the piece of paper that I'd torn out of the back of the log. Gramps and Dad would freak if they knew I'd ripped something out of their precious book, but unless my plan worked, this log wasn't going to be anything but a sad reminder of what the McNeils used to be. Or, I remembered, Exhibit A in the trial to put us all behind bars for fraud. But if my plan actually worked, which was the longest of long shots, then my page tearing would be more than forgiven. I glanced at the clock. It was already four in the morning, but if I hustled, I'd have just enough time to pull off the biggest McNeil hoax yet.

Adrenaline pumping, I bounded to my feet and opened the fridge in search of some caffeine and maybe a dish of rocky road. Five minutes later I sat down at Dad's computer armed with a Coke and a dish of ice cream as big as my head. I wiggled the mouse to wake up the computer and saw my notebook, still open to my list of lame ideas for the scholarship essay. My heart sank. The scholarship essay. The one that was due by Wednesday. The one I hadn't even started yet and would have no chance of finishing if I implemented my plan to save the McNeils' hoaxing career. I'm not sure how long I sat there, maybe a minute, maybe a lifetime, as I played out both scenarios in my mind. Culver vs. Cryptids. Hoaxing vs. Happiness. But as I wrestled with the decision, I remembered those words in the front of the logbook. If my family's legacy was making sure that the legends stayed alive, who was I to stand in the way of that? I was torn from my debate by something buzzing under my hand, and I jumped and looked down to find Curtis's cell phone plugged in next to the keyboard. Its screen was flashing blue with a new text message, and I picked it up. The text was from a strange number, and I opened it, already thinking up the excuse I'd tell Curtis for snooping around his phone without permission.

Hi Curtis This is Grayson's friend Clare Mayfield. Mallory's little sister. Grayson gave me your number. I hope that's ok. Anyway, I just wanted to make sure you guys were ok after everything that happened at the bonfire. That was crazy. If you could have Grayson text me back, that would be great. Thanx.

I reread the text and then sat back. In the chaos of waking up in jail I'd completely forgotten about giving her Curtis's cell number. I glanced at the clock. It was almost five a.m., but I decided to text her back anyway.

Hi Clare. This is Grayson. We are okay. Thanks for checking.

Setting the phone down, I turned back to the computer and pulled up the website for discount airplane tickets my dad always used. The shrill ring of Curtis's cell phone sliced through the sleepy silence of the house a moment later, and I jumped about a foot. Clare's number was flashing on the caller ID. I picked up the phone and stared at it for a second. Was Clare really calling me? At five a.m.?

I slid my finger across the screen to accept the call and held the phone to my ear.

"Hello?" I whispered.

"Grayson?" came Clare's voice.

"Um, yeah," I said. "Hi."

"What are you doing up so early?"

"Why are *you* calling so early?" I countered.

"Right," she said, then hesitated. "Well, I just wanted to apologize."

"For what?"

"For the bonfire," Clare said. "For ditching you like that. Mallory totally should have waited for you to get in the car."

I paused at this, remembering how Clare's sister had peeled out of that cornfield without a backward glance. In hindsight that was pretty crummy, although I remembered feeling only relief at the time that they were out of the fray.

"It's okay," I said.

"I heard you were arrested," she said. "I'm actually kind of surprised you were able to answer the phone. I figured you'd still be at the police station."

"Oh," I said, feeling my face flush red. "That. Um, I'm not sure we were actually arrested. They didn't take mug shots or anything, but yeah, we were at the police station."

"I can't believe they let you go with your dad and grandpa out of town," she said. "Aren't you both minors? I figured they'd detain you both until your dad or grandpa came back."

"Curtis did some fast talking," I said. "He's good at that."

"I believe it," Clare said. "So what are you doing up so early if you're not in jail?"

My brain scrambled for something cool or interesting I could possibly be doing at five in the morning. "Looking at airplane tickets," I said, because the truth was as good as anything right now. Besides, what was the harm in telling her?

"Tickets?" she said. "Why?"

"Thinking about going to Vermont," I said as I consulted the page I'd torn from the log for the correct address, then typed it in.

"Really . . . ?" she said, her voice trailing off. "When are you going?"

"Tomorrow," I said, then glanced at the time on the computer. "Scratch that. Today."

"You shouldn't go," Clare said suddenly.

This brought me up short, and I stopped typing in our billing information.

"Why?" I asked, even though if I was honest with myself, I wasn't fully committed yet. My Culver essay prompt—*What Does the World Need?*—was still leering at me from my open notebook, so I shut it.

"I just don't think you should," Clare said. "Especially by yourself."

"Who said I was going by myself?" I asked. There was an awkward pause, and I wondered if I'd offended her somehow.

"You did," she finally said.

"I did?"

"Yeah," she said. "You told me that Curtis would have to drive you to the bonfire because your grandpa and dad were out of town. I assumed that if you were leaving today they wouldn't be with you?"

"Oh," I said, feeling exceptionally dumb. "Right. Well, don't worry about me. I'll be fine. Curtis is coming."

"I'm serious, Grayson," she said. "Don't go." And there was something different about her voice, a seriousness that usually wasn't there. But before I could think too much about it, I heard the creak of Curtis's door opening down the hall.

"Sorry, Clare," I said. "I gotta go. Bye." I hung up

and hurriedly deleted our text messages as well as her number from the recent call list before plugging Curtis's cell phone back in and putting it back exactly where I'd found it. I shouldn't have worried, though, because a second later I heard the flush of the hall bathroom's toilet, followed by Curtis's door shutting again. I sagged in relief, feeling a little guilty for hanging up on Clare like that. I quickly brushed the feeling aside and focused back on the computer screen, my mind made up. It was time to buy some plane tickets to Vermont.

CHAPTER FIFTEEN

"Something better be on fire," Curtis groaned when I charged into his room and turned on his lights a few hours later.

"Get up," I said.

Curtis glared at me. "Remind me again why Mom and Dad didn't drown you at birth?" he asked.

"Shut up and get up," I said. "We can fix this. We can pull off the Grand Slam."

Curtis shoved aside the tangle of blond hair that had flopped over his forehead, and he narrowed his eyes at me. "What are you talking about? You need a sea monster to pull off a sea monster hoax. A really good sea monster, and last I checked we were fresh out."

"Then we should probably go get one," I said, not even bothering to keep the smugness out of my voice.

"And where are you planning on getting a gigantic sea monster decoy on short notice? Walmart?"

I inspected my nails nonchalantly. "I was actually thinking we could get one from one of the annexes."

"The annexes?" Curtis repeated, and then sat bolt upright. "Holy crap! The annexes!"

"Actually, just the Vermont Annex," I said. "Annex V. Keep up. We don't have a lot of time if we're going to catch a flight to Vermont this afternoon." Curtis looked like he was about ready to say something, then he just shook his head and motioned for me to go on. So I did.

"You and I are going to finish the Grand Slam. And when we do, we are going to take our great big check and trade it straight up for Gramps and Dad."

Curtis stared at me for a second, and I felt my triumphant smile of moments before begin to slip at his expression.

"Great plan," Curtis said. "But we don't know where the annexes are."

"Correct," I said, using my best game-show-host voice that I knew annoyed him. "But you are forgetting about one thing. The logbook!"

"You mean the log the Gerhards took?" Curtis asked. He flopped backward in his bed and threw his covers over his head.

"Nope," I said. "I mean the logbook they didn't take." Curtis sat up, his eyes wide as he took in the logbook perched in my hands. "Turns out the Gerhards didn't get everything. I never put it back in the safe after our fight the other night, and I've been up all night reading it. And when I got to the very back, I found this," I said, pulling the page out of my pocket and handing it to Curtis. He took it gingerly, as though I'd just handed him a live snake.

"Wait a second," he said before he'd even unfolded it the whole way. "Did you tear this out of the log? Dad's gonna kill you."

"Prioritize," I said. "The log is a glorified paperweight unless we do something. Now, look."

Curtis looked, and his eyes grew big. I knew the feeling. I'd felt the same shocked surprise when I saw the map displaying the multiple locations of the McNeil family annexes. Curtis studied the map for a while longer before setting it down to look up at me.

"These annexes aren't what you think they are. I went to the Iowa one with Dad once. They are basically stashes of old cryptid crap—broken decoys, half-decayed costumes, rusting gear—a whole bunch of junk that no one wanted to throw away."

I brushed his comment off with a wave of my hand. "Did you see this?" I asked, leaning over his shoulder to point at the address I'd circled. "There's an annex in Vermont right by Lake Champlain. I guarantee there is an old Champ decoy in there. And an old decrepit Champ decoy is better than no decoy."

Curtis stared at the address, and I could almost hear his brain clicking.

"So what do you think?" I asked. "Do you still want to call the police? Or do you want to beat the Gerhards at their own game?"

"I want to beat the Gerhards," Curtis said.

"Good. Then get up. We have a lot to get done, and I already booked our tickets to Vermont for this afternoon. Nonrefundable."

"How did you manage that one?" he asked. "The Gerhards grabbed the rest of the Altie cash."

"Dad's credit card information was saved on our computer," I said while processing the new bit of information. I'd been banking on using that two hundred bucks for travel expenses. Now what?

"Well played." Curtis nodded, swinging his legs out of bed. "And you're sure this plan is good?"

"I'm not," I said, deciding that now was not the time to bring up our lack of funds. I'd just have to figure it out, that's all. "But it's all we've got."

"Fair enough," Curtis said as he grabbed an abandoned T-shirt off the floor, gave it a sniff, and slipped it over his head. "Wait a second," he said, turning to me.

"What about school? I thought you couldn't miss any more days if you wanted to get into that fancy boarding school?"

I felt my guts twist a little at his words, but I clenched my hands into fists. I'd made my choice, and even though my stomach felt like I'd swallowed a family of snakes, I knew that I'd made the right one.

"I can figure out a way to be a photographer without Culver," I said, wishing I felt as convinced as I sounded. "Family is more important."

Curtis studied me for a second longer, then nodded and clapped me on the shoulder. "It's about time you figured that out."

We had to hustle, but we made it to the airport that afternoon in plenty of time for our flight. At least I thought it was plenty of time until we hit airport security. I fidgeted uncomfortably as the attendant gave us the stink eye before turning back to our passports.

"And you're sure you're eighteen? You have to be eighteen to fly with a minor," he said to Curtis.

Curtis nodded. "Yes, sir."

"When is your birthday?" the man asked.

"July 21, 2001," Curtis said without batting an eye. It was an admirable performance. Curtis might be a C student in school on a good day, but he could lie with the best of them. Which was lucky, because he was no more eighteen than I was.

The airport attendant nodded, then looked back at Curtis from the passport. "It says here that you're both not checking bags? Seems odd."

Curtis nodded. "That's correct. Our dad and grandfather are already in Vermont, and they shipped our bags over with their research equipment."

"Research equipment?" the man asked.

"They are studying the effects of maple syrup consumption on the brain development of groundhogs," Curtis said, and I almost choked but held it in.

"Is that right?" the man said, then with a shake of his head he handed Curtis back his passport, gave mine a cursory glance, and waved us on.

"Maple syrup and groundhogs?" I whispered a few minutes later as we walked toward our gate.

Curtis smirked. "It's all I had. If that didn't work, I was going to start pretending you were the long-lost child of a Vermont mountain hermit."

"Just call me Heidi," I said.

"Huh?" Curtis asked.

I just shook my head. "You really should read more books," I said. "*Heidi* is a classic."

"Unless the Heidi you're talking about is Heidi Klum, I couldn't care less," Curtis said as he gave two college-age girls walking by his ear-to-ear, *Aren't I cute?* smile that showed off his dimples. I decided that pointing out that the literary Heidi was nothing like Heidi Klum would be a wasted effort.

"Thanks," I said, shaking my head as Curtis gave the girls an overexaggerated wink that made them giggle.

"They're too old for you," I said.

"Not today they're not." Curtis smirked. "Today I'm eighteen, and I have a passport to prove it and everything."

"We're just lucky that worked," I said.

Curtis scoffed. "Luck schmuck. Gramps is one of the best paper forgers in McNeil history. There was no way it *wasn't* going to work."

I rolled my eyes. "You know what I meant."

"Should we grab something to eat?" Curtis said.

I nodded. "That's a good idea. It's a long flight."

"That's an understatement and a half," Curtis said. "I may actually *be* eighteen by the time we finally get to Vermont."

Ten minutes later we were sitting down at our gate with small greasy cardboard boxes in hand. Inside were pizzas that smelled heavenly but cost more money than an extra-large pizza at the place we usually ordered from at home.

"Do you know what this reminds me of?" I asked,

and then took a sip of the bottled water I'd paid almost five dollars for—airports were a real rip-off.

"No clue," Curtis said, taking it from my hand and taking a long drag before handing it back.

"Traveling with Gramps," I said, wiping off the lid with the sleeve of my shirt. "I think the last time I was in an airport, he was taking us to Scotland."

"Ah," Curtis said. "I remember that trip. The flight of the never-ending barf bags. Good times."

I made a face at him, wishing I'd thought to grab some motion-sickness medicine at the little kiosk where I'd bought my water bottle.

"But seriously," Curtis said. "That was the last time you flew? What were you, eight? Didn't you go with us on the Mongolian Death Worm expedition?"

I shook my head, my mouth too full of pizza to answer.

"What about the Storsjön trip?" Curtis said. "Or the Nandi Bear hunt?"

"Nope and nope," I said. "After Scotland, whenever Gramps offered, I always said I had too much going on at school and that you should go."

Curtis shook his head. "You were already signing out, weren't you? I'm surprised I didn't realize it back then."

"It just wasn't my thing, and you always got this look on your face like Christmas had just come early or something every time Gramps brought up a trip, so I figured you should be the one who went."

"Those trips felt a little like Christmas," Curtis said, taking another bite of his pizza and chewing thoughtfully. "At least Dad isn't here this time to bust you for bringing your camera. Man, I've never seen his face as red as when he caught you trying to turn in that report on Nessie."

"Yeah," I said, swallowing hard. "Lucky." I stared out the window of the airport—looking at all the identical planes that were rolling this way and that—until the pressure behind my eyes went away. Curtis hadn't asked about where I'd found the money for the airport food or the bus we were going to need to take once we got to Vermont. Maybe he figured I'd found it in Gramps's room when I'd dug out our forged passports. You can always buy it back, I reminded myself. The pawnshop a block away had promised to hold my camera for at least a week before they put it out for sale. I'd find a way to buy it back before then. Or, I reasoned, I'd be in jail and wouldn't need it anyway. I was just lucky that the camera had turned out to be an antique that was worth something, or this trip would have been over before it even started.

"That's us," Curtis said a minute later, slapping me on the shoulder.

"What's us?" I asked, confused.

"It's time to board," Curtis said. "Man, you are rusty on airplanes."

"I'm not a big fan of them," I said, my stomach rolling in uneasy anticipation.

"I remember," Curtis said. "Here." He tossed me something, and I grabbed it out of the air as he headed toward the line of people waiting to board our flight. I looked down at the small cylindrical bottle of motion-sickness medicine. The exact kind Mom used to buy me.

CHAPTER SIXTEEN

The flight from Georgia to Vermont is long but not if you take medicine that makes you drowsy. Then it feels a little like a really long blink. A flight attendant woke me up by telling me that I was going to need to put the tray table I'd been using as a makeshift pillow into its upright and locked position. I sat up groggily and made a half-hearted attempt to wipe the puddle of drool off the tray with my shirtsleeve before pushing it shut.

"Morning, sunshine," Curtis said. "Glad to see you're back among the land of the living."

"Did I seriously sleep through the entire thing?" I asked as my stomach let out an angry rumble. "Did I miss the snack cart?"

"Yup," Curtis said. "Don't feel bad. It wasn't that great. Just a few teeny-tiny bags of crackers that wouldn't fill up a chihuahua. I ate yours. You snooze, you lose. Ever since I've been sustaining myself on Skittles and beef jerky."

"So that's the smell," I said, wrinkling my nose.

Curtis nodded. "Beefy rainbows."

"Did you get any sleep?"

He shrugged. "Enough. I've been working my way through this," he said, motioning to the family log that sat across his lap. It was the reason he'd gotten the window seat while I made do with the middle seat. Not that most people would believe what was in the log, but it still wouldn't be a good idea to have someone reading over his shoulder.

"How did you get through it in one night?" he asked. Then he shook his head. "Don't answer that. Now that you're awake, I think we need to go over things one more time."

"Sounds good," I said, digging around in my backpack until I found a granola bar. I really needed to stop staying up all night, sleeping for huge chunks of time, and missing meals.

"So when we land," Curtis said, his voice barely loud enough for me to hear over the roar of the airplane's engines, "the first thing we do is get to the annex. Right?"

"Right. We take stock of what's there, and I really hope it's a workable Champ model or decoy or we are sunk before we even get started. Once we figure out what we can use, we find a way to transport it to the lake and beat the Gerhards to the Champ hoax. This whole thing is going to come down to timing and a lot of luck."

"Which is what worries me," Curtis said, glancing out the window as our plane dipped below the clouds and we got our first view of Vermont. "The McNeils haven't had much of that these last few years." I nodded, and I wasn't sure if he was thinking about Mom dying, Dad checking out, bank foreclosure notices, or this mess with the Gerhards, but it didn't matter.

"Then it's high time it turned around," I said. The plane's wheels touched down a few minutes later, and I smiled at Curtis. We'd already made it further than I'd thought. Maybe, just maybe, things were going to work out.

"That bus smelled like feet," Curtis said three hours later as we watched the back taillights disappear around the corner.

"It was better than walking," I said. "And I'd say the smell was more a combination of old sweat and rubber."

"Somehow I pictured everything in Vermont smelling

like maple syrup," Curtis said. "Which sounds dumb now that I hear it out loud."

"Come on," I said. "We only have a half hour until the storage center closes."

"I can't believe the annex is at a self-storage place," Curtis grumbled as he readjusted his backpack and followed me down the street.

"Why not?" I asked.

Curtis shrugged. "Seems anticlimactic? When Dad took me to the annex in Iowa, it was in this sweet old cave with a hidden sliding panel and a combination lock. I felt like I was in a spy movie. I kinda thought they'd all be like that."

"I bet most of them are," I said, thinking of some of the notes I'd seen scribbled in the margins of the logbook, "but apparently old barns and hidden caves are getting harder and harder to come by. Gramps wrote a note in the log that the Vermont annex had to be moved because a developer bought the land the old annex was on and was putting in a subdivision. He also included some interesting words about how he felt about things like developers and subdivisions." Curtis snorted and I smiled, imagining how irate our grandfather must have been when he had to move generations' worth of junk into an expensive storage unit until he could find someplace better. I didn't mention to Curtis that I suspected Gramps had never actually found someplace better because Mom had died then and he'd moved in with us.

"I guess that makes sense," Curtis said. "But it's not nearly as cool."

"Not nearly," I echoed, not really paying attention as I consulted the map I'd picked up at the bus station. The tiny different-colored lines crisscrossing and intertwining across the page reminded me of tangled spaghetti, and I was really hoping that we'd just gotten off at the right stop.

"We have my phone," Curtis said, holding it up. "We don't really need that bus map anymore. I still say we should have just taken an Uber and been done with it."

"Ubers are expensive," I said. "Buses aren't. Just plug the address in. If I got us off at the right stop, we should be in walking distance." Curtis looked over my shoulder and quickly typed in the numbers.

"Which way?" I asked.

"That way," he said, pointing to the street on our left. "Think there is a McDonald's around here? I'm starving."

"I doubt it," I said, glancing down at the quaintly cobblestoned street and the brick storefronts. "This doesn't seem like that kind of place." Although, with only twenty bucks left to our names, McDonald's was about all we were going to be able to afford. Bus rides were cheaper than an Uber but not as cheap as I'd hoped.

"Well, let's go, then," Curtis said.

Our luck held, and a ten-minute walk later we were in front of the self-storage building with a few minutes to spare before closing time. Unlike the charming town we'd walked through to get here, the storage facility stood out like a sore thumb, which was why it probably lurked on the edge of town. Curtis was now holding a brown paper bag from one of the bakeries we'd passed, and the smell wafting out of it was making my stomach snarl hungrily, but I'd been too nervous about making it here before closing to stop somewhere and eat.

"Now what?" Curtis asked. "Do we just walk in and say we have a storage locker here?"

I glanced up at the tall chain-link fence with its scary-looking barbed wire strung across the top. It seemed like overkill for protecting the extra junk people didn't have room for in their basements. Although, I considered, that was probably why this place had been chosen for the annex: the extra security.

"Got any better ideas?" I said.

"Not even one," Curtis said. "Let's do this." He squared his shoulders and marched into the self-storage office like he was the president entering the White House. I followed, the passcode for the storage locker clutched tight in my hand.

The man behind the desk looked up when we came in, wearing a polite expression that changed to slightly annoyed when he saw two kids.

"How can I help you?" he asked. I pulled out the folded-up paper from the logbook and consulted it again just to make sure I had the number right.

"We need to get in unit number 5630," I said.

The man nodded and typed something into the computer. Whatever he saw there sent both of his eyebrows shooting upward toward his perfectly combed brown hair.

"Do you have the passcode for the unit?" he asked, his tone clearly implying that he doubted it.

"We do," I said, waving around like a flag the piece of paper I'd ripped from the family log.

"Well," the man said. "Then I need to see a form of identification. The only individuals allowed to access the unit must be members of the McNeil family." We both produced our passports, and the man studied them more carefully than the guy at the airport had before handing them back to us.

"This all looks good," he said. "Be advised that our facility closes in thirty minutes, and you must be off the premises before then."

"Yes, sir," Curtis said, and I breathed an internal sigh of relief that we hadn't needed to resort to the maple syrup and groundhogs story we'd used in the airport.

"You know," the man said. "This particular unit hasn't been opened in years. Tons of security on it, though, best we offer, plus a few extra features we don't. It's a bit of a mystery around here, but the payment shows up every month so we mind our own business."

He looked at us expectantly, as though we were about to solve the mystery for him by revealing what was in the storage unit. But Curtis and I stayed silent, waiting. If there was one thing a McNeil did well, it was keep his mouth shut. After another few seconds the man shrugged and showed us the location of the unit on the large map behind him. The facilities layout looked like a cross between the squares of a crossword puzzle and a Pac-Man game. The man watched us suspiciously as we left the office and entered the labyrinth of storage lockers stacked side by side like matching LEGOs. Not that I blamed him. We had the passcode, thanks to the family log, but two teenage kids showing up a few minutes before closing was weird.

"We're number 5630," I reminded Curtis, glancing down at the piece of paper that contained all the information we'd need to gain entrance to Annex V.

"This way," Curtis said, taking a sharp right and heading down the row of storage lockers at a trot, his brown pastry bag still clutched in his hand as he read the numbers above each of the large garage-style doors. By the time Curtis found the five thousand section, I was breathing hard and my backpack felt like someone had snuck a hippo inside it. In an attempt to relieve the pressure, I hooked my thumbs underneath the straps, lifting the weight momentarily off my shoulders to give my screaming muscles a break, and ran full force into Curtis's backpack.

I hit face-first, getting a nose full of buckle and backpack strap before tipping backward and onto my butt. Curtis didn't even acknowledge it—instead he was staring up at the number 5630 above what had to be one of the biggest lockers in the entire place. The door was wide and tall, big enough for a semitruck to park with ease, made of a thick corrugated metal that looked like it meant business. Unlike the door, which had a feeling of age to it, the locking mechanism was anything but old. A keypad sat on what looked like a small computer, and I glanced at it nervously as I got to my feet and dusted myself off. With shaking hands I unfolded my page of information and glanced down at the fifteen-digit key code that had to be entered. Fifteen digits seemed like overkill, but overkill was all part of the McNeils' legacy, so I shouldn't have been all that surprised. I lifted a trembling finger toward the pad.

"Move over, shakes," Curtis said. "If you screw this up even once, that twitchy guy at the front desk might get an alert."

"Right," I agreed, and handed over the piece of paper. My hands were sweating, and I rubbed them against my pants as Curtis shoved his pastry bag into my arms, glanced at the paper, and tapped in the numbers. The job done, he hit the Enter key, and the lock gave a very satisfying click.

I was just bending down to haul the door open when Curtis's hand on my shoulder stopped me.

"What?" I asked, the word coming out much harsher than I'd intended. This annex was going to make or break our already risky plans, and my insides felt like an overstretched rubber band ready to snap. Curtis didn't respond. He didn't have to. Voices were heading our direction, and to my horror I realized they were voices that I recognized. The Gerhards had found us.

CHAPTER SEVENTEEN

My first instinct was to duck inside the unit to hide before the Gerhards rounded the corner, but Curtis had other ideas. He smashed his hand onto the Rearm button on the storage locker before he practically dragged me twenty yards to where a large blue dumpster sat. Before I had a chance to duck behind it, Curtis had me by the back of the sweatshirt and was shoving me bodily inside the rusty container. It was either help with the effort or lose my front teeth on the thick metal side of the dumpster, so I helped, sliding headfirst into the thankfully mostly empty container moments before Curtis came flying in after. He pulled the lid shut over the both of us so that we could just see out through the one-inch gap provided by the dumpster's ill-fitting plastic lid.

If you'd asked me what I thought the inside of a dumpster would smell like, I probably would have guessed that it smelled like the trash can in our garage, rank and slightly rotten. Instead it had the musky smell that I associated with thrift stores, old clothing, and mold. Which I guess made sense considering we were currently crouched on boxes full of what appeared to be someone's old T-shirt collection.

"Why didn't we just hide in the locker?" I whispered. "It at least had a lock on it and didn't smell." I felt vulnerable inside the dumpster, and having a thick steel door between us and the Gerhards would have been nice. If they were in fact the Gerhards, I reminded myself as I strained my ears to hear the voices that had set off the alarm bells in my head in the first place. Maybe we'd been mistaken.

"Shut it," Curtis whispered. "For all we know they are going right to our locker and we'd have been trapped."

Just then two figures rounded the corner, and I felt my stomach sink even further than it already had. They *were* the Gerhards, no doubt about it.

"Our locker hasn't been opened in years," I whispered back. "Remember what the guy said? They can't be going for our locker. This must be a coincidence."

"There is no such thing as coincidence," Curtis muttered back. "And speaking of our guy, check it out."

A third figure had just rounded the corner, and I recognized the clerk from the front desk. Unlike the Gerhards, who seemed annoyed and impatient as they stomped down the row of storage units, he seemed twitchy and anxious, his gray shirt now sporting dark sweat rings under the arms that hadn't been there when we'd talked to him earlier.

The group stopped in front of our unit and Axel turned to the store clerk and asked him something we couldn't hear.

"Dang it," Curtis muttered, and I felt my heart, which already was doing something similar to the bongos on my ribs, give a sickening lurch. I looked at him wide-eyed. When you were hiding in a dumpster from two guys, the last thing you wanted to hear was "dang it."

"What?"

"Look," Curtis said, jerking his head toward the group. "You dropped my pastry bag." I followed his look, and there on the ground sat the brown paper sack that Curtis had been carrying around. I frowned at him. Typical Curtis to be worried about his doughnuts.

The clerk was fumbling to reply to Axel, who was scowling at him.

"Let me say it again since you are obviously dense," Axel said in his thick accent. "Open the unit. The boys must be inside it."

The clerk shook his head. "I can't," he stammered. "And they aren't in it. The units are programmed not to lock if someone is inside."

"What do you mean 'can't'?" asked Clive, who somehow managed to be just as intimidating as his uncle, despite the fact that he couldn't be much older than Curtis.

The clerk spread his hands wide and looked at them helplessly. "Look," he said. "I fulfilled my end of the deal and called you when someone showed up about this locker. I never promised to deliver them to you or open top security units and lose my job."

"No one will know it was you," said Axel. "Open it."

"Oh, really?" he said, pointing above his head to where two large security cameras perched. Of course a place like this would have cameras, I realized. And then swallowed hard, realizing that all that clerk would have to do to figure out where we'd gone was to review the footage and watch us swan dive into a dumpster. Curtis must have realized the same thing because I felt him stiffen beside me.

Clive looked up at the security cameras, appearing unimpressed, and without hesitation he reached up and ripped them down like they were balloons at a birthday party.

"Clive!" Axel snapped. "What do you think you're doing?"

"What's it look like?" asked Clive. "Fixing the problem." He tossed the camera on the ground and stomped on it for good measure. Axel scowled at his nephew, clearly disapproving, but did nothing to stop the destruction.

The clerk watched Clive's performance with an open mouth, but to his credit, he was smart enough not to say anything.

"Problem solved," said Clive a moment later as he kicked the busted camera toward the clerk. "Happy?"

"Not exactly," the clerk said as he stared at what was left of the cameras.

Clive looked up and down the row of units as though we might just pop out at any second. "Hey," he said, bending to grab the pastry bag on the ground. "What's this?" He opened the bag and pawed around inside, pulling out a chocolate croissant. He sniffed it and broke it in half before holding it out to Axel. "This is fresh," he said. "Think they dropped it when they heard us coming? They won't have gotten very far."

"Get that thing out of my face," said Axel, not taking his eyes off the clerk. "The boys are a waste of time. Just a couple of kids. I'm more interested in finding out what those bloody McNeils have been stashing in here all these years."

"But Grandpa always told us that it wasn't worth the risk to poke around in the McNeils' annexes," said Clive with a sideways glance at the clerk, who was carefully inspecting his shoes as though he'd gone temporarily deaf. "You know," he prompted. "Exposure? Besides, we got everything we need for this job."

"Don't pretend you know this business better than I do," Axel said. "I do not need your lectures on exposure. And that was easy for your grandfather to say. He never knew where one was. Thanks to nabbing that old duffer, we do. Big difference."

I sucked in a breath just as Curtis dug his fingernails into my arm. Gramps. They had found out about the annex from him, which I guess is the only way they could have found out since the family log in my backpack was the only other place that information could be found.

The clerk cleared his throat. "Maybe I didn't make myself clear," he said. "It's not that I *won't* open that unit, it's that I *can't* open that unit. It requires a passcode that I don't have access to."

"So use some bolt cutters," said Clive.

The clerk shook his head again. "This unit would

require more than a set of bolt cutters, and my manager is the only one who has access to that equipment."

"Then get your manager," Axel said, his voice tight with annoyance.

"I'm sorry," the clerk said, taking a step back. "He's not here this week. He has a training conference in New York."

Clive huffed in annoyance and glared at our unit for a moment before giving it a swift kick accompanied by something in German that I had a feeling wasn't very polite. Suddenly both Gerhards' heads snapped up, and they turned simultaneously as the distant sound of a police siren drifted down the row of units.

"What's that?" Axel asked, turning to the clerk. The clerk pointed weakly at the spot where frayed wires protruded from the eaves of the building.

"Built-in alarm system," he said.

"Now see what you've done!" Axel said, rounding on his nephew. "How many times must I tell you? Finesse is always greater than force. Discretion greater than destruction. Sometimes I think I took on the wrong apprentice!"

"We'll be back," Axel said to the petrified clerk as he turned to run.

"But what about the McNeils?" asked Clive.

"Forget 'em," called Axel as he disappeared around

the corner. Clive stood a half second longer, still torn, before racing off. The sweating clerk opened his eyes as the Gerhards disappeared around the corner, his whole frame sagging in relief before he turned to stare down at the mangled and discarded security camera. He bent to pick up the broken equipment, turning it over in his hands momentarily. With a sigh, he turned and walked directly toward our dumpster.

CHAPTER EIGHTEEN

Curtis and I ducked simultaneously, hunkering down into the boxes of old clothes and who knew what else as the footsteps got closer. I didn't dare even to breathe as the lid above us was raised. The broken camera hit my back a half second later, and I bit my lip hard to keep from making any noise. It thankfully wasn't that big or heavy, but that didn't mean it didn't hurt. I felt Curtis's hand on my arm, squeezing as though I needed the reminder to be quiet. A second later the lid clanged shut and the clerk's footsteps faded as he made his way down the row of units. Neither of us moved, and I kept my head ducked, breathing in the musky smell of forgotten clothes as my heart slowly settled into a somewhat normal rhythm.

"We have to get out of here," Curtis whispered a minute later, tugging on my arm as he raised the lid of the dumpster.

"And go where?" I asked, rubbing my throbbing back as I clambered to my knees to look out at the deserted row of units. The wail of police sirens was getting closer by the second. We weren't the ones who had destroyed the security camera, but I still felt as though we were about to get caught mid-hoax or something.

"The unit," Curtis said, as though this should have been obvious information. "Come on." He vaulted out of the dumpster, the paper with the code still in his hand. I followed, not so much vaulting from the dumpster as flopping over the side like a fish. Curtis was already punching in numbers, and I glanced up at the wires that used to control the security camera and felt a small rush of gratitude to that gorilla Clive for ripping it down. Without it, we could enter the vault unseen and unrecorded, and as an added bonus, it had called the police and made the Gerhards scatter like the cockroaches they were. Win-win.

The loud beep and clunk of the unit unlocking drew my attention back to Curtis, and he grunted as he lifted the heavy door. I hurried to help him, the cold metal of the handle biting into my hands as I pushed. The door groaned and creaked in protest and the sounds made me wince as they grated against my ears, almost drowning out the approaching police sirens.

"Inside, quick," Curtis commanded, holding the door at chest level so I could duck underneath. I did, my backpack catching on the door and bringing me up short. "Wait a sec," Curtis said before I managed to unstick my backpack.

"What now?" I said, backing up. I unhooked the backpack straps and threw it under the door ahead of myself.

"Grab the bag," Curtis said, gesturing with his head to where Clive had dropped his pastry bag, not bothering to replace the croissant that lay discarded next to it. I turned to stare at him in a *You can't be serious* kind of way, but he just shrugged and jerked his head impatiently toward it again.

"What?" he said. "I'm starving. Grab it."

"Un-freaking-believable," I muttered, bending to scoop it up before ducking, this time successfully, under the door. Curtis slipped inside a second later, and with a grunt slid the door back down, leaving us in pitch darkness.

Before we could do anything, the sound of voices coming our way made us freeze. For a half second I worried that the Gerhards had decided to come back, but the voices sounded too official for that. A moment later I recognized the clerk's voice, and I realized he was with the police officers who had accompanied the sirens I could still hear blaring somewhere nearby. He was saying something about vandalism. The footsteps stopped outside our door, and the clerk went on and on about how he was sure the damage was done by some teenage kids. He wasn't a complete liar, I thought darkly. Clive was a teenager, although with those broad shoulders and his general lack of a neck, he had more in common with a gorilla. I glanced over at Curtis, but in the dark the only thing I could make out was the faint outline of his silhouette. All the officers would have to do to find two guilty-looking teenagers was to slide up the door they were standing three feet from. A door that was now unlocked. The dumpster was starting to look pretty good in comparison. My breath sounded loud inside the unit, and I wondered momentarily how big the space behind me was. It felt cavernous. Five minutes later the officers left, accompanied by the clerk, who thanked them over and over for their prompt arrival and for their willingness to patrol the area regularly for the next few days. For the second time in less than ten minutes, I sagged in relief.

"We have the worst luck ever," I whispered to Curtis.

"Or the best," came Curtis's voice from somewhere in the dark to my left. "They left, didn't they?" A second later the light of his cell phone lit up his face as he held it out like a flashlight. "Found it," he said, and there was a faint buzz as above us large fluorescent lights clicked on. Their sickly yellow glow was faint at first but slowly grew stronger until the entire unit was illuminated. I felt my jaw drop like a cartoon character's as I took in the storage unit where members of my family had been stockpiling the castoffs of hoaxes and hunts for who knew how long.

"Whoa," Curtis said, his voice echoing the same awe I was feeling. He walked up to stand beside me, and shoulder to shoulder we took it all in. The space was huge, twice as large as our basement at home, and with good reason. In the very center was a gigantic sea monster twice the size of our go-to sea monster decoy that was currently at the bottom of Loch Ness. Unlike our other one, which stopped just below the shoulders and was mainly head and neck, this monster was the whole enchilada. It had a gigantic head that resembled something between a dog and a horse with a tumbling mane of silvery hair that rippled halfway down the long snakelike body that lay sprawled across what looked like large wooden shipping crates.

"What is that?" I asked, taking a few steps forward

to get a better look at the thing's head. It was made out of some kind of carved wood that had been painstakingly hand-painted to resemble slick bluish-gray scales.

"Looks like Selma to me," Curtis said, bending down to inspect the serpentine body. "But then again, it could be Gryttie, the Stronsay Beast, Veasta, the Storsjön Monster, or even Champ in a pinch." He stood up, his hand on his chin as he looked at it. "How in the world did they transport it? Do you see any buckles where the thing breaks apart? There has to be. No way they lugged this guy all over in one piece." I wasn't really paying attention, though. After the initial shock of seeing a twenty-foot-long, fully-assembled sea monster had worn off, I'd finally started noticing the rest of the unit.

Large shelves stretched across the entire length of all three concrete walls, their wood construction hefty and thick to support the myriad of cryptids clustered in almost every nook and cranny. I guess I should have expected something like this. I shouldn't have been shocked—after all, I grew up with a basement full of this kind of stuff—but I was. Large sea monster fins sat in piles on one shelf, while others held stacks of black-and-white photographs and jumbled heaps of moldering fur in various shades of brown and white that must have once been part of various Bigfoot or

Yeti costumes. Tools—some familiar, some not—also lay in haphazard piles in various states of rusting away.

I walked over to the closest shelf and picked up a long pole with a large metal foot welded to the end. The right foot, I noted as I glanced around, finding a moment later the left foot of what had to be the Gray King of Wales. It had been snapped off its pole at some point, the left toe smashed as though something had run it over.

Castoffs, I reminded myself as I set the two pieces down—equipment that had been retired for one reason or another over the last two hundred years. I paused a second as I thought about that. How much did it cost to keep all this junk hidden? Suddenly our empty bank account seemed slightly less mysterious.

"Check this out," came Curtis's voice from behind me, and I turned, setting down the box of gigantic fanged plaster teeth I'd been inspecting, to find him standing over one of the wooden packing crates.

"What?" I asked, walking over to look into the crate. Two large green-glass eyes stared up at me out of the face of a ferocious-looking sea monster, its mouth open in a snarl that revealed a line of sharp white teeth.

"Ha!" Curtis said, grabbing me suddenly by the shoulders. I yelped, jumping about a foot. He laughed and punched me playfully on the shoulder as I glared at him, my heart once again hammering hard in my chest. "Too easy," he said. "Been doing that to you since you were five. Never gets old."

"Neither do you," I said, scowling back down at the sea monster head. "It's not like we haven't had enough terrifying things happen today." I glanced over at the thick steel door of the unit, the clerk's words about not being able to lock the door once we were inside coming back to me as I remembered Axel's glowering face. Curtis must have followed my line of thought because he walked over to the door, running a hand down the side and inspecting what looked like a metal box just to the left of the door. A second later there was an audible click, and he turned back to me with a smug grin.

"Locked," he said. "With as paranoid as we McNeils are, I knew there had to be a way to secure it from the inside. Now even if the Gerhards or that slimy clerk do come back, it should look like no one entered the unit."

"Was the Iowa annex you went to this big?" I asked, spinning again in a circle.

Curtis shook his head, "Not even close. The only Iowa cryptids we still hoax are the Lockridge Monster and that gigantic snapping turtle. What's its name again?"

"Big Blue," I said. "The snapping turtle the size of a car that lives in that rock quarry outside Mason City."

"Right," Curtis said. "Big Blue. But that decoy is just a head and a shell, and the shell breaks down into pretty small pieces, and the Lockridge Monster is just a suit. There was a really old model of the Van Meter Visitor there too, but when Great Grandpa did that hoax in 1903, it got blasted with so many bullets that it will never fly again. This place is way bigger. Less spiders too. What time does it close again?"

I glanced down at my watch, my eyebrows jerking up in surprise when I saw how late it was. "A half hour ago. I guess time flies when you're terrified."

"It does at that," Curtis agreed as he turned back to me and shrugged. "It looks like we're sleeping here tonight." I glanced around the storage unit with new eyes. None of the things my ancestors had decided to store in boxes and crates frightened me, but I still couldn't really imagine sleeping here. But Curtis had a point. Between the police officers, the Gerhards, and that clerk, getting out of here undetected was unlikely. Besides, we'd come here to do a job, and after hearing what the Gerhards said about Gramps, I was more determined than ever to make this work. I wanted him out of their hands sooner rather than later, and that wasn't going to happen if I just kept standing here like an idiot.

"Right," I said, turning back to the open crate. The

sea monster head leered up at me, and I bent down to pull it out of the box. Slightly larger than a horse's head, it was surprisingly light. Made of the same thin wood as the larger version, this one looked more like a prehistoric plesiosaur than the weird doggish horse-faced version that still leered over the top of us.

"There's a different head in here too," Curtis said from my left, pulling out a snakelike one with yellow slit eyes. He turned it this way and that, taking in the flat head and open jaws that appeared to be on some sort of hinge. He gingerly touched the long sharp fangs of the creature before shutting the jaws again.

"Think this one bites?" he asked, grinning.

"Ha-ha," I said, flexing the fingers on the hand Altie had attempted to take a chunk out of. "You're hilarious." There were seven other crates of equal size scattered around the floor of the unit, each with various degrees of dust and cast-off bits of hoaxing junk stacked on top. Curtis and I stood there a moment, each examining our own respective sea monster head. Our lives were weird.

"Does your head have a hinge?" I asked, flipping over the gigantic head in my hands with some difficulty to inspect the hollow interior.

"Nope," Curtis said, mirroring my movements with his own grotesque sea monster.

I ran my hand down the inside of the head, feeling

slight grooves like the kind on the end of a hose. "Got it," I said, walking over to the assembled monster. On its neck was a thin, almost invisible line. Gingerly setting down the head in my hands, I climbed up onto the nearest crate, grabbed the horselike sea monster on either side of its grizzly face, and gave it a firm twist to the left.

"What are you doing?" Curtis asked.

"Righty tighty, lefty loosy," I said, my teeth gritted against the effort. For a moment the head didn't budge and I thought my theory might be wrong, but then with a creaking groan it unscrewed, coming off in my hands.

"Bloody brilliant," Curtis said, walking up with his own snakelike sea monster head still in hand. "One body with interchangeable heads. I was wondering how in the world we were going to pass that ugly thing off as Champ. What do you want to bet his ugly mug is hanging out in one of these crates just waiting for us to use him to save Gramps?"

I grinned. "I'll take that bet," I said.

"Our ancestors kept a lot of crap," Curtis complained two hours later. I snorted, my mouth too full to talk.

"This is amazing," I said, holding up my half of the remaining chocolate croissant. Despite being smashed in a paper bag, dropped, and almost forgotten on the ground, I was pretty sure that if heaven had a flaky, buttery crust with a soft chocolate-filled inside, it wouldn't taste as good as this croissant. If I didn't already hate the Gerhards for stealing our stuff and kidnapping Dad and Gramps, I would hate them for ripping apart that other croissant and throwing it on the ground. I wondered momentarily if it was still salvageable. I wasn't above eating something off the ground if it was filled with chocolate and not too many ants. It took me longer than was probably normal to discard the idea. I was *that* hungry and the croissant was *that* good, but we needed to stay inside the unit, out of sight and off the radar, at least until we got a bit more organized.

"This is better than amazing," Curtis agreed, chewing thoughtfully. "Think everything in Vermont tastes this good?"

"No idea," I said. "But if it does, I'm moving."

"You mean after you graduate from that fancy Culver Academy?" Curtis asked. I looked over at him, surprised by the tone of his voice. The last time he'd said something about Culver, it had sounded like an accusation, something I should be ashamed of for wanting. Now he'd sounded almost sincere.

He wasn't looking at me, too concerned with licking his finger and poking it into the contents of the paper bag in search of any stray crumbs we'd overlooked.

I watched him for a moment, jealous that he'd thought of that first. "Well, that's not going to happen anymore," I said, doing my best to content myself with sucking the last of the chocolate off my fingers.

"Why not?" Curtis asked.

I shrugged. "I'm here, aren't I?"

"So?" Curtis said.

"So there is no way I'll ever get that scholarship essay done now. It's due Wednesday, and I don't even have an outline done. Not that it even matters because Mrs. Howard is sure to report my absence today to the scholarship board." I tried to say it like it didn't hurt, like the decision was one I wasn't still second-guessing even as I sorted through the piles of hoaxing castoffs in search of the tools we'd need to pull off the biggest hoax of our lives.

"Oh," Curtis said, and I purposefully didn't look at him this time because I could feel tears of disappointment pushing against the backs of my eyes. "What do you suppose this was used for?" Curtis asked, holding up a large fake eye the size of a basketball.

"Your guess is as good as mine," I said. "Is it hand-painted too?"

Curtis looked down at the eyeball, his brow furrowed. "Looks like it."

"Can we use it?"

"Not sure what for," Curtis said, tossing it behind him, where it landed with a clattering thump on the pile of other discarded hoaxing junk we'd uncovered in the crates and boxes that lay scattered around us. "To be honest," he said, inspecting what looked like the hairy right arm of a gorilla before adding it to the pile, "I'm not really sure what they used half of this stuff for."

I glanced back at the pile. It had seemed fairly impressive moments ago, but compared to the stuff that had been stolen, well, it looked like the castoffs from a really weird garage sale. With a sigh I turned back to the crate in front of me.

"Curtis?" I said, glancing over at him. "Do you think this is going to work? I mean, really?"

He sniffed. "I hope so."

"Me too," I said. We worked in silence for a while longer, the only sounds the clatter and creak of hoaxing junk that we sorted into piles. My eyes hurt from being open for too long, but I pushed exhaustion aside. It could wait until I went through just one more crate, one more shelf, one more box. . . . It wasn't until I whacked my head on the model of a Piasa Bird that I realized I'd started to nod off. Curtis was already asleep, curled up on the furry pelt of what was probably supposed to be a Yeti before mice had gotten ahold of it. He made it look surprisingly comfortable, and with one last look around the messy locker, I lay down next to him with a sigh. He was snoring, but the noise was comfortingly familiar in such a strange place, and I felt myself slip into sleep.

CHAPTER NINETEEN

"**D**o we really have to steal a truck?" I said.

"Yes, although I prefer the term *borrow*. We will return it tomorrow and pay our friend the U-Store jerk for it, so don't get yourself all worked into a moral tizzy over it," Curtis said, and I could tell from his tone that I shouldn't ask the question again. I sighed and bit my lip as I looked at the pile of stuff by the door of our unit. I wasn't sure what money Curtis was planning to use to pay for the truck, but I pushed that particular problem aside. He was right. There was absolutely no way we'd be able to carry it out of here in our backpacks. For one thing the Champ head we'd finally found probably weighed almost fifty pounds and was roughly the size of a German shepherd. Which was completely beside the point because, even if we *could* walk out of here carrying everything we'd need, we wouldn't get far without drawing some major attention to ourselves. Disembodied sea monster heads tended to have that effect.

"I'm not sure why you're dragging your feet," Curtis grumbled. "You knew we'd need a truck if the storage locker wasn't an absolute bust. Remember, this was your brilliant plan. I was all ready to call the police."

I swallowed hard. "Don't remind me."

Curtis glanced around the unit again. "Not that all this old crap isn't great and all, but our gear was about a million times better."

"And lighter," I said, grabbing the last sea monster segment so I could add it to the pile with the rest.

"I know," Curtis said. "Lucky it's hollow or we'd never be able to move it."

"I'm just glad we don't have to be inside it to pull off the hoax," I said, holding up the segment in my hands so I could peer through it at Curtis. "Can you imagine being stuck in this thing at the bottom of a lake?"

Curtis smirked. "Even your skinny butt would have a hard time fitting inside that." He gave a mock shudder. "Seriously, though, that's the stuff nightmares are made of." I knocked on the side of the part I was holding, still amazed that someone in my family tree had taken the time to hand carve this beast out of wood.

"You know," Curtis said, hefting the original sea monster head we'd discarded in favor of the Champ head, "this one might not be Storsjön. It's too horselike. Maybe Caddy?"

"A wooden horse," I murmured as I turned the piece over in my hands again. "I hope ours works out better than the Trojans' did."

"What was that?" Curtis asked, looking up.

I shook my head. "Nothing. Just thinking about the history test I'm missing today. I would have aced it. But if we have any hope of beating the Gerhards, we have to get to Lake Champlain and get our geriatric Champ under water."

"And to accomplish that, we need a truck." Curtis said, rubbing his chin. "The question is do we borrow the really big truck, the sorta big truck, or the weeny truck that would probably fit everything but requires some major skills to pack?"

"Not the weeny truck," I said, thinking of the three trucks we'd spotted on our way into the storage facility the night before. "It didn't look much bigger than Dad's kidnapper van, and we are going to need some room to maneuver."

Curtis sighed. "Never thought I'd miss the good old kidnapper van. Funny but, you know, *not*, all at the same time. Anywho, the sorta big truck it is," Curtis said. Just then his cell phone vibrated, and he picked it up to read the text message. His eyebrows rose, and he looked over at me. "Why is Clare Mayfield texting to see if you really went to Vermont? When did you tell her we were coming here?"

"Clare texted?" I asked, my hand automatically reaching for the phone. Curtis jerked it back out of my reach.

"Yeah, she texted," he said. "On *my* cell phone. Why does she know we're in Vermont? What gives?"

"She may have called the other night to see if we made it home okay from the bonfire," I said. "And I may have mentioned Vermont."

"May have?" he said.

"Yeah," I said, biting my lip. "What's the big deal?" Even as I said it, I knew exactly what the big deal was. I'd broken a hoaxing rule: never be associated with the location of a hoax. It would be too suspicious if everywhere a McNeil went strange things seemed to happen. We'd had this lesson drilled into us over and over again.

"Grayson," Curtis said, my name a warning and a reprimand all at the same time. It was just the way mom used to say it when I'd left my toy trucks in the hall.

"My bad," I said because, really, what else could I say?

"It's fine," Curtis said, glancing back at his phone. "It's your first experience having a girl pay attention to you. I should be glad you didn't do something even dumber."

"Just don't respond," I said. "This place opens up in ten minutes, and I want to be out of here before the Gerhards come back."

As though we'd summoned them, there was suddenly a knock on our storage unit's door, and I jumped about a foot, dropping my section of the sea monster so it clattered across the floor.

Curtis turned wide, frightened eyes to me, and I gave myself a solid mental kick for not insisting that we get the heck out of there earlier. Why had we slept? Why had we wasted any time when we knew the Gerhards could be back at any second?

"Grayson? Curtis? Are you guys in there?" came a female voice.

"*Is that Clare?*" Curtis mouthed to me, and I shrugged, feeling a rush of relief that it wasn't Axel or Clive—although, I reasoned, they probably wouldn't have knocked.

"I know you're in there," came the voice again. "Now open up. It's freezing out here."

"No one's here. Go away!" Curtis yelled, and I rolled my eyes at him.

"*Really?*" I mouthed silently. He shrugged.

"Let me in, or I'll post all over social media about the sea monster hoax that is getting pulled off this afternoon."

Curtis turned to me and glared. "Anything you want to tell me?" he said. I must have looked as gob-smacked as I felt because he just shook his head in disgust before bending down to unlock the mechanism that had kept us secure through the night. It gave a dull click, and he slid the door up a foot to reveal a familiar pair of brown snow boots with pink laces. I cranked my head so I could see under the door and looked up into Clare's flushed face.

"What are you doing here?" I asked. "And how in the world do you know about that?"

"I'm here to help," she said, ducking under the door before I could stop her. She stood up and came face-to-face with the open-mouthed Champ decoy. I waited for her to scream or jump or faint or something. Instead she just looked at it, sniffed as though completely unimpressed, and turned back to us.

"Is this what you're using?" she said, jerking a thumb at Champ. "It looks more like San Clemente than Champ, but if it's all you got, it will work in a pinch. You'll just have to hope your EWs are near-sighted with outdated iPhones."

My jaw dropped, and Curtis and I stared at her like she'd just sprouted an extra head. After a moment Curtis turned to me, his expression furious. "What the heck, Grayson!"

"I didn't," I stammered. "I mean, I *may* have mentioned something about a sea monster biting my hand, but I never . . ."

"Relax," Clare said, turning back to us. "Grayson didn't have to tell me anything."

"Then how . . . ?" Curtis said.

"You McNeils really need to work on finishing a complete sentence," Clare said. "You may not be the dumb crooks my uncle and cousin made you out to be, but you aren't exactly impressive."

"Your uncle and cousin?" I asked.

"You met them the other night," Clare said. "Axel and Clive?"

CHAPTER TWENTY

"What?" Curtis yelped.

"You're a Gerhard?" I said. "But you can't be a Gerhard. You're a Mayfield. That's why we sat next to each other in homeroom!"

Clare waved a hand dismissively. "I am a Mayfield," she said. "But my mom was a Gerhard before marrying my dad." She tucked a stray curl behind her ear and raised an expectant eyebrow at me.

"But you're black!" I said, thinking of the very, very white Gerhard brothers with their icy blue eyes and blond hair who couldn't be any more different from Clare with her dark curls and warm brown skin.

"Don't be dumb," Clare said. When Curtis and I

didn't say anything, she rolled her eyes. "Sorry. Apparently you two can't help it. My dad's black. My mom's white. I'm freaking awesome."

"And a Gerhard," I said, feeling stupid. "So Axel Gerhard . . ."

"Had a sister. Two, actually. One of them is my mom," Clare said. "Keep up, Grayson; we don't have a lot of time. My uncle Axel and my creep of a cousin Clive will be here within the hour."

I stared at her a second longer, trying to make all the pieces of this bizarre puzzle fit together.

"If you're here to steal everything, you're out of luck," Curtis said, his voice hard and angry. "We aren't going to let that happen." He sniffed. "Again."

"I'm not going to steal your stuff," Clare said, giving our disassembled Champ model a look that made it clear our stuff wasn't worth stealing. "I'm here to apologize, and to help you if I can."

"What do you have to apologize for?" Curtis asked. "Besides being a stinking, filthy Gerhard."

"Ouch," Clare said. "Although not completely undeserved. What my uncle and cousin did to you guys, stealing all your stuff, wasn't very nice of them. And I feel really bad about the part I played in it."

"What part was that?" I asked, although I had a sneaking feeling that I already knew.

"Getting you to that bonfire," Clare said, confirming my suspicions as I remembered the out-of-the-blue phone call to my house to confirm I'd be there and how antsy she'd been that night, checking the time every five seconds. She'd been waiting for the stolen Shunka Warak'in to show up. And, I remembered, it was her sister who'd run screaming out of the woods. We'd been played.

"And spying on you guys all year," Clare finished, and I felt like I'd swallowed a snake as I stared at the girl I'd counted as one of my only real friends.

"All year?" I repeated.

Clare nodded. "It was just dumb luck that I ended up in your class. And I really regret telling my uncle about it, but I couldn't believe I'd landed in the seat right next to an actual McNeil. Honestly, I'd heard so many stories about you guys, it was hard to believe you really existed."

I shook my head as I listened, this whole thing feeling surreal. My one true friend wasn't. She was a spy, and she was here, in Vermont, wearing a red stocking hat that smooshed her normally springy curls down around her shoulders.

"Anyway, my uncle asked me to keep an eye on you, so I did. But then he asked for my help getting you to that bonfire. He promised not to hurt you, and

I had no clue he was going to call the cops or steal all your stuff. And I feel really bad about what happened with your dad and grandpa. I wouldn't have helped if I'd known they were going to do that."

Curtis snorted in disbelief.

"I swear I didn't know," Clare said. "Gerhards don't need to play dirty to beat the McNeils."

"Then why *did* you help them?" Curtis asked.

Clare shrugged. "Because I wanted to apprentice with Uncle Axel in Germany this summer," she said. "I've been researching cryptids my entire life, and all I've ever done is hear stories at our family reunions about all their adventures. My mom isn't in the business, but Uncle Axel promised that if I helped them, he would train me."

"And?" I asked, feeling like there was more to this story.

"And," she said, looking up, her eyes angry, "he went back on his word. Apparently being a Gerhard doesn't mean squat if you're a girl, so he took my cousin Clive on as his apprentice instead. Never mind that he's a jerk with rocks where his brains are supposed to be. Uncle Axel just gave me some lame excuse about how I wasn't old enough yet and let me come along on this hoax as a consolation prize. But," she said, sticking her chin out, "I don't accept consolation prizes. So I'm here to help. Uncle Axel doesn't deserve to collect that check, and I'm going to make sure he doesn't." Curtis and I stood there staring at her a moment longer, and I wondered if his brain felt like it had just gotten squished like mine did.

"What do you think, Grayson?" Curtis said finally. "Can we trust her?"

I shook my head. "Obviously I'm not the best judge of character, considering she's been sitting next to me all year and I thought she was actually my friend."

"I am your friend," Clare said.

"You're a Gerhard," I said, and I actually felt angry tears pressing against the backs of my eyeballs. I blinked hard.

Clare sighed and rolled her eyes. "If I wanted to screw you guys over, I would have done it already. My sister installed a tracking app on Curtis's phone at the bonfire, and once you gave me his cell phone number, I was in business. I've known exactly where you were ever since, thanks to the GPS on Curtis's phone. If I wanted to, I could have my uncle and cousin here right now."

Curtis turned to me. "Don't give my cell phone number out anymore."

"Don't let girls install apps on your phone," I shot back.

"Good point," Curtis said, and we both scowled at Clare.

"Don't look at me like that," she said to me. "You'd do anything for your family, or you wouldn't be in this stupid storage locker full of junk instead of in first period taking a test on Greek history or working on your scholarship essay. I know all about Culver and your attendance issues."

I threw my hands up in the air. "What the heck? What are you? Sherlock Holmes?"

"No," she said. "I'm better."

"I like her," Curtis said with a wide, approving grin. He held out his hand. "Welcome to the team."

"No," I said. "She's not on our team."

"Grayson," Curtis said. "We don't have time for this. We could use all the help we can get. And she seems to know what she's doing."

Clare looked at me expectantly, and I stood there a moment longer, arms crossed defiantly over my chest before I sagged in defeat. "Fine," I said. "But I still don't trust you."

"Fair enough," Clare said, throwing her arms around my shoulders and giving me a hug I didn't return. She stepped back, her hands still on my shoulders. "My uncle asked me to keep an eye on you, not to befriend you. That happened because I think you're funny and creative, even if you did make up a stupid story about a sea monster biting your hand to impress me the other day."

"A sea monster did bite his hand," Curtis said. "A fake one. Not even a little bit impressive." Clare laughed as he clapped his hands together, the sound echoing in the cavernous storage locker. "Now then," he said," I'd love to stand here and watch you make Grayson's face turn even redder, but we have work to do."

"My face is not red," I said.

Clare looked at me and scrunched her nose. "I'd say it's closer to purple, actually."

Curtis snorted and shook his head and then turned to Clare. "You said Axel and Clive are coming back here?"

She nodded, glancing at her cell phone to check the time. "In the next half hour or so."

He nodded. "Then it's time to *borrow* that truck." He held up his fingers and put air quotes around the word *borrow* before reaching down and picking up the thin piece of metal we'd brought with us from home. Curtis made breaking into cars look as easy as tying his shoes. I knew how to do it too. Gramps was an excellent teacher, and he was right: you never knew when you might need to "borrow" someone else's car if a hoax went south. I took a deep breath that did nothing to calm my churning stomach and glanced over at Clare, who didn't look at all surprised to see a burglar's tool in my brother's hand. This was going to take some getting used to.

"Let's get this over with," I said.

Curtis slid the door up a couple feet, and all three of us ducked underneath it. Curtis slid the door back down, leaving it open a crack so we could get back in without the complicated passcode. It made me nervous to leave it like that, but really, we were about to steal a truck, and it was just one more calculated risk in a whole spiderweb of risks surrounding this whole mess.

The air was crisp and goose bumps immediately prickled up my arms and neck as I hunched my shoulders and followed Curtis at a run down the alley. Clare kept pace beside me, and I glanced at her out of the corner of my eye, still not quite believing that she was here. Even as I came to terms with that, though, I realized that the only girl who'd ever paid any kind of attention to me had only done it because she was prepping for a hoax. The irony was not lost on me. Before I could think about it anymore, we rounded a corner and saw the trucks. There were three of them, and maybe it was because they were all a really unattractive brown color or because they sat side by side—large, medium, small—but the whole thing reminded me of Goldilocks and the three bears. Curtis signaled for us to wait, and Clare and I ducked into the shadows of the nearest storage unit while Curtis ran up to the driver's-side door of the closest truck.

"I wouldn't have used a Slim Jim, but I guess it will work on short notice," Clare said as we watched Curtis maneuver the thin piece of metal into the gap between the window and the doorframe.

"This is so weird," I said. "How do you know about any of this if your mom doesn't do hoaxes?"

Clare shrugged. "Mom wanted a normal childhood for me and my sister, so she left hoaxing behind when she moved to the United States and married my dad, but I've been picking her brain about the whole cryptid business ever since I can remember. She knows it inside and out, even if her family never let her do much actual hoaxing. Honestly, I'm a little obsessed with it all."

Listening to Clare felt a little like looking in a funhouse mirror. She'd grown up surrounded by all sorts of normal, and she wanted nothing more than the exact life I would give anything to escape. I shook off the thought. I wasn't going to escape this life. In fact, I was currently watching my older brother break the law, yet again, to save the McNeils' hoaxing legacy and future. I glanced back at Clare, who was watching Curtis work in a way that made it clear she thought she could do better.

"Like I said, so freaking weird," I muttered, and forced myself to refocus. If we didn't get out of here and beat her uncles to the Champ hoax, none of the weirdness would matter one bit. Less than a minute later Curtis was inside the truck, and I let out the breath I'd been holding and waited as he messed around with the wires beneath the steering wheel. The truck roared to life and lurched into motion a second later. Its headlights snapped on, spotlighting us in the dark. I jumped guiltily. Which was dumb, because I'd known it was coming. Clare, I noticed, didn't jump. She just leaped neatly onto the back of the still-moving truck. Did the girl have ice in her veins? Telling myself to get a grip, I ran and jumped up next to her. We held on tight as Curtis maneuvered his way back down the rows of storage units. I half expected security alarms to start sounding, but we made it back unscathed.

Curtis pulled to a stop and jumped out of the cab. "Pick the padlock on the back hatch," he instructed, tossing me the small leather case that held our lock picks. I caught it and flipped it open, eyeing the tools and the lock a second before selecting what I needed. Behind me I heard the grate of metal as Curtis threw open the door of the unit. Clare jumped down to help him. My hands were sweaty and slick, and I wiped them on my pants before bending down to work on the lock. I heard Curtis huff impatiently a moment later as he dropped a pile of stuff by the still-closed hatch before jogging back for the next load.

"Want me to do it?" Clare asked.

"No," I said through gritted teeth.

Willing my hand to steady, I shut my eyes, feeling for the locking mechanism the way I'd been taught. Two minutes and a few twists of my lock picks later, it was unlocked. I slid the door up, feeling a wave of relief.

"Took you long enough," Curtis grumped as he threw Champ's disembodied head up to me. "Pack that carefully," he said. "If it breaks, we're screwed." I nodded, deciding not to point out that he was the one who'd just thrown it to me like it was a dollar-store beach ball. It had taken hours to sort through the storage unit the night before, sifting out the useful from the junk, but we had the truck loaded in less than five minutes.

"That's the last of it," Curtis said, handing me up the last crate.

"What do you mean that's the last of it?" Clare asked, looking back at the empty shelves of our storage unit and the pile of hoaxing castoffs we'd heaped in the middle of the room.

"We can't take it all," I said. "The rest of that stuff is just junk."

Clare shook her head. "That can't be everything. Where's your scuba equipment?"

Curtis's eyes narrowed at her. "You probably know that answer better than us, seeing as it's your uncle and cousin who stole it all."

"Oh," Clare said, looking sheepish for the first time since entering our unit. "That. Sorry."

"We will just have to find a dive shop on the way," Curtis said, sounding much more positive than he looked. "The important thing now is to get out of here and get to the lake. Who knows? Maybe once we get our Champ assembled, we won't need scuba equipment."

"A dive shop," Clare repeated, "in Vermont. Good luck with that."

I was still staring at our van full of sea monster and absolutely zero air tanks when the clicking rasp of a lighter made me turn back to the unit, my heart in my throat. The last time I'd heard that noise had been when Axel Gerhard was lighting a cigarette. And I was right, at least about the Gerhard part. Clare was holding a lighter up to a thick wad of brown packing paper I recognized from one of the crates that had contained a strange collection of plaster Bigfoot feet we'd deemed unusable.

"What are you . . . ?" I started to ask, then stopped as Clare lit the paper and tossed it into the pile of hoaxing castoffs we'd left behind. It caught fire almost immediately, one of the hand-painted wooden eyes we'd found igniting like a tiny sun.

"What are you doing?" Curtis exclaimed, flapping his hands at the fire, his cheeks puffed out as he tried to blow it out like the candles on a birthday cake.

"Making sure my uncle and cousin don't have anything to find when they show up here," Clare said, turning to us, eyebrows raised. "Your hiding spot's obviously been compromised. There is more than one way to ruin a hoaxer's career, and if we succeed at beating them to the Champ hoax, I'd hate for them to drag a news crew back to this unit. Besides, what better way to hide a stolen truck than to distract everyone with a fire?"

"What if it spreads?" I yelped as I glanced around the unit for a fire extinguisher I knew didn't exist. "This could burn down the whole place. People could get hurt!"

Clare rolled her eyes. "Relax. It's a pile of stuff on a concrete floor. It has nowhere to spread. Now stop worrying and let's get out of here!"

Curtis waved his hands at the fire a moment longer before giving up and running for the truck. I stood frozen for another second, watching as the fire gained momentum, eating up the discarded wooden crates that had held sea monster heads for who knew how many years.

"Get in!" Curtis yelled as he threw himself into the driver's seat and slammed the door. The blare of the fire alarm jolted me into action, and I jumped out of the truck, pulling the sliding door of the truck down behind me. I ran for the passenger side of the truck cab, making it only halfway inside before Curtis threw the truck into drive and floored it. Clare grabbed my shoulder and hauled me the rest of the way in, and I just managed to slam the door behind myself.

"Why did you do that?" I asked Clare. "That was never in the plan!"

"Had to," Clare said.

"Did you?" I asked, my voice squeaking as it hit a register only dogs could hear. "Because I thought the plan was to get out of here as quietly as possible so we'd have a head start before the police showed up to investigate the truck we just stole."

"Borrowed," Curtis said. "We borrowed the truck." His mouth was set in a grim line as he took a turn so fast the back end of the truck almost slid into storage unit 764.

"Well, good luck explaining that to them!" I said.

"Put your seat belt on," Clare instructed, leaning over me to grab the shoulder strap. I grabbed the belt out of her hand and clicked it into place.

"We'll have a head start at least," Curtis said. "Now

shut up a second. This thing is like driving a bus, and I need to get us out of here."

"Go left," I said, and Curtis cranked the wheel as we went down yet another long alley of seemingly identical lockers. This is what a mouse in a maze must feel like, I thought as I watched the lockers whizzing past us.

"Where is the entrance?" Curtis asked, his knuckles white on the steering wheel. "I thought you knew how to get us out of here."

"I thought I did too," I said, "but then Clare set our storage locker on fire, and I kind of forgot to pay attention to where we were going!"

"That was dumb," Clare said, and I almost laughed. Because it was dumb. This whole plan was dumb. The police, the fire trucks, and the Gerhards would be here any second and find us driving around in circles in a stolen truck full of dismembered sea monster parts. We'd never get Gramps and Dad back, and even if we did, we'd all be going to jail forever. I snorted. Just one big happy criminal family. Yeah, dumb didn't even begin to cover it.

"I'm starting to think all the stories I've heard about the McNeils might have been a tad exaggerated," Clare said, her knuckles white on the dash of the truck as Curtis took yet another hairpin turn. "I thought your hoaxes were supposed to be planned down to the very last second? That you were sticklers for rules and details."

"This isn't our best day," Curtis said through gritted teeth.

"You think?" I said as I glanced out the window, trying to get some idea of where we were in this storage locker labyrinth.

"Do you even *have* a strategy?" Clare asked. "It seems like you're pulling this entire plan out of your—" Her sentence was cut off sharply by her scream as Curtis rounded another corner and immediately slammed on the brakes. In front of us was the chain-link fence that surrounded the entire storage facility, complete with a thick rope of barbwire winding across the top like twisting metal snakes. We'd reached a dead end.

"Turn around. We took a wrong turn," I said.

"No kidding," Curtis said, cranking his head in an attempt to see far enough in the rearview mirror to turn the truck around. But it was pointless. The space was too narrow, the surrounding lockers pressing in on us from both sides.

"It's too tight," Clare said. "You'll have to reverse out." Curtis turned back and looked at me in the dim early-morning light. My breath felt caught inside my lungs, like pure panic and adrenaline had frozen it into a block of ice inside my chest. Curtis and I stared at each other for a moment before his jaw clenched, and he threw the truck out of reverse and back into drive. And before I could stop him, he was flooring the truck straight into the chain-link fence.

CHAPTER TWENTY-ONE

I think I screamed, although maybe it was Clare, or even Curtis. Someone did, but the sound was drowned out a second later as we hit the fence. Hard. There was a loud grating crunch as it bulged outward, the chain link bending around the nose of the truck. After a moment of resistance the engine of the truck gave an angry roar, and the entire section of fencing popped loose and clattered out of our way. We were free. The truck squeezed through the opening in the chain link, and we decimated some very well-trimmed shrubbery before bumping hard over a curb and onto the road.

"We made it!" Curtis said, glancing back at the mangled fence. "I can't believe that actually worked!" All I managed was a half-articulated grunt as I sagged backward in my seat. My bones felt like limp noodles, and my heart was hammering so hard I could feel it in my nose.

"Is it too late to change my mind about helping you?" Clare asked, her voice sounding shaky for the first time since she'd ducked under our storage unit's door.

"Way too late," Curtis said. "You are officially on Team McNeil." When I still didn't say anything, Curtis looked over at me and grinned. "You still breathing?" he asked, reaching over Clare to thump me hard on the chest. "You look a little green! Are you a McNeil or not?" He let out a victorious whoop and pumped his fist in the air.

"My grandpa was right," Clare muttered, "you McNeils are nutty."

"As squirrel poo, baby!" Curtis crowed, and I felt a smile creep onto my face against my will.

"Just do me a favor," I said to Clare. "Next time you're going to change the plan by lighting something on fire, just give us the heads-up, okay?"

"Deal," Clare said. "It's for the best. You'll see."

"You'd just better hope that unit burns well," I said. "If a half-burned piece of hoaxing gear gets pulled from the ashes, we are in big trouble."

Clare flapped a hand dismissively. "That won't happen."

"Try telling my great uncle that," I said. "He tried to burn his sea monster decoy in a hotel after a Silver Lake Serpent job, and when the fire burned down, there sat a gigantic sea monster decoy."

"In 1855?" Clare asked, and I blinked at her in surprise.

"Yes?" I said, wondering how in the world she could possibly know that.

"Wanna know a secret?" she asked, her honey-colored eyes practically sparkling with mischief.

"Always," Curtis said.

"The decoy that was found in the ashes? *My* great grandfather stuck it in the burned-out attic of that hotel for everyone to find. He was trying to knock the McNeils out of the hoaxing business. Didn't work, though."

"Good to know some things never change," Curtis said, shaking his head. "Now, grab my phone and start navigating. We have a sea monster hoax to pull off and apparently some history to repeat." I dug out Curtis's cell phone with fingers that still shook and then glanced over at Clare, remembering that she'd somehow used his number to track us down.

"Is this safe to use?" I asked her, "or is your creepy uncle somewhere waiting to follow us to screw up our hoax?"

Clare rolled her eyes. "It's safe," she said, "and Uncle Axel isn't creepy. Kind of a grouch but not creepy. Clive, however, is a Grade-A creep with a side of brat thrown in for good measure."

"I disagree," Curtis said. "Creepy is way too nice of a word for him. Your family is something else entirely."

"Hold it right there," Clare said. "I'm helping you to prove my uncle wrong, that a girl can hoax just as well as a boy, better even. But I'm not bashing my family. However, I will agree that they went about this all wrong. They shouldn't have stolen your stuff."

"Or Gramps and Dad," I said. "They stole them too."

"You can't steal someone, dork," Curtis said. "You kidnap someone. They *kidnapped* Gramps."

"They didn't kidnap them," Clare said, rolling her eyes. "That sounds so dramatic. They just detained them to keep them out of the way until after this hoax was pulled off. Besides, neither of them are kids. They're adults. So they adult-napped them, which I don't even think is a thing."

"Whatever, same difference," I said, glancing back down at the phone. "You need to take a left in one mile, and if you want to step on it, I won't complain. We didn't exactly make the discreet exit we were hoping for back there."

Curtis nodded. "Done and done."

The drive to Lake Champlain took only about twenty minutes, and even though I checked our slightly mangled rearview mirrors every few seconds, I never spotted a police car. It seemed like Clare's plan to distract everyone from a stolen truck by lighting our locker on fire had actually worked.

"Time to get set up," Curtis said, all business as we pulled off the main road and onto a smaller dirt one that curved through the woods toward the lake. Around us mountains towered, casting their reflections onto the blue water. It would be a nice place to visit someday under different, less dangerous circumstances.

Curtis put the truck in park and leaned forward on the steering wheel, staring out at the lake. "Dad always promised I could come with him on a Champ job," he said. "But then he'd change his mind when it came time to book the plane tickets."

"It's expensive to fly to Vermont," I said. "He may croak when he sees how much I paid for same-day flights for both of us."

"If we can pull this off, it will be worth it," Curtis said as we climbed out of the truck. The beach leading down to the lake was covered in smooth, flat gray and white stones, and all three of us walked down to stand on the rippling edge of the lake. It really was beautiful.

"A perfect sea monster lake if I ever saw one," Curtis said, and he picked up a rock and skipped it neatly across the lake. "I'm surprised you don't have your face pressed into that camera of yours, Grayson. This place is awesome. You know, they say it's over four hundred feet deep in some places."

I winced at his mention of my camera. Luckily Curtis was still staring out at the lake and didn't notice. I rearranged my expression and stuck my hands in my pockets.

But once again I'd forgotten about Clare, and her honey eyes were narrowed in on me as I squirmed. "Yeah," she said. "Where *is* your camera? I know Uncle Axel didn't take it. I checked."

Leave it to Clare to shine a spotlight on something Curtis probably never would have noticed. Curtis turned to look at me, eyebrows raised expectantly.

"I sold it," I muttered, not taking my eyes off the sand under my feet.

"You what?" Curtis said. "Why?"

"Because buses are cheaper than Ubers, but they aren't free," I snapped, my embarrassment morphing quickly into anger. "Neither is airport food or parking."

"Oh," Curtis said. "I never realized . . ." He trailed off, and I wished that this conversation wasn't happening in front of Clare of all people. Not only were we the pathetic family that had gotten all our stuff stolen, but now it was obvious that we were broke too. Great. Just great.

"Sold it where?" Curtis pressed, and I gritted my teeth, wishing more than anything that he'd just drop it.

"The pawnshop off Fifth," I said. "Now, can we just focus on Champ? It's not a big deal."

Clare and Curtis shared a look that made me feel about five years old, and I momentarily considered throwing myself into the lake and swimming away.

"My grandfather spotted Champ here when he was twenty," Clare said, her arms crossed against the chilling breeze coming off the water. My insides relaxed as the spotlight she'd thrown on me was diverted back to the lake and the task at hand. "He said Champ's head alone was almost as long as his boat. If he hadn't dropped his camera, he'd have gotten one of the best close-up shots of the century."

"If," I said, and sniffed. "Have you ever noticed that there is always an *if* when someone tells a story about spotting a cryptid?" When she just stared at me, I shrugged. "You know. '*If* I'd been closer, the shot wouldn't have been so fuzzy.' '*If* I hadn't stopped for lunch, I would have stumbled right on the Orang Pendek instead of just finding a footprint.' '*If* I hadn't made so much noise, I wouldn't have frightened the Mothman away before I could turn on my video camera.'" Clare laughed, and I smiled.

"Sometimes it's not an *if* on a cryptid hunt. It's a

but," I went on, really on a roll now. "Like, 'I would have caught Megalodon, *but* I forgot to bring a gigantic net capable of holding a shark the size of two school buses.'"

"Yeah," Curtis said, "and sometimes the butt is your little brother who stands around talking when the clock is ticking down to the biggest hoax of our lives."

That really made Clare laugh, and I gave Curtis a dirty look even though he was right.

"Did your uncle and cousin already sink their Champ?" Curtis asked Clare.

She shook her head. "They always sink the hour before a hoax."

"We usually sink at least twelve hours in advance," I said.

"Do you think that hunk of junk in the truck is actually going to sink?" Clare asked. "It's made of wood, and it looked hollow."

"Time to find out," Curtis said, turning back to the truck.

When fully assembled, our Champ model was somewhere between pathetic and downright sad. The bumping ride in the back of the truck and our run-in with the fence hadn't done it any favors either. Paint was chipped, buckles were busted, and hinges were loose.

"Did it look this bad in the unit?" Curtis asked, wiping sweat out of his eyes as he tried to manually bend a hinge back into place.

"No," I said, glancing at my watch.

"If we don't have this hoax pulled off before sundown, we forfeit our contract and Axel and Clive are going to get the contract by default," Curtis said, sitting back. He hadn't mentioned our lack of scuba gear again, but I knew it had to be gnawing at him. Gramps would skin us alive if he knew how stupid we'd been.

"This thing isn't going to fool anyone," Clare said. "It might have worked back in the nineteen fifties before everyone had high-resolution cameras and iPhones. Face it. You're screwed."

"Why do you sound so mad?" I snapped. "This isn't even your hoax. You lose nothing if this doesn't work. We lose everything."

"I'm mad because you guys were my chance to prove myself," Clare said. "My chance to be taken seriously. Had I known you were working with this thing"—she gave our Champ model a kick—"I never would have showed up at your stupid storage locker."

"Then why don't you just call your uncle to pick you up!" I said.

"Maybe I will!" she yelled back. "At least his Champ model doesn't look like a dumb horse!" She threw down the piece of Champ she'd been trying to put together despite two broken buckles and stomped off toward the lake.

"Good one," Curtis said. "Now we're never going to get this thing together." I dropped my head into my hands and shut my eyes. My brain hurt. This whole plan was stupid. I should have just stayed home and taken my history test instead of flushing my entire future down the drain in some harebrained attempt to save a family business I didn't even like. I sighed and looked back up at our Champ. Clare was right. It did look like a horse. I thought about going after her to remind her that another name for Champ and Nessie and half the other sea monsters out there *was* a water horse, thank you very much, when something clicked. I picked up the piece of Champ I'd been holding and looked through it at Curtis, who was still doggedly trying to assemble Champ's left fin.

"I just had an idea," I said.

Curtis looked up at me with exhausted eyes. "If it's all the same to you, I'm going to pass on your ideas, seeing as I'm still trying to assemble your last one."

"This one is good. I promise." I turned to the lake and cupped my hands around my mouth. "Clare!" I called. "Come back. I need you to call your uncle!"

"What?" Curtis said. "How is that an idea? That's suicide!"

I looked at him and grinned. "Trust me?" I asked.

He glanced down at our sad Champ and grimaced. "Do I have any other choice?"

I shook my head, and he sighed as Clare walked up, a confused look on her face.

"Change of plans," I said. "We are going to upgrade our Champ model. Are you sure you're on Team McNeil?"

Clare shrugged. "Temporarily for this hoax. I owe you that much. Afterward all bets are off."

"Fair enough." I nodded. "Remember in history class? The story of the Trojan horse?"

"No," Curtis said at the same time that Clare said yes.

"The Trojan horse is famous," I said. "And really, if you think about it, it's one of the first hoaxes in recorded history. According to legend, the Greeks had been in a battle with the city of Troy for years, so in one last Hail Mary attempt to win the war they constructed a hollow wooden horse. Then they hid a group of soldiers inside it before leaving the horse outside the gates of Troy and pretending to sail away. Feeling pumped over their victory, the Trojans pulled the horse inside to keep as a trophy. That night, the Greeks came out of the hollow horse and threw open the gates so they could finally infiltrate the city and win the war."

"So?" Curtis said.

"So we are going to take a page out of the ancient Greeks' hoaxing playbook," I said, holding up my hollow section of Champ again. "Except we are going to use a water horse. It's time to hoax some hoaxers."

CHAPTER TWENTY-TWO

Next thing I knew, I was hiding inside a sea monster, this one substantially less spacious than our high-tech Nessie decoy Dad had taken with him to Scotland, and my shoulders pinched painfully at the close quarters. The Greeks' Trojan horse *had* to have been roomier than my water horse, but room or no room, what mattered was that my attempt at recreating the famous hoax was as successful. Curtis had wanted to be the one to hide inside Champ, but he was way too broad shouldered—a point I'd made when I'd explained my plan to him and Clare. He'd listened, his lips compressing into a thin worried line, and he'd argued with me.

It was too dangerous.

It was too risky.

It could all go horribly, horribly wrong.

It was just plain dumb.

I was dumb.

Et cetera.

But it was our only option. So eventually he'd had to agree. Our Champ model was junk. That fact was obvious to all of us, and even though this plan was a long shot if I'd ever seen one, we were going for it.

"They took our stuff twice before," I said, hoping to ease the worried look on Curtis's face. "They stole Dad's Shunka Warak'in, and then they turned around and cleaned out our basement. They won't pass up the chance to steal our Champ decoy, even if it is a hunk of junk, and when they do, we will have our very own Trojan horse, or water horse, or whatever. Trust me. Stealing stuff is kind of the Gerhards' sleazy MO. No offense, Clare."

"None taken," Clare said. "If I had my way, the Gerhard family would run their whole business a lot differently. My grandpa would have a fit if he knew what Uncle Axel and Clive did to you guys. Gerhards are too good to cheat."

"Debatable," Curtis muttered, and Clare stuck her tongue out at him.

"But Grayson's right," she said. "They'll take it. If for no other reason than to make fun of how pathetic it is." I glanced over at our sad Champ and had to agree, pathetic pretty much fit the bill.

So she'd made the call. I'd shimmied into the Champ model, and Curtis had dragged it, me inside, into the first few inches of water of the lake. We had to make this believable.

"They're here," Curtis said from where he stood three feet away in the lake holding Champ's long slightly warped tail.

"Is Clare with them?" I said.

"Shhhhh," Curtis said. "It's showtime." I heard the crunch of tires over gravel and the sound of car doors opening and shutting.

"Well, Clare Bear," came Axel's voice. "I sent you out to get coffee, and you managed to snag a McNeil. Nice work."

"Does this mean you didn't get the coffee?" Clive asked, and I heard Clare huff indignantly, and despite my current cramped situation, I smiled. Clare was good. Really good. She was currently playing her uncle and cousin like fiddles, and they thought she was only good for picking up Starbucks. Their loss. Our gain. I heard Curtis yell something inarticulate as though the Gerhards had just caught him mid-hoax, and the

265

Champ model I was in shifted as he pretended to attempt to push it into the water. I gritted my teeth as the inch of water inside the model became three in an instant. There was the sound of splashing and a scuffle as Curtis let himself get caught.

"Let me go," Curtis yelled, and something hit the side of Champ with a thump that sent it another inch into the water. Not good. Why had I insisted Champ be on the beach so it looked convincing?

"Where's your sniveling little brother?" Clive said.

"At the hotel," Curtis said. "I didn't want him getting wrapped up in this if it went wrong." My stomach churned from the raw nerves zinging through my body, and I wondered momentarily if I was going to puke. I glanced around at the narrow tube I'd shoved myself into and pressed my lips together. Vomiting in here would be bad news.

"Did you really think you could pull off this big of a hoax with that thing?" Axel asked a moment later. "Was this monstrosity in that storage unit you torched this morning?"

"And what if it was?" Curtis asked. "Even with this thing we could pull off a better hoax than you two idiots."

"Watch yourself, boy," Axel said, his voice low. "We should have done more than get you arrested back in

Georgia. This time we won't make that mistake. Clive, get him in the car. I don't want him mucking up our hoax."

"What are you going to do to him?" Clare said. "You promised on the phone that you wouldn't hurt him."

"And we won't," Axel said, and I heard him slosh over to inspect Champ. "Yet," he muttered just loud enough for me to hear. "By the way, dear niece," he said, and there was something about the way he said it that sent warning goose bumps rippling down my arms. Although those could have been caused by the icy water I was lying in. "It seems awfully convenient that you just *happened* to go for a walk to town for coffee and passed by young McNeil here about to sink his sea monster. Is there anything you'd like to tell me?"

"No," Clare said, and to her credit, her voice didn't waver even a little. "Except that you shouldn't have sent me to get your coffee. You told me I could help with the hoax."

Axel snorted. "Just like your mother. Either way I'm keeping you close until after this is all over. This hoax is worth too much for a woman to mess it up."

"Whatever," Clare said, and this time her voice had a bitter edge to it. She hadn't been lying about her uncle being old-school and not letting girls hoax. Which I found totally weird because, even if I'd been born a girl and not a boy, I was positive that Dad and Gramps would have had me hoaxing and cryptid hunting just the same.

"What about this thing?" Clive asked, giving Champ a firm kick that sent me rocking.

I heard Axel sigh. "Just throw it in their truck. We'll hide it until after our hoax."

"Are you serious?" Clive said. "It looks like it weighs a ton." Champ lurched as he gave it a shove.

Axel paused for a second, considering. "On second thought it might just be easier to sink it in the lake," he said.

"No!" Curtis and Clare yelled at the same time.

"Why not?" Axel said, and I felt my stomach clench at his tone. He suspected something.

"Because it's just too ugly not to keep," Clare said. "Besides, it looks like it's solid wood, and you don't have the weights here to sink it."

"Good point," Axel said. "How were you planning to sink it, kid? And where is your scuba equipment?"

"I, um, hadn't gotten that far yet," Curtis said, his voice tight with nerves. Nerves that I knew had nothing to do with being caught and everything to do with the fact that his little brother might be drowned right before his eyes. Should I just make a break for it now? I was wedged inside Champ like a cork in a wine bottle, and if they sank it. I was pretty much screwed. But I gritted my teeth and waited for the verdict. We'd come too far for me to chicken out now. Besides, if they decided to sink it, screaming bloody murder was a completely viable option.

"You've got a point," Axel finally said. "Once we pull off the hoax tomorrow morning, we can burn it, but I don't want it anywhere some stupid tourist is going to stumble across it. That includes in the lake."

"Great," Clive grumbled. "If I screw my back up and can't play football next year, I'm blaming you." I smiled and braced myself inside my very own Trojan water horse as the Gerhards hauled our Champ model up onto the beach and toward our waiting truck. My plan was actually working.

CHAPTER TWENTY-THREE

Five minutes and a long string of what I could only assume was some impressive swearing in German and Champ was loaded into the truck. I let out a sigh of relief. So far my plan was working. One short but bumpy ride later, we stopped. I heard the sounds of muffled voices outside the truck and then the slamming of some doors followed by silence. I waited, unsure what was happening. Was someone going to come unload me? Were Curtis and Clare okay? Where were we? I didn't know how long I lay there inside the belly of an antique sea monster and straining my ears for some hint of what was going on, but it felt like hours. Finally I decided that it was time to make my move.

Besides, if I stayed inside Champ much longer, I was going to be too stiff to run, let alone pull this off.

Getting out was easier said than done. I wasn't sure if Champ had shrunk or I'd swollen since I'd wriggled inside, but I finally managed to squirm out of the ancient decoy, sweaty and with more than one bruise and splinter to show for it. The interior of the truck was dark, and I crept over to the door, grateful to find it unlocked. Good job, Clare, I thought. So far everything was working out just like I'd hoped. It was kind of shocking. Don't get ahead of yourself, I mentally reprimanded myself. All I'd actually managed to do was get Curtis and me purposefully caught. Unless I pulled off part two of this and stole the Gerhards' Champ to complete the hoax by the deadline tonight, then all I'd have accomplished was taking us out of a frying pan and throwing us into a fire. Not real impressive.

I pressed my ear to the truck door for another minute, triple checking that I wasn't going to waltz right into a waiting Gerhard, before easing the door open and poking my head out. I was in some kind of warehouse. The corrugated metal walls surrounding me looked beat-up and rusted, and I changed my evaluation from warehouse to old crappy barn. The fact that when I jumped out of the truck I landed in a pile of horse poop reaffirmed that guess. I wrinkled my nose

271

and did my best to scrape the yuck off the bottom of my shoes. Leave it to a Gerhard to choose a place like this to park our truck.

As relieved as I was to be by myself, where was everyone else? I crept around the side of the truck and came face-to-face with two huge bulbous eyes, and I leaped backward, stumbled, and fell butt first into the same pile of horse poop I'd just stepped in. Although this time I didn't even notice because I was staring up into the familiar face of the sea monster I'd helped assemble and disassemble more times than I could count. Burnished gray-green scales rippled over the light chicken wire frame with a realness the wooden hunk of junk in the truck behind me couldn't hope to achieve. The eyes that had frightened me were the size of tennis balls and painted with a special paint so they glowed in the dark like two small moons. I'd had to repaint them just two weeks ago before helping Dad and Curtis break her down and pack her carefully in crates for the long trip to Scotland, where she would make an appearance as the infamous Nessie before coming back to the States for the final Champ hoax. It was one of the more convenient things about sea monster hoaxes: most of them were similar enough in description that you didn't need ten different decoys.

"How in the world did you get here?" I murmured

as I scrambled to my feet and ran my hand over her smooth snout. My vague plan of finding the Gerhards' sea monster and stealing it to pull off the hoax evaporated as I walked around our decoy, making sure nothing was damaged.

"They must have stolen you from Dad when they stole his Shunka Warak'in," I mused as I gripped the edge of the monster and tilted it up to check the gear underneath. There sat two scuba diving rigs, complete with air tanks and wet suits. Jackpot. I was about to pick up the closest air tank to check whether or not it was filled when I heard voices approaching. I dropped it and quickly replaced Champ back on top before glancing around frantically for somewhere to hide, which is when I finally noticed what was surrounding me. Stacked up against the walls, sometimes two or three deep, were bins. Our bins. I whipped my head in the other direction, recognizing more familiar shapes of decoys and costumes and props.

"Holy crap," I whispered, spinning around again. It was all of our stuff, and I meant *all* of it. The more I looked, the more I saw: from the Yeren suit that itched and smelled like cat pee inside to the large glider that Dad had been working on transforming into a working Thunderbird decoy. The voices were getting louder, and I realized that in my shock at finding the entire

McNeil hoaxing stash, I'd run out of time to find any-where decent to hide. In desperation I tilted the Champ decoy back up on her side and slid underneath just as the grating creak of a barn door being opened ripped through the air.

I lay still, trying my best not to make a noise as I heard Axel and Clive enter. My lungs burned as I held my breath, praying that they weren't coming to dis-assemble for their hoax the very decoy I was hiding underneath. And even though I was beyond terrified and I felt like my heart was about to leap out of my chest, I had to admire them for the sheer arrogance of their plan. They were going to steal our hoax from us using our own equipment. But even as I thought it, I realized that it was exactly what I'd been planning to do to them—that is, if I could ever stop hiding inside sea monsters.

A moment later one of them let out a shout of sur-prise.

"What is it?" I heard Clare say as the barn door grated shut behind her.

"Did you open up the truck for something?" Axel asked, and I had to stifle a gasp. Had I left the back of the truck wide open? Was I that dumb? I couldn't stand not knowing what was happening, so I pressed my eye to the small crack between the bottom of the decoy and the floor and peered out. Clive and Axel were standing at the back of the truck, looking in. Clare stood behind them, and even with my limited vantage point I could tell she'd just gone rigid, her muscles tight with nerves. She was probably calling me every name in the book right about now, I thought. Because, seriously, what kind of epic moron leaves the back of the truck open?

A moron who jumped out and landed in horse poop and got distracted, I remembered, mentally kicking myself. I might as well have put up a sign that said, "HEY! SOMETHING IS GOING ON HERE! YOU SHOULD PROBABLY INVESTIGATE!"

"What happened to their Champ? It's been busted open," Clive said as he clambered into the back of the truck. "Uncle Axel, you're going to want to come look at this. The stupid thing is hollow!" he called a second later.

Axel grabbed the side of the truck and heaved himself inside. It was all over. Any second now they were going to put two and two together, and I was officially dead meat. Game over. The McNeils' entire hoaxing future evaporated before my eyes.

But I'd forgotten about Clare.

At first I thought she was going in the back of the truck too, probably to admire how completely and totally I'd screwed this up, but instead she leaped onto the tailgate like some sort of ninja, grabbed the handle to the back of the sliding door, and jumped back down, slamming it shut. Before her uncle and cousin had even realized what was happening, she was sliding the metal locking bar into place. She turned and looked frantically around the dim interior of the barn as Axel and Clive went berserk inside the truck.

"Grayson!" she said in a loud whisper yell. "Where are you?"

"Here," I said, rolling out from underneath Champ and scrambling to my feet. "That was brilliant." She held a finger to her lips and shook her head with a nervous glance behind her to where the truck was rocking violently as Axel and Clive tried to Hulk their way out.

"That's more than I can say for you," she whisper-yelled. "That was so incredibly stupid!"

"You aren't wrong," I said. "Where's Curtis?"

She jerked her head toward the barn door that stood open about a foot. "They're in the house. Hurry. I don't know how long this truck can hold."

"Thanks!" I said, and sprinted through the door and out into the afternoon sunlight, where I slid to a stop, my head turning this way and that in an attempt to get my bearings. I spotted a small cabin to my left, and it wasn't until I was hurrying up the steps that I registered what Clare had said. She'd said that "they" were inside. What *they*? My question was answered a second later when I burst through the unlocked door and found my entire family sitting side by side around a battered wooden table. It took me a second to register that it wasn't just Curtis tied hands and feet to a chair but Gramps and Dad too. All three of their heads whipped around guiltily at my entrance, and Gramps dropped from his mouth the small pocketknife he'd been using to saw at the ropes tied around his wrists and grinned at me. But Gramps wasn't the only one I was shocked to see.

"Dad?" I said. "I thought you were in Scotland!"

"It's about time you showed up!" Curtis said. "What did you do? Take a nap inside that thing?" His words didn't match his tone, and I saw the wrinkle of anxiety across his forehead ease. He'd been worried about me. Very worried.

"Where are Axel and Clive?" Dad asked, and I took my first really good look at him. The Gerhards had obviously taken more care in shipping Champ back to the States than they had Dad. His clothes were rumpled, ripped, and stained, and one side of his face sported a pretty spectacular black eye. Gramps wasn't much better.

"Grayson!" Dad said again, his voice sharp. "Where are Axel and Clive?" I shook my head and refocused, grabbing the small pocketknife and getting to work on Gramps's ropes.

"In the barn," I said. "Clare locked them in the back of our truck."

"Nice," Curtis said. "I knew having her help was a good idea."

"I'm not convinced yet," Dad said. "She's a Gerhard."

"A Gerhard who's currently saving your butts," Clare said, coming in behind me. I got Gramps's hands free and moved over to Curtis while Gramps quickly untied his legs and began working on Dad's hands. Clare bent to untie Curtis's feet, and within a minute everyone was free.

I'd expected Dad to rush out the door to check on all our hoaxing equipment or to immediately start talking about the logistics of finishing the Sea Monster Grand Slam, but instead he turned and wrapped me up in a hug. He squeezed so hard that my ribs creaked in protest, releasing only momentarily to pull Curtis into the hug as well. Curtis and I stood there like blocks of wood, looking at each other with the same expression of "*What the heck is going on?*" on our faces. I honestly couldn't remember the last time Dad had given us hugs like that. We both looked to Gramps for guidance, and he flapped his hands at us, clearly directing us to hug back. So we did. And it was familiar and strange and wonderful.

"I'm so glad you boys are all right," Dad said, his voice choked, and when he finally let us go, I was shocked to see tears in his eyes.

"We're fine, Dad," Curtis said. "But what about the hoax? The Grand Slam? We don't have much time left if we're going to pull this off."

"Forget the hoax," Dad said. "It doesn't matter. What matters is that you two are okay."

"I'm okay too," Gramps piped in with a grin.

Dad laughed, wiping at his streaming eyes with the back of his hand. "You're always okay, old man. You're like a cockroach."

"I'm going to choose to take that as a compliment," Gramps said.

"All our stuff," Curtis began, "the Gerhards—"

"It doesn't matter," Dad said again. "They can have it. Ever since those two knuckleheads cracked me over the head in Scotland and dragged me back here, I've been doing nothing but thinking and worrying about you two. I realized that I had no idea if you'd be okay or not. I haven't been paying much attention to anything but hoaxing ever since . . ." He trailed off, but we all knew he was talking about Mom. He shook his head. "Not anymore, though. I can promise you that."

"This is touching and everything," Clare said, and we all jumped a little. I guess I wasn't the only one who'd forgotten that she was there. "But are you guys seriously going to blow off this hoax after all this?"

"Yes," Dad said.

"No," Curtis and I said at the same time.

"It's not worth it," Dad said.

"It is to me," I said. "Our family has been in charge of keeping the legends alive too long to let something like this put us out of business. Besides, we could really use the money." When Dad and Gramps shot each other a look, I groaned and rolled my eyes in exasperation. "We aren't dumb, guys," I said. "We know about the bank notices and the foreclosure warnings."

"And," Curtis said, "it could also come in handy when we send Grayson to that fancy school he's been dreaming about."

Dad shot me a questioning look before glancing down at his watch and frowning. "I'm not sure what school you're talking about, but we have only one hour left or we forfeit the contract. I don't know if it can be done."

"Oh, yes it can," I said, already heading for the door. But I paused when I saw that Clare wasn't following us. "Aren't you coming?" I asked.

She shook her head. "I'm going to stay here," she said. "In fact, if one of you would be kind enough to tie me up to this table, that would be great."

"What?" I asked, confused.

Clare sat down and started expertly wrapping the rope around her wrists. "If they ask—not that I think you'll have any friendly conversations with my uncle and cousin any time soon—but if you do, just tell them that you are the one that shut them in that truck. Then you grabbed me and tied me up. I'm only a girl after all," she said, and winked.

Gramps was looking at Clare with a raised eyebrow, then he looked back at me and Curtis to see what we were going to say.

"If that's what you want," Curtis said, grabbing the rope. "You can come with us, though, help us with the hoax."

"That's okay," Clare said, settling down at the table. "I'm guessing that truck holds them for about another ten minutes, and I'm not ready to flush my entire hoaxing career down the drain by letting them know I locked them in so you guys could escape. Thanks but no thanks."

"Are you sure?" I asked.

She nodded. "Positive. I owed you one, but you've got your dad and grandpa back, and if you hurry, you can still pull this off. We're even. Don't expect me to help you out again."

I was still mulling this over when Curtis finished off the last knot on her wrist and stood back. "I tied this loose enough that you can wiggle free if you need to. But we'll come check on you after the hoax just to be sure," he said. "Your uncle and cousin might not be as adept at getting out of that truck as you think."

Clare shrugged, unconcerned.

"Let's go," Dad said. "We have a Sea Monster Grand Slam to finish." He headed out the door, Curtis and Gramps hot on his heels, but I hesitated another second in the doorway and looked back at Clare.

"You know," I said. "The McNeils and Gerhards don't *have* to be in competition."

She glanced up. "Don't take this personally, Grayson, but you guys really aren't what I would consider competition. I helped you out this time. But after this it's every hoaxer for herself."

"I don't want to be a hoaxer," I said. "I want to be a photographer and document my adventures."

"Why can't you be both?" Clare asked.

"Because the number-one rule of cryptid hunting and hoaxing is that they are secrets," I said.

Clare leaned forward, eyebrows raised. "It's called publishing anonymously, Grayson. People do it all the time. It's called a pseudonym."

I opened my mouth to respond, then shut it again. Was that possible? Could I be a photographer *and* a hoaxer? Did I want that? Dad's shrill whistle came from behind me, and I jumped guiltily and turned at the door before stopping and turning back one last time.

"Clare?" I asked, and she looked up from studying Curtis's sloppy knot job on her wrists. "Were we ever really friends?" I asked.

"Of course," she said. "My uncle asked me to keep an eye on you. Not be your friend. That was all me."

"But you're a Gerhard," I said, because really that fact kept gumming things up for me.

"I can be more than one thing too, you know," she said. "Now get out of here. I didn't lock Uncle Axel and Clive in that truck so you and I could have a chat." She had a point, so I turned and raced for the barn.

The Gerhards had their own truck parked outside, and Gramps already had the door open as Curtis tossed the long neck of our Champ up to him to load. I clambered into the back, and with all four of us working together we had Champ and the scuba gear loaded in a matter of minutes.

Axel and Clive must have realized what was going on, because the banging and cursing from the inside of the battered self-storage truck were getting louder by the second. Clare's estimation that it would take them ten minutes to bust out of there might have been a little high, I thought. I'd have put money that they'd be out in two more. Dad motioned us into the truck as he and Gramps climbed into the cab. Curtis and I threw ourselves into the back, barely getting the sliding door down before Dad was peeling out of the driveway and onto the road.

"Suit up," Curtis said, tossing me my wet suit as he pulled on one of his own. "Dad and Gramps are going to have to hustle to get the EWs in place, so it's up to us to get Champ sunk and into position."

My insides clenched nervously as I double-checked the air tanks. Dad took a tight turn, and Curtis and I grabbed on to Champ as she went sliding and clattering across the cavernous interior of the truck. Dad straightened the truck back out, and I sat down to pull off my shoes and start yanking on the wet suit. I looked across at Curtis, who was doing the same thing.

"Do you really think we can pull this off in time?" I asked.

"We've made it this far," Curtis said. "We have to at least try, right?"

I yanked my air tank across my back and tightened the straps as I felt the truck leave the smooth pavement and bump onto a gravel road. We were getting close.

"Ready?" Curtis asked, tossing me a pair of goggles.

I nodded. "I was born ready."

Curtis snorted in surprise and shook his head. "Cheesy," he said, "but I like it."

The truck screeched to a stop, and the back hatch

was opened, letting in the last rays of afternoon light. I could see the sun, huge and orange as it made its descent toward the lake. We were going to cut it close, really close.

Dad was inside the truck a moment later, and Champ was out and assembled in record time. There was no time for our usual safety checks. With Curtis and me on the front ropes and Dad and Gramps pushing from behind, we had her in the water. Without even waiting for us to submerge her, Dad and Gramps were running for the truck to get into position. The hoax only counted if the eyewitnesses saw it.

"Is the pager on?" I asked Curtis as I waded deeper into the water, Champ bobbing between us.

"You mean the pager we couldn't find in the five minutes we had to get our gear together? No. That's not on," Curtis said.

"Then how will we know the eyewitnesses are ready?"

Curtis held up his cell phone, which he'd sealed inside a Ziploc bag. "Gramps is going to call me when they're ready. It's not great, but it's all we got."

"I hope that bag doesn't leak," I said, eyeing it nervously.

"You and me both, little brother," Curtis said. "You and me both."

We were up to our necks in the water and just about

to depressurize Champ so she'd sink to the bottom with us when I heard the crunch of truck tires on gravel.

"Did Dad forget something?" I asked, turning to look back toward the beach. But the truck that was barreling down the rough gravel road through the woods was not the pristine white-and-orange one we'd stolen from the Gerhards. It was the battered and beat-up U-Store truck that we'd left behind, and instead of the Gerhards being locked in the back, they were sitting in the front, and they looked mad.

"No way," Curtis said.

"Sink it," I said. "Now!" Curtis hit the button on the side of Champ's neck, and there was an audible hissing sound as the air inside of her escaped and water pumped into her cavernous interior. She sank, but not before I saw Axel and Clive vault out of the truck and run for the water, slinging on their own air tanks as they went.

"Dive," I yelled, and Curtis and I both jammed our regulators in our mouths and went under, forcing Champ under so fast that air bubbles burst out of the vents on her side and rippled up to the surface above us. The water of Lake Champlain was freezing cold, but I barely felt it as I paddled for all I was worth toward the middle of the lake. All I could think of was putting some distance between us and the Gerhards.

We had a head start, but they weren't attempting to tow a two-hundred-pound sea monster with them. Thankfully Curtis was able to think and panic at the same time and remembered to switch on the sea scooters Dad had built into the bottom of Champ that acted like tiny little propellers to make our progress much faster. Lake Champlain was murky, so we only had to dive around fifteen feet down to avoid detection before heading toward the middle of the lake, and I prayed that same murk would make it that much harder for Axel and Clive to find us. A quick glance over my shoulder showed me nothing but blue-black water, but not knowing where they were was almost worse.

Dad had shown us on a map where we needed to put Champ, and I prayed that we were still headed in the right direction despite our rocky start. The only sound in my ears was the hiss of my regulator as I tried not to use up all my air by hyperventilating. Ten minutes later I spotted a familiar metal contraption protruding up from the bottom of the lake. Unlike the portable anchors we'd used for the Altamaha-ha hoax, this was one of four permanent structures the McNeils had installed in the bottom of Lake Champlain long before Curtis and I were born. We swam for it, hauling Champ along behind us, and within five minutes we had the ropes unfurled from inside her hollow interior and in the correct position around the metal bars. I glanced at Curtis, who gave me the thumbs-up signal. We were ready. We may actually pull this off, I realized with a nervous glance behind me at the impenetrable water where somewhere the Gerhards were looking for us. The thought made nervous goose bumps ripple up my cold-deadened arms.

And then, after what felt like a lifetime of rushing and hurrying and going at a breakneck speed, we had to wait. And it was the worst. I could see Curtis's Ziploc-bagged cell phone glowing like a lightning bug in the dark water, and I clenched my teeth into the rubber of my regulator to keep them from chattering.

Then a few things happened at once. The first was that Curtis's cell phone turned blue as he got the signal for us to make our move, and he slammed his hand down on the button that repressurized Champ. The other thing that happened in the same instant was someone snaking their arm around my neck and squeezing. The Gerhards had found us.

CHAPTER TWENTY-FOUR

I let go of Champ to clutch at the arm around my neck, and I saw Curtis's eyes go wide inside his mask. A second later he was battling his own Gerhard—Axel, I think, although it was hard to tell in full scuba gear— and Champ, no longer being held by either of us, started a slow ascent upward. I drove my elbow backward into Clive's gut, felt his grip loosen momentarily, and sucked in a much-needed breath. Locking my teeth around my mouthpiece in case he got any funny ideas about yanking it out of my mouth, I writhed and squirmed like a snake, doing everything in my power to free myself. And all the while I fought off Clive, Champ was still heading toward the surface. This was bad. Without Curtis and I to control her, she was going to pop out of the water like a gigantic bath toy, and the hoax would be an utter flop or worse. Clive grabbed my arm and attempted to twist it behind my back, and I stopped worrying about Champ and started worrying about myself.

Suddenly Curtis was in front of me, wrenching Clive off me, and I looked over to see Axel struggling with the rope Curtis had somehow managed to wrap around his ankle and the metal brace we used to anchor Champ. I turned back to help Curtis, but he motioned frantically upward toward our escaping sea monster. I got the picture.

Champ was only ten feet from the surface when I finally caught up to her, and I grabbed the loose ropes in both hands and hauled backward, kicking for all I was worth, but it was like trying to stop a runaway bull or an escaped hot air balloon. Champ was going to surface and fast. Using every trick I'd ever been taught, I leaned back and leveraged Champ so that she'd at least breach the water more like a rampaging whale and less like a rubber duckie. She needed to emerge with a realism that, when seen through the fog of sunset, would make any eyewitness an immediate believer in the impossible. The On button for the head and neck was mounted to my left, and I hit it, grateful that Dad was the one with the remote control on land. With the way my hands were shaking, there was no way I'd be able to control Champ's facial features in any kind of believable way. And then she was on top of the water, and I felt her neck move above me, the animatronic eyes blinking. A second later my head broke the surface inside of Champ's hollow interior as it filled momentarily with air. My heart was hammering from the heady combination of adrenaline, exertion, and pure terror, and I spit out the mouthpiece of my regulator so I could gulp a lungful of fresh air. Well, maybe not fresh—the inside of the decoy smelled of rotten rubber, but it was still an improvement.

I quickly checked the ropes that I'd need to get her back underwater. That done, I waited, suspended inside the body of a fake sea monster. A second later I realized that I had no idea how long I should wait. Curtis was the one with the cell phone, and without some way for Dad or Gramps to signal me I was essentially flying blind. Had they even succeeded with the eyewitnesses? My breath echoed eerily off the walls of Champ's body, reminding me of the time I'd flipped a kayak and come up underneath it instead of beside it. I put my face underwater to try to catch sight of what was happening with Axel, Clive, and Curtis, but the lake was getting more impenetrable by the minute as the sun sank toward the horizon. I pulled my face back out of the water and bit my lip.

I'd just decided I would count to ten and then re-submerge Champ when something grabbed my ankle and yanked me underwater. I struggled to put my regulator back in my mouth and turned to come face-to-face with the furious eyes of Axel Gerhard and a lethal-looking scuba knife. He motioned with it for me to get out of the way, his eyes already flicking upward to Champ and the ropes that were keeping her level. Ropes he was obviously intending to cut. His message was clear: if he couldn't get the money for this hoax, then no one could, and at least he'd have succeeded at ruining the McNeils' hoaxing reputation.

I looked past him, panicked at the sight of that knife, and noticed that he had a pretty impressive underwater camera strapped around his neck, probably to take blackmail pictures of us pulling off the hoax. Leave it to me to be in a crisis and notice a camera, I thought in disgust. Where was Curtis? Was he okay? Axel motioned again for me to move it as he picked up the camera to take a picture of the ropes trailing from the underside of our Champ model.

And I thought my last sea monster hoax had been bad, I thought grimly, remembering my near-death experience at the bottom of the Altamaha River when our decoy had succeeded in ripping off my goggles and nearly removing my right hand.

That was it, I realized. I may not have a knife, but I knew all too well that even a knife wasn't very useful if you couldn't see to use it. Before I could second-guess myself, I'd reached out and ripped his mask off his face. He dropped the camera and made a grab to stop me but overshot it, and I spit out my regulator to clamp down hard on the hand holding the knife. Hey, if our Altie decoy could do it, so could I. Axel's yell was nothing but a burst of bubbles, and the knife fell out of his hand and sank, disappearing into the murk of Lake Champlain.

Curtis was there a moment later, his arm around Axel's neck, and he jerked his head upward to where Champ was still bobbing on top of the lake. I nodded and paddled toward the surface, my lungs burning at the lack of oxygen, and came up gasping inside Champ's hollow interior for the second time. Reaching up, I smacked the button that would allow her to sink again. I waited a half second until I heard the distinctive hiss of escaping air that let me know it had worked before grabbing the front ropes and diving back underwater, working them this way and that in an effort to make our hasty descent look as natural as possible, all the while fumbling for my regulator. I finally found it and popped it in my mouth just as Champ made it completely underwater.

I left her to sink on her own and swam over to help Curtis with the blinded but still flailing Axel. Together we wrestled him down to the bottom of the lake, where Curtis already had Clive neatly tied to the metal brace. Axel fought us every step of the way, but eventually we managed to get him tied to his nephew. If Champ hadn't almost landed directly on our heads a moment later, I would have completely forgotten about her in the chaos. As it was, Curtis barely avoided getting brained by her left shoulder. I hurried to grab the trailing ropes so I could tie her up next to the fuming Gerhards.

It wasn't until the last knot was tightened, securing Champ, that I felt the wave of exhaustion hit. The adrenaline of the last few days seemed to drain out of me like air from a balloon, and my muscles screamed in protest at the combination of exertion and freezing cold. I looked over at Curtis to see if he was doing any better, but he was looking down at his bag-encased cell phone. A moment later he looked up at me, and even with a regulator shoved in his mouth, I could tell he was grinning. He gave me a thumbs-up, and I knew that we'd done it. The Sea Monster Grand Slam was a success.

* * *

It took another full hour before I was trudging out of the now-black lake and back onto the beach. Axel and Clive Gerhard had been gigantic pains to get off the bottom of the lake. Which seemed unfair, since we could have just made life a whole lot easier and left them down there. After everything they'd done, they'd have deserved it. They hadn't even kicked a fin to help as we hauled them the quarter mile back through the nearly pitch-black water to where a very worried Gramps and Dad were waiting beside the battered self-storage truck.

Gramps let out a yelp of surprise when he saw us emerge trailing Axel and Clive behind us like two bedraggled and very angry dogs.

"Are you boys okay?" he asked, sloshing into the water to help.

"Fine," Curtis said with a grin at me. "Nothing a couple of McNeil brothers couldn't handle."

"You shouldn't have had to handle it," Dad said, coming over to take charge of Axel's ropes. "This whole thing has been such a mess."

"You can say that again," Gramps agreed. "I haven't been part of a hoax this hairy since the Yowie mix-up of seventy-six with your great-uncle Bernie and that wackadoodle moose."

Clive made a lunge for Gramps, apparently intending to head butt him since his arms were still tied

295

behind his back, but before I could even yell a warning, Gramps had neatly sidestepped, allowing Clive to face-plant into the water. Gramps muttered something under his breath and pulled Clive up out of the water by the back of his shirt.

"You need to learn some respect for your elders, young Gerhard." He turned to Axel. "This is how you raise the next generation of hoaxers? Like common criminals? Your father would be ashamed of you," he said. "I bet old Humphry is rolling in his grave right now at the foul play you two have cooked up."

Axel yelled something in German that sounded bad, and Gramps chuckled.

"Not anatomically possible, my boy, but thanks for the suggestion." He ripped off two large chunks of fabric from his tattered shirt and gagged each of the Gerhards. "I think it's high time you both stopped talking."

"You knew his dad?" I said to Gramps, this nugget of information too interesting to pass up.

"I did. And a sneakier son-of-a-gun you'd never hope to meet." Gramps sniffed. "Ugly too. Biggest schnoz this side of the Mississippi and teeth like a woodchuck's. But if he knew his son was relegating the next generation to picking up his Starbucks instead of hoaxing just because she was a girl, he'd have walloped him from here to next Tuesday. From what I saw when I was tied up in that minuscule cabin of yours, that little girl had twice the brains of this youngster. You chose the wrong apprentice, Axel." Unable to answer because of his newly tied gags, Axel just grunted angrily as we hauled him and a fuming Clive the rest of the way onto the beach. Gramps stripped them of their air tanks while Dad deftly secured them to a tree.

Dad tightened the last rope and then stepped back. "Not exactly how I envisioned this hoax going," he said. "But nice work."

"So did we really do it?" I asked. "Did we complete the Grand Slam in time?"

Dad shrugged. "I think so, but I won't know for sure until I get confirmation from the client. Even if we didn't succeed, though, you two just saved us from exposure." He shook his head at Axel and Clive. "Unbelievable, the lengths these two went to just to steal a job I outbid them for fair and square. Did they get any photos?" he asked, unhooking the camera from around Axel's neck and handing it to me.

"I don't think so," I said, quickly looping the strap over my neck so I could check the camera without worrying about dropping it from my wet hands. I flipped back through the memory card and deleted a few blurry shots of Curtis and one of my left elbow before lowering

297

the camera down to look back at Axel's furious face. "He didn't get anything good," I said. "Nothing a magazine or tabloid would pay money for at least."

Dad nodded. "Good. Now that these two are settled, we need to get Champ off the bottom of the lake. Grayson, I know how much you hate this kind of stuff, so why don't you strip off that wet suit, and I'll go with Curtis to bring it in."

"That's okay," I said. "I'll go with Curtis. You and Gramps can stay here."

"Are you sure?" Dad asked, the surprise obvious in his voice.

"Positive," I said, checking the levels on my air tank before turning to Curtis. "Ready?"

"Born ready," Curtis said with a grin. Dad tossed us both a pair of headlamps, and we strapped them on and headed back toward the water.

"Hey, Grayson," Gramps called as I was about to follow Curtis into the water.

"What?" I called back.

"Keep an eye out for Champ," he said.

"That's what we're doing," I said, confused.

Gramps shook his head. "Not our Champ. The *real* Champ. After sundown is the perfect time to spot her."

"Right," I said, hoping my mask hid my eye roll.

"You know," Curtis said as we waded deeper into

298

the lake. "I'm kind of surprised at you."

"Why's that?" I asked.

Curtis shrugged. "What you said back at that cabin, to Dad and Gramps about our family being the one who keeps legends alive."

"What about it?" I asked.

Curtis shrugged again. "I guess it was just surprising coming from the kid who doesn't believe in any mysteries."

"Hazard of the hoaxing business, I guess," I said, thinking back to the Loch Ness Monster project and the camera Dad had thrown in the trash in Scotland when I was eight.

Curtis snorted. "That and frostbite. Let's get this over with. I'm worried about my toes."

I laughed as we slowly sank under the surface of the water, following Curtis's headlamp as it cut a swath of light through the dark. I barely felt the cold, still riding on the success of the hoax. For the first time I actually felt like I belonged with my family, and it was a feeling I thought I could probably get used to, especially if Dad was going to tune back in and actually be a dad again.

The swim back to Champ felt fast without a sea monster or two thugs to tow behind us. She was still floating where we'd left her, and Curtis and I began untying the knots by the gleam of our headlamps. Suddenly something grabbed my arm, and I jumped, my heart hammering. But this time it wasn't Axel Gerhard; it was Curtis, his eyes wide. I scowled at him. Was he really playing one of his dumb pranks to scare me after all this? I brushed him off and turned back to untying the knot I'd been working on when he grabbed me again. I jerked my head up, all the warm, fuzzy feelings I'd been having about my family evaporating quickly, and I noticed that he was pointing. I turned, following his finger and the beam of his headlamp but saw nothing but dark lake water. I was about to brush him off again when I saw it. Something massive and black, its skin smooth like a whale's, glided past us, visible for only a second in the thin beam of light before disappearing into the pitch-black water.

Was that? Could it be? No. Freaking. Way. A second later the thing circled back around. This time I could make out a long slender neck and large paddle-like fins that reminded me of a seal's. Curtis was gripping my arm so hard I was losing feeling in my fingers, but I couldn't have cared less. The thing, and it could really only be one thing, made one last pass in front of our Champ decoy, turning large round eyes on us. Our headlamps illuminated a flash of curved sharkish teeth before it darted forward like a striking snake to grasp our Champ decoy around the neck.

Curtis and I threw ourselves backward in the water as the thing vigorously shook our poor Champ decoy like a wolf trying to break a rabbit's neck. The thin wires inside our decoy buckled and crumpled like a cheap tin can in the thing's powerful jaws. Finally, determining our decoy was good and dead, it turned to look back at us just as I remembered Axel Gerhard's camera still hanging around my neck. With hands that felt like they belonged to someone else, I grabbed it and snapped a picture just as the thing disappeared into the pitch-black water faster than I would have thought possible. Curtis and I floated there for a second, frozen, as we watched the spot where it had disappeared. Then we both turned to look at our mangled Champ decoy that now sported large puncture holes the size of quarters where the thing had latched on. We looked at each other, and I felt something bubbling up inside my chest. Champ was real.

CHAPTER TWENTY-FIVE

We hauled our poor mangled decoy through the black water and back toward shore. After we'd gotten over our shock at the Champ sighting, Curtis and I had hustled, both of us anxious to get the heck out of that dark water. The puncture holes in our crumpled Champ were no joke, and as we paddled, I tried not to think about what those teeth could do to a leg or an arm. I also tried really hard not to play the *Jaws* theme in my head, my heart already hammering so hard it felt like someone was pounding a drum in my chest. After what felt like an eternity but was really only a few minutes, we were out of the water and hauling what was left of our decoy onto the dark beach.

Curtis yanked his regulator out of his mouth and

called, "Gramps! Dad! You aren't going to believe what just happened!" I pulled my own regulator out and slipped my fogged mask onto my head, wiping at my eyes as I hustled the last few feet out of the water. I may never go swimming again, I thought grimly as I hauled on Champ's rope so she slid up onto the beach. I was about to check the camera to see what kind of picture I'd managed to snag of Champ when I noticed how quiet and empty it was.

Where were Dad and Gramps? And where were the Gerhards for that matter? I looked over to where we'd tied them to the tree, and one of the mysteries was answered. There sat Dad and Gramps, tied and gagged and looking exceptionally sheepish. Curtis spotted them at the same time, and we dropped the ropes and ran over. Curtis beat me there, sliding the gag out of Gramps's mouth. I was about to remove Dad's when I saw the piece of paper stuck to the tree above their heads. I grabbed it, noting the bubbly, girlie handwriting I'd seen on a pink planner in homeroom more times than I could count.

Sorry Guys,
They are family after all. Don't worry. I won't let them torch the barn full of your stuff like they wanted to, but if I were you, I'd change the locks on your

doors. Don't feel too bad. Life is better
with a little competition. Keeps you from
getting sloppy. Although you guys aren't
much competition.

No offense,

Clare

PS You owe me one.

Curtis read over my shoulder and snorted. "I knew I liked her." He turned to Dad and Gramps and grinned. "Let's bypass for a second that somehow a twelve-year-old girl got the best of two veteran hoaxers, because you are not going to believe what just pulverized our Champ decoy!"

I just shook my head as I bent down to untie Dad and Gramps. I had a lot to think about.

Two days later I was back in Mrs. Howard's office as she looked at me in the classic "*You've disappointed me*" way that they must teach guidance counselors in college.

"I'm sorry, Grayson," she said, "but after our talk last week I had high hopes of your turning things around. But a three-day trip to Vermont?" She shook her head as she looked back at the note my dad had written for me explaining my absence. She sighed and set it down, forcing a smile onto her face. "Did you at least turn your scholarship essay in on time? What did you end up writing about? What did you decide that the world needed?"

"Mystery," I said, remembering how I'd worked on my essay in our Vermont hotel room up until two minutes before it was due and then never sent it in.

"Mystery?" she said.

I nodded. "The world needs a little mystery. Everyone thinks they have everything figured out these days, and that's no fun. It takes the magic out of things. The world needs mystery."

Mrs. Howard looked at me for another second and then shrugged. "If you say so, Grayson. Although I'm afraid that your attendance might knock you out of the running for that scholarship."

"That's okay," I said. "I actually withdrew my application."

"You did?" she said. "Why?"

"Because I realized that I didn't need to go to Culver to be a photographer. I can do that right here."

"Really?" she said, eyebrows raised.

"Really," I said. "Besides, I wouldn't want to be away from my family."

I walked out of her office a few minutes later after listening to her lecture on the importance of a good attendance record and almost ran into Curtis.

"How did it go?" he asked.

I shrugged. "Fine. Is the blog ready to go live?"

He held up his phone. On it was the home page of our new adventure blog with the picture I'd taken of Champ and our name, Cryptid Clues, above it.

"Are you sure you want to do this?" he asked. "If Dad or Gramps finds out, they'll disown us."

"Are *you* sure the blog can't be traced back to us?" I said.

Curtis nodded. "One hundred percent anonymous."

I took a deep breath and then nodded. The world needed some mystery, and for generations my family had been behind the scenes making sure that no one forgot about legends like Bigfoot or Nessie. I'd sat in that tiny hotel room writing an essay for a scholarship I didn't even want, listening to my dad and grandfather tell stories so fantastic that no one would believe them except for maybe a kid who had just come within a few feet of a living legend. I shuddered, remembering the teeth of the real Champ in that dark water. It was true what Gramps always said: it only took one eyewitness account to make someone a true-blue believer in the impossible. That essay hadn't been wasted, though. It had become the very first article for our new blog. I wanted to be a photographer, to tell stories to the world through my pictures, and I couldn't think of a much cooler story than a sea monster encounter—especially

306

since I'd managed to capture a picture of Champ's right fin and most of her torso. I looked at Curtis and nodded. "Publish it."

Curtis hit a button and and slid the phone back in his pocket. "Done. The first installment of Cryptid Clues is ready for its virtual debut. Let's just hope that the world wants to read about a mysterious monster swimming around in Lake Champlain."

"They will," I said.

"I still say that if you'd let me include some of your pictures of our decoy's mangled neck, we really would have made a splash with our first post. Maybe even gone viral. Those teeth marks are probably the most conclusive evidence ever collected to prove that Champ exists, and we can't show anyone."

I nodded. The irony wasn't lost on me, but even without that photo, I was ridiculously proud of our first article. Clare might be right. I might be able to be a photographer and a McNeil. It was an idea I was still getting used to.

Together Curtis and I walked down the hall and out to the parking lot, where Dad and Gramps were waiting to take us out for pizza to celebrate our big payday. I glanced at Clare's newly emptied locker as we passed, and I shook my head. She'd transferred to a different school across town. Probably because her family didn't want her sharing a homeroom with a McNeil anymore, especially not after the mess in Vermont. I felt a tug of worry for my friend, wondering how much trouble she'd get into if her family found out how she'd helped us. Because despite everything, I was pretty sure she was really my friend. And that wasn't just because I'd opened my locker on Monday to find Gramps's old camera sitting there, the pawnshop receipt tucked in the case showing that it had been paid for in full.

"What is it?" Curtis asked, looking at me.

"Nothing," I said. "I'm just thinking about how Clare said we aren't real competition."

"Well." Curtis grinned. "We will just have to prove her wrong. How did you put it in your essay? Something about mysteries being magical?"

I shook my head. "I said that mysteries are like magic. They teach us that it's okay to believe in things that we can't always see."

"Bingo," Curtis said. "And that is why you write the blog, and I just publish it."

"We're a good team," I said, and smiled.

Curtis threw an arm around my shoulders and squeezed as we walked out of the building and into the bright sunlight. "It's about time you figured that out, little brother. It's about time."

AUTHOR'S NOTE

Dear Reader,

What do you get when you sew the back half of a dried-out fish to the front half of a mummified monkey? If you answered "ugly," you'd be right. This was the exact reaction the public had when they first saw P. T. Barnum's Feejee Mermaid on display in 1842. Lucky for Walt Disney and his plucky mermaid heroine, the Feejee Mermaid turned out to be a hoax. (Even Disney magic couldn't make *that* particular mermaid into a princess.)

What the Feejee Mermaid did prove, though, was that we are intrigued by the mysterious and the unknown. The idea that a body of water might be hiding a sea monster or that a huge ape man might be traipsing around the woods sets our imaginations on fire. And that's where my original idea for *Hoax for Hire* began.

I knew my way around cryptids (those creatures that live only in legend . . . at least for now) thanks to teaching a nonfiction book titled *Tales of the Cryptids: Mysterious Creatures That May or May Not Exist* during my six years as a seventh-grade Language Arts teacher. We were only supposed to spend a few days pulling the book apart like a dissected frog so that we could work on "analyzing nonfiction texts," but I lingered. I dug up video clips about Champ and Megalodon for my class to marvel over, we picked sides and debated whether or not the evidence for Bigfoot was enough to prove his existence, and we poured over grainy Loch Ness Monster photographs. And it was during this time that I jotted down an idea in the margins of my lesson-plan book: "What if one family was responsible for it all?"

Hoax for Hire was born.

We humans have ourselves convinced that every mystery can be answered with a quick Google search or a deep dive into Wikipedia. But can it? While I was researching this book (and let me tell you, that was some *interesting* research—talk about falling down the rabbit hole) I stumbled across so many amazing stories that made the unimaginable seem completely possible. I wove some of these into the McNeils' family history—from the story of the U-28 Monster that was blasted into the air by a World War I submarine to the remnants of the Silver Lake Serpent decoy found in a burned hotel in 1857. The problem was that I had more cool cryptid sightings than I had McNeil relatives to hand them off to!

The more I researched, the more I found that cryptid stories march through hundreds of years of our history with a regularity that would probably surprise even the most cynical skeptic. Do I have *you* convinced yet? Personally I can't wait for the day that we find an actual Bigfoot or that Nessie gets herself tangled in a fisherman's net long enough to get a decent picture so that the true believers in the impossible can have their "I told you so" moment. I'll be right there cheering them on—and probably handing out bookmarks for this book, because, hey, a girl's gotta do what a girl's gotta do. Right?

As for me? I'm not a conspiracy theorist, but I *do* believe that the world is chock-full of mystery if we just open ourselves up to the possibility that there are still discoveries to be made and creatures to be found.

Still a skeptic? It's okay. Bigfoot doesn't believe in you either.

CHAPTER ONE

REGAN

April 14, 1865. Gosh, I was sick of that date, and it wasn't just because that is when our sixteenth president was assassinated. Nope. I was sick of April 14, 1865, because I kept getting sent back to it for training purposes. Although training purposes was just code for, *You screwed up again, Regan; get it right this time.*

I materialized in the back row of Ford's Theatre for the fifth time this year just as the play, *Our American Cousin*, began. I always materialized into seat 10B when I did this particular practice simulation. It was supposed to contain Mrs. Margaret O'Hana, but she'd gotten sick with the measles and hadn't been able to make it to the performance that night. Her change of plans had left a convenient place for time travelers, or Glitchers, as we're called now, to slip in and out of history on the infamous night Abraham Lincoln was shot by John Wilkes Booth.

I'd see Booth momentarily, but I wasn't here to fix him. He would be allowed to murder our president without any interference from a Glitcher like myself. Interfering with him is against the law. Interfering with him was why I was here on a training mission in the first place.

I opened my eyes and looked around. Because I'd been here countless times before, I barely noticed the immaculate and stately Ford's Theatre, the theatergoers around me wearing their best dresses and suits, or the smell of a generation who handled body odors by covering them up with heavy colognes and perfumes. Even though I'd done this a lot, I still couldn't stop my eyes from automatically going up to the balcony where Mr. and Mrs. Abraham Lincoln would be taking their seats any minute. They would arrive late to the theater tonight and would be safe until the intermission, when their bodyguard would decide he'd rather go sit at a saloon and have a drink instead of protecting the president. There wasn't such a thing as the Secret Service yet. Although, in a weird ironic twist, Abraham Lincoln would sign the document that would create the Secret Service right before he left for the theater tonight. With some reluctance, I tore my eyes away from the balcony. I had less than ten minutes to find the Butterfly and complete the mission. It was time to get to work.

The last time I'd done this training mission, I'd immediately stood up and made my way to the lobby of the theater, sure that the Butterfly would be in wait there to waylay Booth. Unfortunately, I'd thought wrong.

I hated this simulation. It felt ten kinds of wrong to allow something horrendous like an assassination of arguably one of our greatest presidents, but it was all part of the job. It was why *this* particular simulation was so important to our training. We had to learn that what *we* thought about right and wrong didn't matter. At least not when it came to changing history. As a Glitcher, it was my job to make sure things stayed exactly the way the history books described without interference from a Butterfly.

The term Butterfly had thrown me for a loop when I'd first heard it. It seemed too, I don't know, fluffy to describe a time-traveling criminal the same way you describe a really pretty bug. I mean, a time-traveling criminal is usually someone attempting to manipulate history with the full intention of screwing up the future, and there was nothing fluffy about that. But I learned quickly that the term Butterfly did not come from the beautiful insects I saw landing on the flowers outside my window. Instead, it referred to the butterfly effect.

In 1963, this guy named Edward Lorenz presented a theory to the New York Academy of Sciences that "a butterfly could flap its wings and set molecules of air in motion, which would move other molecules of air, in turn moving more molecules of air—eventually capable of starting a hurricane on the other side of the planet." And everyone thought he was crazy for thinking something as small as a butterfly could start a snowball effect capable of wiping out whole cities.

He was laughed at.

He was called a fool.

And then thirty years later, they realized he was right.

So we called time-traveling criminals Butterflies, despite the fluffiness of the word, because they traveled back to the past to change something. They were the people who believed Hitler should have won World War II, that slavery should never have been abolished, or that women shouldn't have been given the right to vote. That's where Glitchers come in.

I glanced down at my watch. It was the exact same one the woman three rows up and two over was wearing. Everything from my light blue dress with the ten crinolines underneath to the way my hair was curled

4

and pinned up to the back of my head like a poodle was historically accurate, down to the last piece of lace trim. Of course, I wasn't exactly historically accurate, since unchaperoned twelve-year-olds weren't a common sight at Ford's Theatre, but that didn't matter for a simulation. If I ever actually did this Glitch for real, I'd be an adult with years of time traveling under my belt. I swallowed hard and ignored the fact that the thought made my stomach feel like I'd swallowed a bucket of live snakes.

Shaking my head, I forced myself to focus. I looked just like anyone else at the theater. The problem was that the Butterfly, wherever he or she was, did too. There was movement in the balcony to my right, and I glanced up to see the president and his wife taking their seats with their friends Clara Harris and Major Henry Rathbone. Those friends were one of the reasons they were late; they couldn't get anyone else to come with them tonight. Had Ulysses S. Grant's wife not been mad at Mrs. Lincoln, he would have been here instead of Rathbone, and Lincoln's wouldn't have been the only assassination.

A movement to my right caught my eye; a slim man, probably thirty or so, had just stood up from his seat. I watched him leave, looking for a clue that would let me know he was the Butterfly. Because if he wasn't, and I took him down, then I would cause even more damage to the future. It was one of the biggest rules of Glitching: you could not, under any circumstances, accidentally become a Butterfly. You had to be in the past, but not interfere or interact with it in even the tiniest, most inconsequential way. I had to make sure I touched no one, talked to no one, and didn't change the course of anyone's future by my actions. I was here to take down the Butterfly. That was all.

The man in question paused to talk to someone sitting in the aisle, and I immediately dismissed him. Butterflies never knew anyone from the time period they were messing with. Then I saw her. Two rows up on my right, a woman got up and made her way quickly down the aisle toward the exit. She was the Butterfly. Don't ask me how, but I knew it instantly at a bone-deep level, but because I'd have to give a concrete reason for the identification in my debriefing, I took the extra half second to identify where she'd gone wrong. Like me, she wore an elaborate dress trimmed with lace and her hair was twisted back into a knot at the base of her neck. I bit my lip; nothing was out of place there. Then I saw it. In her ears was a set of delicate hoop earrings, completely on era, but behind them were second and third holes. No one in 1865 had multiple piercings. She was it.

I carefully got up and made my way down the aisle, never taking my eyes off her as she slipped out the exit doors. I had two options. Option One—I could follow her into the lobby and take the chance of her making a scene. Option Two—I could intercept her somewhere out of the way before she made her move to take down Booth. Option One was easier, but I really didn't want to have to redo this simulation for the sixth time, so Option Two it was.

I slipped out the side door and into one of the theater's many hallways. It felt narrow and dark with its thick velvet draperies and busy wallpaper. Suddenly there was a noise to my left, and I saw a flash of blue skirts. Turning, I walked quickly in that direction. I'd have liked to run, but running wasn't something a lady did in a gigantic dress and ridiculous shoes that pinched. I had to blend in on the off chance that someone noticed me. Rounding the corner, I hurried up the narrow stairs toward the second floor. My lungs fought to expand inside the stupidly tight dress as I looked left and right down the empty hallway. To my left I could see the curtain that hid the president from view. According to my watch, I was minutes away from John Wilkes Booth coming up the same staircase I'd just used, gun in hand. I felt my first flutter of panic in my chest. Where had she gone? Should I go back down to the theater and risk missing her or stay where I was and hope I saw Booth before she did?

As I stood there, frozen, trying to decide which was the right answer, I heard a small sound directly behind me. It was the sound of someone unwrapping something covered in plastic. Plastic, a material that wouldn't be widely used until the 1960s. I whirled and saw the curtain behind me quiver just as the sound of booted feet on the stairs came from below. John Wilkes Booth was on his way up. Without stopping to think, I threw myself behind the curtain and wrapped my arm around the startled woman's neck. She let out a muffled gargle, and I saw the long lethal-looking syringe in her hand. She stumbled sideways, throwing us out into the open, and I fought to keep my balance without losing my grip.

Her eyes went wide as she realized that her opportunity to change history was about to be taken away. Her fingernails and teeth dug into the arm I had wrapped around her neck, but it didn't matter; I had her. The thump of Booth's boots was getting louder, and I knew I had mere seconds to get this done. If he came up the stairs and saw a woman and a twelve-year-old girl brawling like a couple of ultimate fighters in big frilly dresses, it might be enough to deter him from his plan and forever change history. I reached for my belt with the arm that wasn't getting gnawed on and grabbed my Chaos Cuffs. It took a second or two of fumbling, but I got them on her wrists just as the handsome face of John Wilkes Booth made it up the stairs. A heartbeat later and we'd disappeared, leaving him free to commit one of the most heart-wrenching crimes in history.

CHAPTER TWO

REGAN

My eyes snapped open inside the narrow white simulation room, and I immediately became aware of how bone-numbingly cold I was. Large computer monitors lined the walls around me, and I could see the frozen image of the woman and me mid-struggle with Booth's surprised face staring right at us. I almost groaned out loud in exasperation, but I swallowed it at the last second. The commander's daughter wasn't allowed to whine like that.

"So I failed?" I asked. "Again?"

"That's right, cadet," said Professor Brown with a sympathetic smile as she leaned down to remove the probes on my arms and legs so I could sit up.

"By how much?" I asked, glaring at the screen.

She consulted the slim black tablet she held for a moment and then sighed. "One second."

"You're kidding," I said.

"I'm afraid not," she said. "In that second, Booth saw you disappear in front of his eyes, and it was enough for him to call off the plan. As you may recall, he'd already gotten cold feet once in his attempted kidnapping of Lincoln, so it didn't take much to spook him that night."

"Well, that stinks," I said.

"One way of putting it," said Professor Treebaun as he looked up from his tablet for the first time. "Although it seems a bit tame considering that if this was a real mission, you'd have just irrevocably ruined the unity of the United States of America."

"I know, I know," I said, really not wanting to hear yet another lecture about all the awful things that happened in the future if Lincoln survived his night at Ford's Theatre. Knowing that something that seemed so 100 percent right, like saving the president of the United States, could actually have catastrophic consequences didn't make it feel any less awful. I'd heard all that before, the last time I'd failed this simulation. But at least last time I hadn't failed by one measly second.

"So, I'm off to the recap review room?" I asked,

silently praying she'd let me off the hook. I mean, how many times could you watch the same recap?

"Correct," said Professor Treebaun, and I stifled a sigh. Five. You could apparently watch a recap for the same simulation five times.

Professor Treebaun scowled at me, as though he'd read my mind. "You will watch your recap, and you will continue watching recaps until you learn the importance of a second. We will get this simulation on your schedule for next week."

"Does my mom already know?" I asked, trying and failing to keep the slight pleading tone from my voice.

Professor Brown nodded. "She watched your simulation live from her office."

"Peachy," I said, shutting my eyes for a second so I could block out the screenshot of my failure for a moment. Professor Brown finished pulling the electrical sensors off my arms and legs, and I barely flinched as the sticky pads yanked out my arm and leg hair.

"What was that, Cadet Fitz?" asked Professor Treebaun sharply, and I snapped my eyes open.

"Nothing, sir," I said.

"That's what I thought," he said as he unplugged his tablet from the main computer and tucked it in his bag. "You know," he went on, eyebrow raised, "it would behoove you to study your history a bit more. There was a different access point to that particular stair-well that would have saved you that precious second. I thought you'd have memorized that by now."

"You and me both," I muttered.

"Enjoy your recap," he said over his shoulder as he left the room, the doors sliding shut behind him with an official-sounding metallic click.